The Wanderer

NORTHWESTERN WORLD CLASSICS

Northwestern World Classics brings readers the world's greatest literature. The series features essential new editions of well-known works, lesser-known books that merit reconsideration, and lost classics of fiction, drama, and poetry. Insightful commentary and compelling new translations help readers discover the joy of outstanding writing from all regions of the world.

Alexander Veltman

The Wanderer

A Novel

Translated from the Russian and with an introduction by
Stephen A. Bruce

Northwestern University Press ✦ *Evanston, Illinois*

Northwestern University Press
www.nupress.northwestern.edu

Map created by John Wyatt Greenlee, Surprised Eel Mapping (https://surprisedeelmaps.com).

Printed in the United States of America

10 9 8 7 6 5 4 3 2 1

Library of Congress Cataloging-in-Publication Data

Names: Vel'tman, Aleksandr Fomich, 1800–1870 author | Bruce, Stephen A. (Stephen Andrew) translator
Title: The wanderer : a novel / Alexander Veltman ; translated from the Russian and with an introduction by Stephen A. Bruce.
Other titles: Strannik. English | Northwestern world classics
Description: Evanston, Illinois : Northwestern University Press, 2026. | Series: Northwestern world classics
Identifiers: LCCN 2025031395 | ISBN 9780810149038 paperback | ISBN 9780810149045 cloth | ISBN 9780810149052 ebook
Subjects: LCSH: Bessarabia (Moldova and Ukraine)—Description and travel—Fiction | LCGFT: Novels
Classification: LCC PG3447.V36 S713 2026 | DDC 891.733—dc23
LC record available at https://lccn.loc.gov/2025031395

CONTENTS

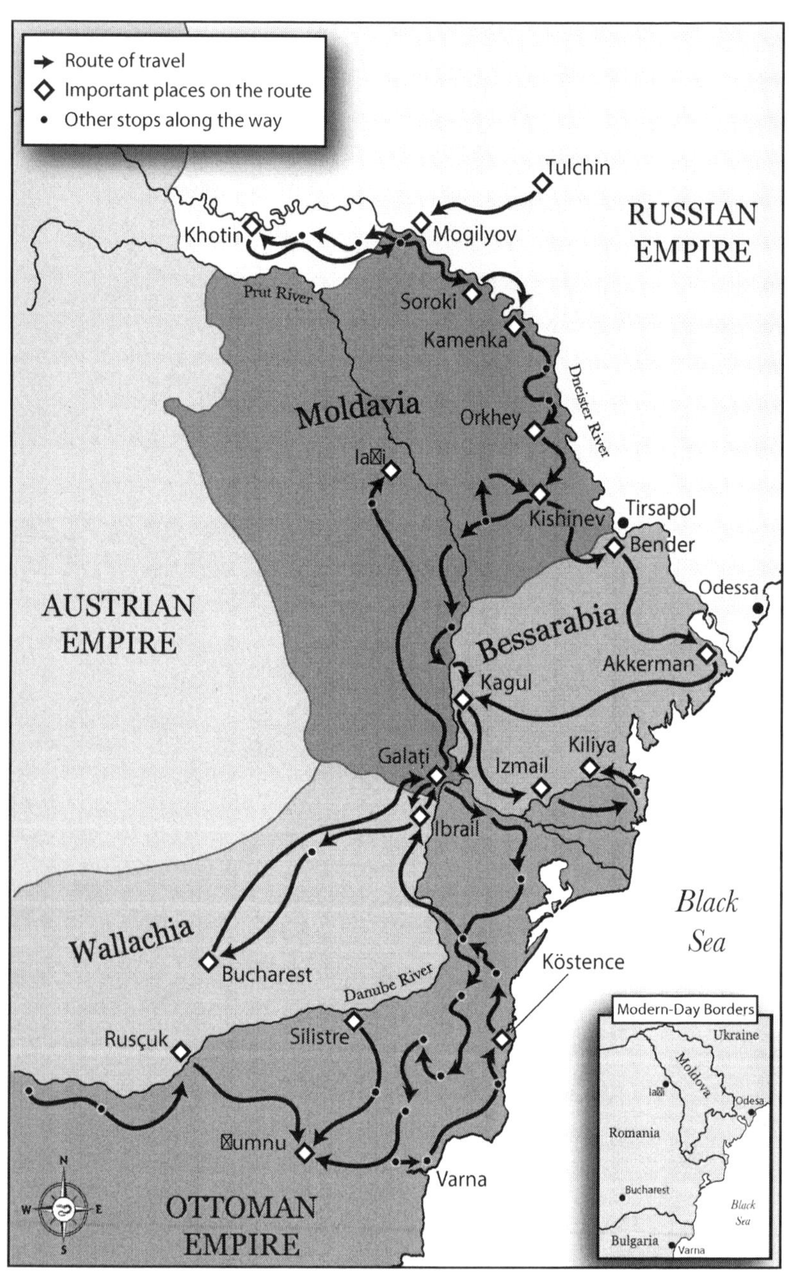

The journey from the Russian Empire to the Ottoman Empire described in Alexander Veltman's *The Wanderer*

TRANSLATOR'S INTRODUCTION

> Here, madame, is the *Wanderer* you asked me for. There is some real talent in this slightly mannered chatter. What's most singular is that the author is already thirty-five and this is his first work.[1]

Alexander Pushkin's brief review, originally written in French, hints at how *The Wanderer* has delighted and confused readers since its first publication in three parts in 1831 and 1832. The book launched its author Alexander Veltman on a brilliant career, but, as the critic Boris Bukhshtab noted, "In the history of Russian literature, there is no other writer who, having enjoyed such popularity in his time as Veltman, fell so quickly into complete oblivion."[2] He was indeed widely read at the time, though not universally praised. Readers at the time recognized his artistic talent and were willing to follow his winding language and experimental devices. But there was also the temptation to see his work, as Pushkin did, as merely extravagant "mannered chatter." Veltman never reaches the lyric intensity of Pushkin, the psychological intricacy of Dostoevsky, or the sweeping philosophical depth of Tolstoy. Yet, as he explains to us in the opening pages of his journey, he is aiming at a different type of truth, the truth about how we tell stories, understand history, and perceive the world through our imagination.

Alexander Fomich Veltman was born in 1800 in Saint Petersburg, the eldest child of an impoverished noble family of partly German or Swedish ancestry. His father was a military officer from Reval (now Tallinn, Estonia) and his mother was a courtier's daughter. His father's career and Napoleon's invasion in 1812 necessitated multiple family relocations, exacerbating their financial struggles and impacting Alexander's education. After graduating from the Moscow Academy of Column Leaders in 1817, he was commissioned as an ensign in the Russian army and soon assigned to the Second Army in Tulchin, southern Ukraine. From there he conducted a topographical survey of Bessarabia (now Moldova), of which he also wrote a history and which lies at the heart of *The Wanderer*. While in Bessarabia, Veltman became known for his humorous verse and formed a friendship with Pushkin, Russia's foremost poet of the time. His military service included participation in the Russo-Turkish War of 1828–1829, earning him the Order of Saint Vladimir (second class) for bravery. He retired in January 1831 with the rank of lieutenant colonel and settled in Moscow.[3] His oeuvre encompassed a wide range of genres, often combining history and fantasy. Parallel to his pursuits in literature, Veltman also forged a career in historical and museum-related work, culminating in his appointment as the director of the Kremlin Armory. Veltman died in 1870 at the age of sixty-nine.

The Wanderer assumes some knowledge of Russian and Ottoman history that would be useful to summarize here. The book was written after the latest outburst of a centuries-long conflict waged between an ascendant Russia and a declining Ottoman Empire, largely over control of the Black Sea region, including southeastern Europe and the Caucasus. In the eighteenth century, the Russian Empire began to exert its influence on the Danubian principalities of Moldavia and Wallachia, which were Ottoman vassals. In 1812, as part of the Treaty of Bucharest that ended the first Russo-Turkish War of 1806–1812, Moldavia ceded part of its territory, known as Bessarabia, to the Russian Empire. Bessarabia's diverse population included Romanians, Ruthenians, Jews, Bulgarians, Germans, Turks, and others, especially in the administrative center of Kishinev.

Because of its frontier position and relative political freedom, Bessarabia was a hotbed of revolutionary activities, housing both Russian radicals who would go on to participate in the ill-fated Decembrist Revolt of 1825 and Greek Hetairists seeking to overthrow the Ottomans. After the Greek War of Independence erupted in 1821, Russia intervened both to defend the Eastern Orthodox Greeks and to advance its long-standing goal of weakening Ottoman power in the Balkans. The Russo-Turkish War of 1828–1829 was fought on two fronts: the Balkans and the Caucasus. In the Balkans, where Veltman served, Russia faced large but uneven Ottoman forces, capturing key fortresses and advancing despite significant losses to cholera and other diseases. The war culminated in the Treaty of Adrianople in 1829, which ceded the Danube delta and sections of the Black Sea coast to Russia outright, while permitting Russian troops to occupy Moldavia and Wallachia provisionally until the Ottoman Empire paid a hefty indemnity. The treaty also confirmed the autonomy of Moldavia and Wallachia, with Russia playing a significant role in their governance.

The Wanderer was Veltman's first published prose work, yet it shares little with the best-known novels of the early nineteenth century, such as the panoramic historical epics of Walter Scott or the realist social chronicles of Honoré de Balzac. Instead of knitting a tightly sequenced plot or charting a hero's interior growth, Veltman sends his narrator and readers on an imaginative "sofa journey" through a map of Europe. The author skillfully interweaves details of a realistic journey, based on his own experiences as a military officer, with philosophical digressions, love poetry, and historical fiction drawing on the lives of Alexander the Great, Ovid, and Augustus. In its fusion of topographical realism, whimsical erudition, and direct address, the work is reminiscent of Laurence Sterne, Lord Byron, Pushkin, and Nikolai Gogol, but Veltman's innovations are surprising even to devotees of nineteenth-century literature.

The linguistic and cultural diversity of southeastern Europe is omnipresent in *The Wanderer*, which contains epigraphs and dialogue in French, German, Latin, Romanian, Turkish, Yiddish, and Greek. Yet the flood of ethnographic color rarely translates into sympathy: The narrator surveys each group with the paternalistic eye of an imperial officer. Moldavian men appear as pompous representatives of an Oriental culture, while their female compatriots—one girl is only fifteen—appear as partly Europeanized, fleeting objects of the narrator's desire. Jewish figures fare the worst, being depicted most often as bothersome hucksters and tavern matrons. Jewish learning appeals to Veltman's antiquarian curiosity, yet his fascination quickly curdles into anxiety. In chapter 262 the very Hebrew alphabet becomes the stuff of nightmare: an uncanny vision sets wizened "Old-Law" patriarchs against a beguiling Jewish maiden, drawing on the legacy of *The Merchant of Venice* and *Ivanhoe.* Such episodes reveal the worldview of a narrator—and in turn an author—who casts himself as the envoy of a scientifically inquisitive European civilization, confronting a frontier whose ethnic, religious, and linguistic variety he finds alternately disturbing and enthralling.

For all these ethnographic descriptions rooted in the cultural milieu of the Russian Empire of the 1830s, *The Wanderer* is striking in its use of intertextual and metafictional devices that are more familiar to readers of postmodernist fiction today. The writer constantly addresses the reader in different ways, even going so far as to form an "Amazon squadron" of his female readers to assist him in a battle. He mixes prose, poetry, and drama. Chapter 178 is left blank, but as the narrator explains in the following chapter, "you cannot call it empty, for nature abhors a vacuum." Different sections of the book refer to each other in sometimes misleading ways, and the book is speckled with epigraphs taken from dictionaries, multiplication tables, and other atypical sources. Throughout his narrative, Veltman plays with time and space, skillfully weaving his fanciful fictional worlds with real ancient and modern history.

For my translation, I have compared the first and second editions published by Semyon Selivanovsky (1831–1832 and 1840, respectively), an edition of part 1 only published by Nikolai Stepanov in 1840, and the Soviet edition published by Nauka in 1977.[4] The "original" text mentioned in the notes refers to the Russian text common to all three editions. Yuri Akutin's annotations to the Soviet edition, providing biographical details and clarifying many of Veltman's obscure allusions, were an indispensable starting point. Yet this edition is marred by some inaccuracies and omissions, leaving out, most strikingly, Veltman's rousing description of the 1828 capture of Şumnu in chapter 260. Benefiting from the increased availability of digitized books and maps, I have added extensive notes that elucidate Veltman's obscure allusions to geography, history, and literature. As a result, I believe that this translation represents a more comprehensive and explanatory edition than has been available in any language. Veltman's own footnotes are reproduced at the bottom of the page; my explanatory notes, keyed to page numbers, are collected at the back of the volume.

The Wanderer switches repeatedly in tone, from sincere love poetry to antiquarian commentary and from Gothic horror to burlesque comedy. All these correspond to specific language registers. I have aimed at balancing the demands of readability with preservation of the author's tonal diversity. I have sought to avoid both modern anachronism and excessive archaism (except when the original text is deliberately archaic). I have chosen to translate the poems with rhyme and meter roughly corresponding to the versification of the original. Here, the possibility for greater literalism in a prose translation was outweighed by the importance of preserving an appreciable distinction between the prose and poetry.

It is difficult to achieve consistency in the transliteration of names, especially when referring to places whose borders have shifted multiple times before and after the work was written. In the end, my solution was to render place-names according to either well-established English tradition or the primary language of the governing power of the time; in other words, transliterating from Russian for places in the Russian Empire, from Turkish for places in the Ottoman Empire, and from Romanian for places in the Danubian principalities. In my notes I have indicated current place-names according to their standard transliterations. I believe this is the best way to provide accuracy while not brushing over the real imperial history of these regions. For Russian names, bibliographical references follow a modified Library of Congress transliteration system. Elsewhere, names are given in forms more familiar to English readers, for example, Yuri instead of Iurii.

Emulating Veltman, I will end this introduction by addressing the reader directly. I encourage you to jump into Veltman's narrative. Navigate the text as you wish, moving forward or backward, as seems to have been the author's intent. This work is a call to active and inquisitive readers, inviting you to join Veltman on his imaginative odyssey and engage, even if fictionally, in a dialogue with the author. Through my translation and commentary, I have inevitably added my own layer of interpretation. Now it is your turn to explore this rich and complex work.

Notes

1. "E. M. Khitrovo," in Pushkin, *Sobranie sochinenii v 10 tomakh,* ed. D. D. Blagoi et al. (Gosudarstvennoe izdatel'stvo khudozhestvennoi literatury, 1959–1962), 10:30.

2. B. Bukhshtab, "Pervye romany Vel'tmana," in *Russkaia proza,* ed. B. Eikhenbaum and Iu. Tynianov (Academia, 1926), 192.

3. For more on Veltman's biography, see James J. Gebhard, introduction to A. F. Vel'tman, *Selected Stories* (Northwestern University Press, 1998).

4. A. Vel'tman, *Strannik,* 3 vols. (Moscow: V tipografii Semena Selivanovskago, 1831–1832), https://search.rsl.ru/ru/record/01003505534; Vel'tman, *Strannik,* 3 vols. (V tipografii S. Selivanovskago, 1840), https://www.google.com/books/edition/Strannik/-0lBV_xV41wC; Vel'tman, *Strannik,* part 1 (Moscow: V tipografii Nikolaia Stepanova, 1840), https://www.google.com/books/edition/Странник/vdz_JPTL6DsC; Vel'tman, *Strannik,* ed. Iu. M. Akutin (Nauka, 1977).

TRANSLATOR'S ACKNOWLEDGMENTS

This translation began over a decade ago as a hobby, a welcome distraction from the rigors of graduate school, rather than a project with a clear path to publication. I owe my initial discovery of Veltman and *The Wanderer* to Stephen Dodson, whose blog *Language Hat* introduced me to this fascinating work. His continued interest, along with insightful suggestions from his readers, has helped clarify some of the book's more obscure references.

I am thankful for my faculty and friends at Columbia University, particularly Irina Reyfman, Liza Knapp, Catherine Evtuhov, and Chris Caes, whose stimulating questions and support enriched my dissertation research on Veltman. I am particularly grateful to Cathy Popkin for her meticulous, sentence-level feedback on a sample of my translation as I prepared it for submission.

I am indebted to my parents, Chip and Susan, and my sister, Emily, who provided unwavering encouragement throughout this long process, including by reading copies of my manuscript during a long camping and canoeing trip in the Adirondacks in our "Van-Again."

I am grateful to the wonderful team at Northwestern University Press, including Faith Wilson Stein, Maia Rigas, Charlotte Keathley, Dino Robinson, Sharon Brinkman, and Connie Richardson, whose care and expertise carried this book from manuscript to publication. Many thanks to John Wyatt Greenlee of Surprised Eel Mapping for creating the accompanying map of the Wanderer's winding journey.

Finally, and perhaps unconventionally, I would like to thank Alexander Fomich Veltman—"Mr. Author," as he would say—whose captivating book, left untranslated for nearly two centuries, I have finally had the privilege to bring into English.

The Wanderer

Sit in this carriage, wing'd and light,
And let us fly, my reader-friend!
You northern resident, turn your sight
South, east, and west—where shall we tend?
To where we've been or where we'll be?
To wondrous, heavenly dwelling places,
The enlightened world or savagery,
To distant stars and unknown races,
Beyond the universe's bounds,
Where light and matter, life and thought
Submissively converge to naught!
Etc.

The Wanderer, part 2

To you

Part 1

Day 1

1

Bored with my sedentary, monotonous life, I said to myself one day, "Let's go, sir! Let's go traveling!"

"What, where, how?" I replied, lying on my large divan, and deep in thought I took a puff on my *dübek*. "We need money!"

"You need a head; you need determination and imagination. Believe me, with this we can satisfy our curiosity; without leaving the spot, we shall be everywhere and learn everything. The difference between us and other travelers will be insignificant: They are eyewitnesses, but you are a clairvoyant. What's the use of seeing everything and doubting everything, like Pyrrho and his followers? Isn't it better to see nothing and doubt nothing?"

2

Firmly resolving is half the work, as the proverb goes. I have firmly resolved to travel around the world and farther, if possible. And now, because of my firm resolution, half the world is already covered: the half of the world that is empty and unremarkable, where I simply will not set foot. This only proves that all proverbs are witty and just.

3

Kindly stand up, take Europe by its ends, and spread it out on a table. Now sit down! There it is—Europe! But don't look at the entire enlightened part of the land all at once. Occupying your eyes, ears, or thoughts with several objects at the same time is terribly harmful to the mental faculties.

4

Now as a foreigner I peer
Into the world of love's delight,
First I admire a rosy cheer
Then marvel at a visage white,
Now I observe the whole creation,
Then take into consideration
Of beauty's whole a single trait,
Then plunge into a dreamy state
And scrutinize the earthly ball
With a triangle set in space,
And you, my reader, like a thrall,
Will follow in my wandering race!

5

So, here's Europe! You've covered Podolia with your elbow. . . . Chase that fly away! . . . Here's Tulchin. From here we shall go to known places, places where we spent the winged time of our life. Go over to the Mogilyov gate!—Listen! Just in time, the post bell outside has begun to ring . . . The whip has cracked; farewell, my friends! *Audaces fortuna juvat!*

6

Instead of a Preface

I am not traveling so that you may read the account of my journey, but if it has already fallen into your hands and you are determined to follow my tracks, from the very point of my departure to my safe return, then upon my arrival in Nubia I will declare to you the purpose of my journey and why I wrote about it; in the meantime I advise you to read *Great Events from Little Causes.* But if you aren't interested in learning how salt was discovered and came into use, then don't read that book—knowing the title is enough.

It is well known to every lover of reading how unbearable any sort of preface is, especially when Mr. Author, still unsure whether people will bother to read his book, begs for mercy and forgiveness and excuses the book's deficiencies by referring to the circumstances of his life. That's why I don't wish to continue this preface.

Although my writing will be unclear in many places, I will by no means agree to explain the true meaning of certain random expressions that will appear along my route like inscrutable meteors of my errant imagination.

Until Hercules finds some means to cross the Atlantic Ocean, let it be written here: *Nec plus ultra!*

7

Coffee with glorious cream and a pipe should always serve as the conclusion to a breakfast before departure. With my morning coffee, I spread Finnish butter on white bread; sometimes it seems to fill not my stomach, but my soul.

We shall not stop at any station until we reach Mogilyov. Too late! My imagination has already rushed down the stone mountain, ridden heedlessly past the city, customs, and quarantine, and crossed the Dniester without moving the ferry from its spot. What speed! Where did those hundred and ten versts go?

8

"Haste bears the semblance of fear; a little slowness has the look of confidence," writes Tacitus, and therefore one should travel more slowly, someone will say. Not so, say I, continuing on my way at the full speed of my imagination. But now my mind has settled to rest upon a little circle on the Dniester, above which the name *Ataki* is engraved. While you walk around the town and a certain portion of the past, I, with your permission, shall read something from a notebook that fell from the shelf right into the Arctic Ocean.

The title is torn off, and there is no beginning, but it seems to consist of diary notes, written in the style of Nostradamus's prophecies. For example:

Apr. 20 Who saw that fair lady and me
When we uttered tearful goodbyes?
Who felt our love's fire burning free
And heard our sad kisses and sighs?
O friend! Never trouble your heart
With tears or a glance all aglow;
Love's kiss is a poisoning slow,
Which lingers since we split apart!

A similar thing may happen to someone not on the twentieth of April, 1822, but on the first, fourth, eighth, or twentieth of May, 1922, and therefore all these words, which were written a long time ago and will come true in the next century, may be regarded as a miraculous prediction.

9

But you are in a hurry to go farther. From Ataki on the Dniester, past the village of Mereshovka, to the mountain, through Oknitsa, to the town of Brichany; from Brichany another fifty versts, and we are in Khotin.

10

Look at this map, as you are able,
Here's Bessarabia, here's the world!
For nigh ten years in it I've twirled—
A ball upon a billiard table!
Only at times a fiendish sprite
Would knock me off, just out of spite!

11

But let us see what Khotin will tell us. The city commands a fortress, citadel, or castle. A ravine runs through the fortress, providing a pathway right up to its walls. The castle is ancient; it was built by the Genoese. Someone has written that this was the castle of the Greek princess Sophia.

The castle, the rocky bank of the Dniester, the sound of the waves, the path up the hill, the thick bushes, the garden, the platform on the slope, the decrepit gazebo—all this merges into a vision of romantic German antiquity.

On the inner walls of the gazebo, wandering knights have scribbled verses in honor of their Rosalinds, Idalides, Idas, and Salomes; they have scribbled memories, thoughts, and other things, e.g.:

> Love is always a mistake!
> Once I happened to partake . . .

The rest has been effaced.

12

But this seems to be enough for the first stage; isn't it time to find our night's lodging? The city is stuffy and dirty! Let's drop in instead at a village on the Dniester, for example, Nedoboutsy or Sharoutsy.

Since one must not judge the customs, the manners, the intelligence, or the abilities of the Moldavian people based on the best village of the Khotin *ținut*, I shall defer my description of them until the first *joc* I happen to see in the Orkhey *ținut*. Meanwhile I now have every right to prefer sleep to everything in the world and to sing:

> You secret sorcerer, O sleep!
> In silent Lethe you reside,
> You come unseen at night to keep
> Me tranquil and stay by my side.
> I love you, gift of languor sweet!
> I love your bed so full of cheer!
> Your irresistible deceit
> Is now the thing I hold most dear!
> I wait for you, do not delay!
> Bestrew me with all magic things,
> Entwine me in a sweet bouquet,
> And hold me in your downy wings!

13

No, I thought, I don't want to sleep, I will not sleep, I shall not sleep! The clock struck midnight. What a familiar hour! It used to mean the same to me as the matin bell does to Arina Makaryevna. Crossing myself, I set off and . . . strolled along the bank of the Dniester. Do you remember?

> The lovely rose, in summer's heat
> Oppressed, inclines its scarlet head
> And luscious stem to grassy bed
> Seeking alleviation sweet,
> Then drunk, with fragrant dew replete,
> It lies, its little leaves thrust open . . .

The subsequent words in the manuscript have been effaced, just as some of Sappho's odes have been effaced on the Parian Marble.

14

To lie down, wait for sleep, and not fall asleep is terrible! . . . She has rushed through my imagination! . . . She seems to have touched my whole being! . . . She has burned me! . . . Ah, an apparition, an apparition!

> Oh, she is blushing and appealing,
> With life and playfulness ablaze,
> She captivates my every feeling
> In gauzy cloth of light and haze.
> I cannot sleep, my soul's in pain
> I wait for her, my heart burns on!
> But jealous men, do not complain—
> For I await the blushing dawn!

Day 2

15

The road had crushed me completely; I woke up about noon and felt a bit unwell. Whoever embarks on such a long journey is troubled by thoughts on the first night. "It's pleasant to travel!" he thinks, but when he comes back to his native country, he is like a shipwrecked man returning to shore. Thus Don Juan, leaving on his journey, could not take his sorrowful eyes off the coast of Spain. Departure is a bitter lesson. It resembles the feeling that entire nations have when going to war. An unaccountable agitation troubles us; our hearts are struck with an unexpected blow. No matter how disagreeable the people and places we left, we cannot look back without emotion at the bell tower looming over the magnificent houses of the city or the peasant huts of the village. I would have felt the same about Saint Dominic's Church, had I been born in Tulchin and been of the Catholic faith, but alas, it made no impression on me, nor did the sermon of the Dominican father, full of appeals to the devout listeners that they should hearken to the truth, keep their eyes from wandering, and let no stray thoughts distract them. "Papa! A teacher told me that the truth lies at the bottom of a well?" "Yes, my friend, *at the bottom of a well, filed away in a long box.*"

16

I wish . . . my journey will bring me glory . . . etc.

Day 3

17

"Time to get up, my dear Alexander, it's almost ten!"

"No, I'll wait a bit; it would be a shame to leave my bed and book . . ."

"What book is it?"

"*The Travels of Anacharsis.* The esteemed author, Abbé Barthélemy, also journeyed across maps and books, traveled all over Greece, and visited remote antiquity."

O tranquil travel! Whither can you not go with a winged imagination?

18

To make a useful journey across the Arctic and Antarctic hemispheres of the globe that represents the earth, one must keep a detailed inventory of all the objects that catch one's eye, for example:

N.B. An example was here, but I erased half of it and scratched out the other half. I did not like how ordinary it was; similar examples, however, can always be found in old calendars, accounts, reports, notes, and memorandum books.

19

Here it would not be improper to warn the reader that he should not expect pure, sonorous diction and exquisite beauty from me. My friend, please copy out this page; these are the words of Aristotle, Dionysius of Halicarnassus, Quintilian, Cicero, and other learned men:

"How unpleasant it is to see a venerable author who degrades himself in pursuit of sonorous style, reduces his art to achieve dignity and elegance of expression, laboriously subordinates his thoughts to his words, avoids the hiatus of vowels with childish affectation, rounds off his periods, and balances his phrases with paltry expressions and misplaced ornaments."

20

If with my work you're not besotted
Still read it once, before you go.
My book has spots, but even so
The sun is similarly spotted.

That was a scrap of one of the ordinary prefaces.

Now we can go further; we're going, going! and here, we have . . . a map. From Khotin to Kishinev, via the Dniester, a road along a steep bank, in some places narrow and dangerous, but our carriage can go anywhere.

21

Without stopping at Nagoryany, Molodovo, Korman, Vasilevka, Verezhany, etc., where the surroundings are sweet, beautiful, and close to the native's heart, but far from my circumstances and affections, I rush on. Let's ride past Ataki, or else you won't be able to make me leave for two months. There's nothing worse than reopening proceedings on an old case!

The sunset now is all aglow,
The woods grow dark . . . alone, we two . . .
The monastery's lamps are low . . .
Let's go! For rumors most untrue
Will cause your modesty to blush;
Guilt on the innocent will rush!

What's this monastery called again? . . . Have you forgotten? What a shame—it's not indicated on the map.

22

The banks of the Dniester are beautiful, steep, rocky, and covered with trees and shrubs, but their uniformity has bored us enough. We will not go into their twists and turns.

This is the ancient Olchionia, which was later Sokol, and finally Soroki. A small Genoese castle, like the ones on coats of arms—that's the only interesting thing in the town of Soroki. Across the Dniester is the city of Tsekinovka, which also is not remarkable in any way.

A few dozen more versts down the Dniester, you will see a beautiful, charming house on the left bank; after it you will see the slope of the bank, regularly dotted with vineyards; then, amid clumps of fruit trees and poplars, there is an arbor; sandy paths stretch to and fro. At the mouth of a ravine flowing down stands a town. This is the Kamenka of Field Marshal Count Wittgenstein, the hero and darling of Russia. This is paradise! A family of angels! "C'est un Dieu consolateur laissé au milieu de ses enfants pour y être une image vivante du Dieu qu'ils adorent," says Lacépède.

23

It is frightening to ride along the bank of the Dniester from the village of Chorna to Sakharna; for several versts the road traverses a rocky slope covered with bushes. The road is so narrow that if you imagined two carriages riding toward each other, the whole mental activity of your brain would suddenly stop, like the Mongols before the Great Wall of China.

24

The popular conveyances in Moldavia are called *căruțe*, of which there are two kinds: horse-drawn and ox-drawn. The former are as small as toys, but the latter are no joke—they are so large that two of them coming together could block not only the ordinary road, but also the road to Tartarus, of which I shall give a particular description later, because Milton and Dante did not provide the route made by Orpheus.

25

When dinnertime comes round and the table is set, a person usually forgets his passions and responsibilities with impunity; at this moment, no one is allowed to reproach him for his indifference to anything unrelated to satisfying his hunger.

I, too, will bring an offering! For hunger, a portion of a calf and the fruits of the earth; for thirst, a drink from the vine!

Every writer should anticipate his readers by having dinner, lest they should not comprehend him, since a well-fed man cannot understand a hungry one.

Leaving my reader on the road, where it is somewhat dangerous and tiresome for him to stand, I shall excuse myself by imparting to him the words of M. Chénier, who said that every person needs indulgence.

26

In early 1828, after a full meal, I was going to sit down and look at a map, but my eyes began to look askance at Turkey, and I fell asleep.

> So listen now to what I dreamed:
> I flew on horseback, so it seemed,
> With fearsome soldiers all around.
> I trampled, slashed, and cut my foes;
> And charging right between their rows,
> With heads and limbs I strewed the ground.
> But suddenly, in armor bright,
> A daring warrior rose to fight,
> I dealt him first a heavy blow,
> Which he resisted, to my woe:
> He flashed his steel with sudden might,
> And sent my severed head in flight!
> I felt my poor soul flit away,
> My very blood turned cold and gray,
> And over me Death spread his cloak!
> I died . . . and gasped, and then awoke!
> And like a madman, in a daze,
> I groped and fumbled in the haze,

I found my head and grabbed it tight,
Then crossed myself in pure delight:
In sleep I'd sunk in death's despair,
But woke to find my head still there!

I would say something here about Turkish horsemen and about how during a war—even a war with the Turks—one needs a good horse, a good saber, a trusty pistol, a keen eye, a steady hand, a fearless soul, and other similar trifles, but Montecuccoli has already hinted at this; therefore I shall turn to what no one has ever suggested, or barely suggested. But is there such a thing in the world? . . . It's only a joke! In the hands of a writer, all words, ideas, and thoughts are like the multicolored pebbles of a kaleidoscope. Every person will take the same thing and turn it over in his own way; a different figure will emerge—and he will be happy, since he will imagine he thought it up himself.

Poor world, everything in you is so old! How many years the sun has chased the earth! There's Platonic love! There's loyalty! What if the earth in its old age should veer from its true course? . . . Humanity would fall from the fiery embrace of the sun!

27

Here, by the way or not by the way, for reasons known to me or for no reason at all, only on a whim—which often happens in the world—I am obliged, or at any rate I should like, to note the following:

1. Alexander the Great, according to all Oriental writers, is called Eskander, or Iskender.

2. According to the same traditions, Alexander is not fully recognized as the son of Philip. Some believe him to be the son of Darab (Darius), who was married to the daughter of Philip. Abul-Faraj and Sa'id ibn Batriq think that Alexander's father was Nectanet, king of Egypt, and some Greek writers say that Nestabanus, a Persian magician, knew Olympias.

3. According to Justin, Philip never recognized Alexander as his own son and confirmed this on his deathbed, after Olympias confessed that she had taken the fruit in question from a dragon.

That's all I wanted to say today.

28

Directing my steps toward my bedroom, I thought: Probably everyone wants to know my reason for writing all this?

The legitimate reason is my will; a secondary reason will be explained in due course. Which is all quite natural.

Day 4

29

What can be better than a detailed, accurate map? For an army commander, to make strategic considerations; for a general staff officer, to decide on the deployment of troops; and for me—to make a peaceful, scholarly journey. I love to take in with one glance the arena where I was, am, and will be!

Having thus expressed my involuntary pleasure in viewing the entire part of the world that is subject to man, I board my boat and float down the Dniester . . .

30

What a terrible bank I see at the turn—a cliff hanging over the river! But what are those dark holes at the very top? I'll satisfy your curiosity, though Horace told us to avoid curious people, as they are indiscreet. Let's go up the hill along the stony road. Catch your breath! . . . Well, farther on there's a path through the garden. The Dniester is meandering like a brook beneath us. We're now at the top of the rock that terrified us down below. Climb carefully down this ladder carved into the rock. Hold on to the railing! Don't look down, or else you'll get dizzy, and, God forbid, you'll go straight down to the source of strength, as the author of *Metamechanics* says.

31

Do you see? . . . Oh, how careless . . . what a terrible flood in Spain and France! . . . That's what happens when you put a glass of water on a map! . . . But I never imagined I'd knock it down from the Pyrenees with my elbow!

In the same way, perhaps—I said with a profound sigh, as profound as my respect for Chaldean traditions—in the same way, the vessel of Cronus's wrath was overturned and the Ocean Sea spilled onto the earth!

The years of nature's infancy flow by;
Contention seethes among the tribes primeval;
The vaults of heaven rage, and waters high
Drown tribes and send the earth into upheaval.
O sun! Upon that horror shone you not,
You cast away the brilliance of your rays!
In sable clouds of sorrow you were caught—
Sorrow for men's and nature's final days.
But now Elaim's thunderous voice is still!
The sunbeams penetrate the sea once dark;
Above the waves is seen Karkura's hill;
And to the earth's first harbor sails the ark!

Everything suffered from the deluge, everything perished; only the innocent fish swam cold-bloodedly in the endless ocean and imagined: Look, the eternal reign of fish has arrived!

Here it is very relevant and necessary to add the following:

. . . and Cronus told Xisuthrus: take down a record about the beginning, continuation, and end of all things, bury it in the city of the sun, Sisparis . . . build an ark, cast yourself into the sea . . . travel to the abode of the gods! . . . And Xisuthrus built an ark five stadia long and two wide and headed at Cronus's command toward the abode of the gods; but probably, being a poor pilot, he lost his way and ran aground on the mountains of Armenia, which, according to the Chaldean traditions, were called Karkura.

32

How unpleasant it is for the curious reader to return from Armenia to Bessarabia, but what can I do? As is my duty, to maintain the general order of things, I shall take him back anyway and, like an eagle carrying a lamb, bring him to the steps in the rock that lead to the Gorodishche Monastery. Here, a board is laid from one projecting stone to another; this is the entrance to an old church hewn into the rock. Thence we descend onto a stone platform. A monk meets us and leads us to the holes that looked to us like the burrows of wild birds. These are the monks' cells. The entire rock, hanging over the Dniester, is the Gorodishche Monastery. The newly carved church consists of three sections. It fits no more than thirty worshippers. Holy thoughts clothe the soul in this peaceful abode. As J.-J. Rousseau said, "The neglect of religion leads a man to the neglect of all duties"!

The Moldavian monk led us through various openings into a rather extensive cave; the outer wall was made of oak planks with rifle holes. "It was a defense against the Tatars," he said, in Moldavian, of course. "And what's this?" "A cannon." "Its length is quite unusual!" After turning it in my hands, I respectfully placed the rusty antique back on the ground. Everyone will agree that it is easier for me to view in one glance the whole universe and the flow of all the worlds that constitute it (I mean in some illustration of the solar system) than to pick up a cannon, but at the time of Stephen the Great, all Moldavian *muscali*, that is soldiers, were armed with cannons, that is rifles.

33

Since a guide is hardly ever necessary on a return trip—I experienced this with the splendid Moldavian chief guide Nicolae Popovici in the last Turkish war—well then . . . but here I must say that this was a well-known character in the army. First, what a portly creature! And second, what an efficient man! Sometimes when the captain of the guides rode next to him, they were like body and soul riding together, and behind them flowed the entire Russian army like the great Ocean Sea!

So a guide is not needed on a return trip. The reader will manage, as he wants and wishes, to leave the Gorodishche Monastery, go up the stone steps, and travel farther, on an invisible stairway or the wings of imagination, to the lands that were promised to the East: Eden and Eiren. For my part I am going to Kishinev and am impatient to go, though as Mademoiselle de Scudéry said, life is so short that being impatient isn't worthwhile.

34

To Kishinev! Here I'm using my compass to measure distances on this plane of paper, with a scale of five versts to one English inch, along the straight road through the villages of Lalovo, Stodolna, Lopatna, Upper, Middle, and Lower Zhora, through Susleny and other settlements not marked on the map, to the town of Orkhey, which lies on the River Reut and which can be passed over without any attention. In this way we have already covered forty versts. Another forty and we shall be in the prosperous city of Kishinev. But since the road goes across a mountain ridge and through a large forest, and since travelers sometimes—though very rarely—encounter mischief there, without further ado I measure forty versts with my compass and with a single step I make a journey that would cost others four hours of travel, with all the foreseen and unforeseen dangers and difficulties. The preceding words, with the weight that I have given them, include damage to the wheels and axles, carriages getting stuck in the mud, horses stopping, and various niggling accidents that exhaust the patience of travelers who have not read the twentieth ode of Horace and do not know that patience alleviates the most intolerable calamities.

Let us pause on this mountain. Here is the city on the rock, there is the Byk, but instead of dwelling on it, let's ride on! Let no one think I'm talking about a *byk* (bull) lying in the road that won't stand up—not at all. From the science called geography we know, among other things, that in Bessarabia there is a river Byk flowing through the city of Kishinev.

The first time I arrived in Kishinev I could have said a great deal about it, but now passing through it for perhaps the last time, I would not say a word—if not for the fact that for us the past often takes the place of the present.

35

"What is the present time?" someone will ask me. The present is food for the heart, the senses, and the mind. We humbly beg for and take what God sends us! . . . And what delicious meat! . . .

36

Following this in my manuscript was a statement of my dinner expenses on the twenty-fifth of July, 1830, but I won't include it, as it is already a thing of the past—though it's never bad to look back at your past expenses. Like a full purse, we too become worn out and exhausted, and after expending ourselves over many years on grief, sensual pleasures, sicknesses, and the like, we are left with a dry, barren land—and nothing more.

When will the dew descend once more
On flowers withered in the sun?
Will it be when the heavens, one
With earth, unveil their mystic lore?
For three full years, I lived carefree,
Without concern or hope, until
A fleshless spirit carried me,
Unceasingly, despite my will,
Through feelings, passions, and desires,
From deep abyss to heaven's height,
From heavenly to earthly fires.
Through every day and every night,
And I myself was that same sprite!

Here, a clever person will have guessed that the day has ended and that we have arrived at our stop for the night, though he still does not know where we have stopped.

Day 5

37

If I were married—or rather, if I had a sweet, pretty, and kind wife—I would not for the world be long separated from her or travel otherwise than how I do now—that is, without leaving my comfortable divan. Here is why: Among my old papers I found a memorandum book that contained the following conclusion: "after a long absence, forgetfulness meets an unexpected return with a look of hatred."

> When Troy was conquered, Greeks victorious,
> Chiefs, mighty kings, and heroes glorious,
> For ten years through the world did roam,
> But coldly were received at home.
> Returning to his native land,
> Even Agamemnon, it is said,
> Came back to find his throne and bed
> Under another man's command.

However, this means nothing. Agamemnon was a great military leader but a poor husband. Ten years! Good God, I shouldn't have the patience! He never went on leave! Never sent any news, and when was that? 1,184 years before Christ. Among enlightened Christians like us, only seven years of absence without news is enough to break the matrimonial bonds; the wife is free to give her hand, heart, and all movable and immovable property to another, and rightly so, and by law! Don't abandon your wife!

38

It is wonderful to get married.

In bliss domestic I would float:
A wife and family—paradise!
Though with a husband and a wife,
The devil often rocks the boat!

This also means nothing: Deficiencies or excesses of a moral nature may be corrected in one way or another; but apart from that, marriage sometimes has quite material disadvantages. Suppose that you contain within yourself the weight or gravity of a one and your partner is as light as a zero. If she is on your left side, then it does not matter—you won't become heavier because of it; but if this zero stands on the right side—that is, if she is united with you according to mathematical and civil laws—then just imagine: it will be ten times harder for you to move from the spot and your needs will increase tenfold. Is this not true? That's what it means to get married, and you thought that you + her = two? No!

A man in military life,
A company officer on campaign
With his incomparable wife
And his two children to maintain,
Replete with honors and self-worth—
This type always excites my mirth!

His orderly, Luká by name,
Is drunk and merry in the morning,
But does his duties all the same;
He woos the maid, his own wife scorning,
Goes to the kitchen, food provides,
Then uncomplaining, in the stable
His master's horse he grooms and chides—
A servant trustworthy and able!

I'm glad to praise this wedded fate;
This lovely pair is quite content,
Especially when they're intent

On safeguarding their peaceful state—
Luká's the one they both berate.

They live in bliss and truth excelling!
All's portable within their dwelling:
The table, looking-glass, and chair,
The samovar and pan and ladle,
And even a folding little cradle;
Cupid himself would slumber there,
That cheeky boy who causes strife,
If he heard this song from the wife:
"Now lullay, lullaby, my dear,
Sleep softly, for mama is near!"

Though help is scarce, she does her best;
She cooks and cleans without a flaw;
She feeds the baby from her breast
And teaches him to say "mama"!

I envy any fellow, therefore,
Who's tied the nuptial knot with ease,
Who has a tender wife to please
And a beloved child to care for!

How oft, when service wearies me,
Desires like these deluge my life!
I think that I as well could be,
A husband to a loving wife—
But this idea's beyond my scope;
I dare not cherish it with hope.

39

If I lost just one day by talking too much about things that don't relate to me—if I lost just one day for nothing, it would be excusable, though the Emperor Titus repeated almost every day: "Amici, diem perdidi!"

40

"Do you know what?" my friend suddenly cried on entering my house. "What?" "Do you know what I heard?" "What?"

"That you are terribly in love!"
  "I swoon!"
"And soon, according to the rumor . . ."
  "Yes, soon!"
"But love's a curse, please do not *rush* in . . ."
  "A curse? . . ."
"The more we prolong this discussion . . ."
  "The worse!"

I cried out, curled my hair, inspected myself in the mirror, straightened my tie, sprinkled perfume on a handkerchief, and left my friend in the dark as to what had happened to me.

41

I was hurrying, and not for nothing, my reader-friends. The evening was racing on. How nice, how pleasant are unexpected, secret pleasures! Just imagine—I was in the kind of cheerful mood in which people in love very, very rarely are. I even decided to sing. For the curious I shall sing through the first and last couplets again.

I

Do open up, my gentle friend!
Tell me the cause of your despair!
Do you, with passion tortured, spend
Your days, like me, in hopeless care?

V

For you will learn love has a price,
And a reward, since for one heart
Only another will suffice,
And for his love, your love impart!

***

Reader, now I cannot keep
Speaking in this subtle way.
I must rush, with pleasant sleep
To conclude my pleasant day.
Paradise I do not need—
Downy bedding suits me well.
Sing me songs, O Lado, Did!
Pamper me, O winged Lel!

Your sweet sounds will travel down,
My impassioned soul to calm,
And my sentiments will drown
In sleep, the all-assuaging balm.

Days 6 and 7

42

Lucullus was just about to join battle with Tigranes when it was reported to him that according to the omens the day was unlucky. "So much the better," he said. "We shall make it lucky through our victory."

A hare ran across the road in front of me. "It's a good sign," I thought as I approached the city. "It's a good sign! Hares must be plentiful here!"—and I rode into Kishinev.

Reason says, "Go ahead!" and prejudice says, "Turn back!" What is prejudice in the face of reason? Prejudice, ladies and gentlemen, is a stone that one stupid person has thrown into the water and ten smart people have not managed to pull out.

43

Thus, word by word, step by step, we made our way at night through the muddy streets of Kishinev. Knowing no one in town, I judged it best to make my way to a roadside inn. "Take me to an inn!" I cried. "*Nu știu!*" answered the *surugiu*. "To a *traktir*!" "*La care fartir?*" "All right, Lakar's then!" "*Nu știu!*" answered the *surugiu*. "Stop, you damned Nu știu!"

Some houses were still lit up; I caught the whiff of Jews. "A factor!" I called out. The response "Factor? Factor?" rang out on all sides. Doors flew open in all the houses, and suddenly, as if by magic, Jews rained down on me. "You want a factor? You need a tavern?" "Yes!" "To Isaevna's, your honor! No better inn in all of Kishinev." "To Golda's, your honor!" cried another group. "Whatever's closer, Golda's or Isaevna's; I don't care!" "Isaevna's is closer!" "Don't believe them! Golda's is closer!" "Not true, not true!" sounded on all sides. Some shouted, "Go left!" others, "Go right!"

Finally both sides in one voice cried, "Here! Go right! Go left!" And I saw that the Jews were pulling the left horse into the gate on the left and the right horse into the gate on the right, from which I immediately concluded that Isaevna and Golda live right next to each other. But the fat Jewess on the left forestalled the fat Jewess on the right by affectionately inviting me into the room, and so I entered Isaevna's domain. They took the things in, and the Jews dispersed like a fog. Out on the street nothing was perceptible now except the lingering Hebrew vapor. The cocks sang out midnight; the dog in the yard yawned for the last time. I stretched out—and fell asleep.

Since dreams are nothing more than insomnia of the imagination, I did not dream, for my imagination had settled down to rest along with me.

44

The day had already held sway in our hemisphere for more than six hours by the time I awoke. As soon as I had dressed, a crowd of Jews flowed into my room with merchandise. "What do you want, damn you?" "Perhaps *you* want something?" they replied all at once. "We have scarves, pomade, perfume! Will you buy some? Towels, napkins, knives! Take a look, if you please!" "Out, you locusts! Go to the devil!" "But where does the devil live?" was the clever Jewish reply. "Hey, take them to the devil!" Without waiting for this guide, the Jews all set off down the road, and all was quiet.

45

The acoustics, or phonics, of the Jewish dialect struck me. There is something original in the pronunciation that could only be imitated with a certain instrument; but this attempt would be in vain, because the *abub,* that ancient instrument that once expressed the Hebrew melody and was kept in the sanctuary of Solomon's Temple, perished with the destruction of the Temple. To devise such an instrument is quite difficult, for the scholarly opinions about its properties are as varied as they generally are about any ancient relic that survives only in name. Kircher in his *Musurgia* says it was an instrument like a trumpet; Calmet concludes that the abub was the same as the *ambubaia*, a pipe previously in use among the Latins; according to the Talmud, the abub was a small horn; and according to others the abub was a cane that made a more pleasant sound on the drum than ordinary drumsticks.

This is very interesting for every lover of pleasant sounds or melodies of expression, especially when they issue from a lovely woman's lips; but this is a special article, which should be included in a chapter *on the harmony of the universe and the choir of genii who carry a righteous soul into heaven.* This is all interesting, but I am already dressed and must hasten to inspect Kishinev.

46

The first step outside in an unknown city is a difficult moment, when a person looks in all directions and usually, after a short or long deliberation, walks inadvertently in the direction where more people are heading.

The first things that struck my eye were the taverns and little sundry shops: in almost every house on the windowsills stood bottles of wine and vodka, and on the wide sliding shutters hung tobacco, sulfur, nails, bullets, rope, *meşti*, *cuşme*, pipes, *caşcaval*, oil . . . "Lord!" I thought. "Here everyone's a seller; where then do the buyers live?" "*Plăcinte, plăcinte!*" a wild voice suddenly called out behind me. "You're a *plăcintă*, damn you!" And exactly: a Moldavian with a toasted face like a piecrust, greasy like a pancake, was carrying a hotcake on a copper pan and crying, "*Plăcinte, plăcinte!*" This is a breakfast for passersby.

47

I came across countless carriages; here, for the most part, everyone drives in calashes, from the last *mazil* with a shaved beard to the first boyar with a long beard. But the Moldavian horses do not suit the Viennese carriages. Like the Tirynthian I burst out laughing when I saw two nags of the kind that usually draw water carts:

With stubborn strain, the jaded pair
Dragged on a Viennese calash;
A Gypsy in a gaudy dolman
Was driving them at plodding pace;
A fat Moldavian, a boyar,
Sat still, just like an ancient idol
Carved with an axe from oak,
Upon his head was a *căciulă*;
He smoothed his beard and thick mustache—
A heavy burden on the springs!
An Arnaut, wearing golden livery,
Stood reverently on the footboard
And held a long pipe in his hands.

Although I was walking slowly, I soon left this procession—a crossing from tedium into idleness—far behind. Having paid the necessary visit and introduced myself in proper form, I next went to the metropolitan church. The liturgy was performed by the metropolitan himself; his advanced age elevated the grandeur of the church rites.

48

The church was crowded; the women stood next to the left side of the choir. Looking at them, I thought, "Pretty!" but lowered my eyes, remembering, you're not in a temple of ancient idols, not a heathen sinner, who would stare at a young sinner praying and would surely have cried out:

Oh, how devout she is, how sweet!
Olympian Zeus, that god severe,
Hearing her sighs, would find it meet
To make her sins all disappear!—
Her shining tears, seen from above,
Would quite disarm the god of lightning;
Instead of bolts of thunder frightening,
He'd cast on her the flowers of love!—

49

Upon leaving the church I had every legal right to examine the worshippers, but a story about them without names would be a treatise on beauty and ugliness. I shall only say in general that the Moldavian *cucoane* and *cuconițe* are outwardly very similar to the Russian *gospozhy* and *baryshni*, the French *dames* and *demoiselles*, the Spanish *doñas*, the English ladies and misses, the German *Frauen* and *Fräulein*, and so on. Their eyes are black, quick, and watchful; their glances ask everyone: "Do you like me? Ah? What? You do? Aha! You've fallen for me!" And then suddenly, yet another sweet look, as if she is saying, "Don't be afraid of me—I'm not cruel."

But this is not the place to speak about the *cucoane* in a clear and detailed manner; besides, anyone who has lived in the world will never be able to speak clearly and in detail about women. I might also mention here that I have made it a rule to see only the best in women.

50

Returning home, I made sure to feed my stomach and sat down at the table intending, after dinner, to seek something for my heart as well. And this is very common. People mostly concern themselves with their stomach and heart, while their mind starves—it is like a dumb and armless beggar who cannot beg or stretch out his hands.

After dinner, I set off again through the streets. Everywhere I met Russians, Moldavians, Greeks, Serbs, Bulgarians, Turks, Jews, etc., but dared not ask them the question, "Why do the nations rage?"

Day 8

51

I suppose you noticed that two days slipped by in the course of the last day? If you didn't, that proves that you're either absent-minded or . . . The latter pleases me more. But time is vindictive—it will ensure that even I am forgotten! Onward!

52

Every learned traveler is bound to give clever and thorough answers to questions about the land he has measured by the breadth of his stride. Even so, if I write about Bessarabia, for example, that it lies between such and such degrees of latitude and longitude, that it borders on such and such states, forests, roads, etc., that it has such and such inhabitants, that it has so many *ținuturi*, or districts—it seems to me that with such a description I should be taking the bread out of the mouth of geography, which I do not wish to do. I shall just say that Bessarabia lies on the globe in the shape of a long female figure, leaning her head on a branch of the Carpathian Mountains and beckoning her native Moldavia into an embrace.

53

The history of a state, a whole entity, is as interesting and instructive as the life of a great man, but the history of a province, especially a province like Bessarabia, is as difficult to write as the history of a finger found after a battle. With all these difficulties, any survey will consist only of the following: "The finger is apparently great and good, though it has entirely lost its elasticity and firmness on account of its lifelessness. According to legends told by Strabo, Livy,

Quintus Curtius, and Ammianus Marcellinus, a similar finger belonged to the left hand of Attila, and it was a ring finger; but if we consult the Greek writers, it belonged to Decebalus in the second century, and being a *measly* little finger, it was employed in building the wall that separates Moesia from Peucinia."

Plutarch very wisely said in the *Life of Pericles* that "it is difficult, or rather impossible, to know and discern the truth in history," and Saint-Réal said even more intelligently that "it is enough to know what such and such historians think about the truth of events."

Had there been as little unanimity among the three hundred Spartans at Thermopylae as among the three hundred historians who have described the Battle of Marathon, Greece would have perished!

54

Deflecting the reader's attention and curiosity from particular and universal history, which in this century of conflict between Classicism and Romanticism is unnecessary, improper, and sometimes shameful to know, I walk down a street in Kishinev.

In ages past, so I surmise,
This common custom did arise:
If you should by a window stride
Of some fine house, then glance inside!
Our curiosity, 'tis true,
Can sometimes rich rewards produce,
A window open to the view
For flirting is a fine excuse.
Thus I, meandering at ease,
Directing glances left and right,
Beheld my darling; truly she's
No maiden, but an angel bright!
No closer did I come, but looking,
I doffed my hat, my mind unsure,
And if I'd been a swarthy Moor,
Then like a crayfish quickly cooking,
I would have turned from black to red;

But all things pass, just as they say!
Though you may clip, though you may shred
Its wings, love's time will fly away!

Oh, dear friend, love is such a wonderful feeling! Do you know what? For a man, love as tempting as a woman, and for a woman it as tempting as a man. Isn't that true?

55

Walking away from the window, I felt as if I were chained to something; the more I moved away, the more I felt a pang of regret, as if I had lost the best part of my being. I wanted to turn back, when suddenly I came across an old comrade. At first he swept me off to his lodgings, and then he took me to be introduced to a noble Moldavian boyar.

Everything in the house was in the luxurious European style. Passing through the hall, my ear was struck with the clapping of hands and loud imperious sounds: "*Iorghi, ciubuce!*" In the next room the master of the house was sitting in all his grandeur on the divan. As soon as we entered, he sat up, took off his fez, and grandly pronounced, "Your servant! *Poftim, şezi!*" and then repeated, "*Iorghi, ciubuce!*" Georgi, an Arnaut, gave pipes to us too. After lengthy greetings, my comrade and the host struck up a conversation. Out of politeness I attentively directed my gaze at the boyar and listened to his flowing speech; looking at me, he turned to my comrade and said, "*Moldoveneşte nu ştie?*" "*Nu ştie,*" answered my comrade. Thus ended his address to me. About the pleasantness of the Moldavian language I cannot say a word, though it always sounded to me as if the host were chopping oak logs and the chips were flying straight into my ears.

56

Since even patience has its limits, and since I was tired of listening to an incomprehensible conversation, I tossed and turned restlessly on the divan, twirled my hat, put on my gloves, stood up, walked about the room, looked out the window, nodded my head at my comrade, gave signals with my eyes but nothing helped! He sat as if chained to the spot. I was already . . . when suddenly the door opened, and a maiden entered.

> This was the boyar's daughter, surely,
> I bowed; she curtseyed, quite demurely,
> Said "*Bună seara!*" soft and warm.
> It seemed as if a sudden storm
> Was brewing in her youthful breast
> And bursting out! Her father said,
> "*Raluca, șezi!*" And she, still red
> With blushing, followed his behest.

57

My comrade did not think long; he concluded his conversation with the host somehow and sat down next to the daughter. A few French words encouraged me; being a gallant gentleman, I too gave my opinion about the weather; but our talk was soon broken off by our mutual consent that the day was beautiful and our conclusion that it was likely to rain because a cloud had rushed in and thunder was rumbling. Meanwhile, I noticed that my comrade's eyes had darkened, his mouth was oozing honey, his entire substance was in some sort of convulsive state and was beginning to express supreme bliss of the soul and an abundance of that sweet fire stolen by Prometheus from heaven. I knew that such a state was long-lasting and could make one forget not only one's comrade but everything in the world. The host of the house, having talked until he was tired, gave himself over completely to the sweetness of silence. Feeling somewhat superfluous, I left my host in the tobacco smoke, my comrade in the fumes of love, and the voluptuous Ralu in some indecision about whether it was better to answer each question with *yes* or *no*, although the words *yes* and *no* were invented by resolute people and for resolute people.

> But here's the problem I must stress:
> When to agreement one is stirred,
> When in the soul there burns a *yes*,
> One simply can't pronounce the word.

My friends, at times I've seen of late
Some charming women in this state.
For them compulsion is a pain;
Love is with myriad signs on show,
Its aspect is so clear and plain;
What need is there for *yes* and *no*?

58

It should be noted here that during the abovementioned adventures my faithful servant moved into the quarters assigned to me. I arrived out of breath at the housewarming, and approaching the front steps, I was already dreaming about how my clothes would fly off me and I would sink into the soft bed, like a drowned man in the waves. But who could have foreseen this new affliction? On the porch I met the mistress of the house—a young woman in a black dress, which adhered to her like springtime to nature. In response to my bow I received an affectionate greeting in French. She herself showed me to my rooms and then invited me into her own apartment.

59

Here I should begin the continued description in the form of some new poems:

The two of us were there . . .

I ought to begin in a different way and in the most modern style. However, I have no time now to continue the story, and the reader, if he is too curious, should know that he that hath a mouth should not always speak.

60

Although I sometimes write short poems, I cannot endure charades, especially the kind presented to the Comte de Lignolle. The best works, in my opinion, are *impromptus,* in which one can perceive true art and the sharp flight of genius. Everything that is well and cleverly made in the world was made *impromptu,* whether in creation, poetry, the art of war, or the unveiling of anything that was previously clothed in mystery.

Here is one of my impromptus:

> My speech was well received throughout;
> Therefore, I brought it to an end.
> "The game's not worth the candle, friend!"
> And so I snuffed the candles out.

Day 9

61

I could not sleep; ere dawn I rose,
By feeble candlelight I read
A chapter of the Alcoran,
Then sank into a death-like doze.
I slept till noon; my dream was sweet—
So marvelous, so deep, so clear:
A houri's shadow, soft and fleet,
Whispered that on my ninth day here
I must, at her behest, unveil
Muhammad's entertaining tale.

And so I did:

Muhammad, or Mohammed, or Mahomet, or Muhammad as before, was traveling on his Al-Buraq like me, without leaving the spot. What a quick and decisive imagination! Where was he not? Reading the book *Azar*, I was fascinated by the description of a journey to Eden. I like the seventh heaven best of all, and who would not like this blessed garden, with its ever-gushing fountains and ever-flowing rivers of milk, honey, and wine? There wondrous trees are always in bloom; there fruits turn into maidens so charming and sweet that if even one of them spat in the sea, the seawater would lose its bitterness! This is matchless, incomparable! But for all these pleasures, imagine also the angels there, with 70,000 mouths each, and each mouth has 70,000 tongues, and each tongue praises God 70,000 times a day in 70,000 different dialects. This is terrible! What a noise, what an outcry! No! It would be a misfortune to be in the Muhammadan Eden, despite the wonderful food and the ever-virgin houris. Do you remember how in the Caucasus the black raven tore at Prometheus's heart every day, and how it would heal by the next day just to be torn again? These things are all possible and understandable.

62

Having descended from the heights of Eden to the heights of the Caucasus, I still wish to cross over to the Arabian Mount Abarim, from whose brow I would gaze at my promised land, into which, across all known seas and abysses, I will bring my few thousand readers. May heaven send us manna and Zamzam on our way, may our path be lit by the moon and the sun, and may we be clothed in shining clothes of glory, girded with honor, and crowned with virtue!

63

But where, where is this promised land in which, after laying off the burden of life, I shall know true peace of mind, infinity of love, and sweetness of friendship? My chosen and only friend will meet me there. So, my dear old friend! Till we meet again I shall be a wanderer; only you can stop my flight and chain me to bliss!

64

. . . . . I love her . . . .
. . . . she loves . .
me! . . . .
. . . . "What?" "Nothing more."

Day 10

65

I spent the morning and afternoon putting my lodgings in order. The table under the mirror was covered with a clean white cloth and my entire *nécessaire* was laid out on it: pomade, perfume, hair-brushes, toothbrushes, nailbrushes, big combs, little combs, tiny combs, *savon à la mousseline*, barber's razors, *cuir de Pradier*, *pâte d'amande*, *pâte minérale*, knives, scissors, a double-faced mirror, etc. The table near the divan was covered with a green cloth, and on it were set, according to their ranks, my books, papers, ink pot, and pens. Having laid everything out, I lay on the divan and mentally admired the orderly arrangement, the apartment, and the mistress herself, who was on the porch and visible through the window. Toward evening my amorous friend came to me.

I

What's wrong? You bear a pall
Of worry. What a graveyard mood!

HE

God knows! I'm not myself at all,
I cannot think of sleep or food!

I

I don't see how I can assist you;
My friend, Raluca has bewitched you!
The dear!

HE

You're joking!

I

No I'm not!
I find her beautiful and kind;
I too could easily be caught
Within her spell, and lose my mind!

HE

So fresh!

I

A wonder!

HE

Eyes so bright!
Have you beheld their radiant glow?

I

Of course! Though it was almost night,
We had no candles with us, no—
No need!

HE

You liar!

I

No, 'twas so!

HE

Enough! You funny man, you grinner!
You haven't felt this sacred love!

I

I haven't? Only God above
Knows who in this is more a sinner!

66

During all this talk we headed toward the Kishinev garden. In less than a quarter of an hour we had arrived. A great many people were strolling about. In the crowd I sought the angel I had seen through the window, but in vain; the lovely vision, like a bright meteor, had flashed by and disappeared forever! Many people were strolling: ladies, girls—my little dears! Who is this darling looking coquettishly at us?

How could she not be a coquette?
She's burdened with a fiery streak!
But scant affection does she get
From her own husband, old and weak.
She finds the ancient stories comical:
From them no pleasure will she reap;
And love that's purely economical
Just causes her to fall asleep!
"And who is that?"
"Matilda."
"Wondrous!"
"And this one?"
"Mashenka."
"A dear!"
"And this one?"
"Pulkheritsa."
"Splendid!"
"And this one?"
"Sashenka."
"A flame!"
"And she?"
"I know not."
"Raphael!
Behold this marvelous creation!

Give me your lightness, Azael!
I'll fly to her in admiration!
What is her chosen destination?
Is she not bound in heaven to dwell?"

67

What happened next, my reader-friend,
I cannot say or comprehend!
My dream was wonderful and bright,
My dream was dreadful, black as night.
I knew true love; I knew the *one*!
She was a goddess manifest!
But where is *she*? Where did the sun
Of all my joy go down to rest?
M——, spirit dear and true!
My eyes and ears are charmed by you!
Let me perceive your passing flight,
Let me behold your spectral light,
Let my devotion be complete!
If life's a dream, then sleep is sweet!

Perhaps premature death is a blessing sent from heaven.

Day 11

68

Enough about Kishinev. I have already said everything about it I wanted to say. I only forgot to inform hunters that near Kishinev there was once a putrid lake where I used to go out of boredom to shoot snipe, wild ducks, and geese. Now this lake has been drained to purify the air. The fowl that inhabited it moved farther to the south, to Budzhak, and also to the Dniester estuary, to the lakes Yalpukh, Kagul, Sasik, etc., and to the lower, swampy part of the river Prut. The native winged inhabitants of these waters—pelicans, swans, and coastal herons—received the immigrants with open wings. During their flight to their new home across the Budzhak steppes, a certain Historian-Goose described in some detail the nomadic camps of great bustards, little bustards, partridges, and black grouse; the merry gypsy life of the cranes; and the dance of their watchful sentinels, who stand on one leg and hold stones instead of guns in the other. He also described the strange custom of the storks, or black rumps, who build their huge nests on village churches and huts and whose children, upon the completion of their education, are sent at a known time to unknown countries. Moreover, he enumerated all the kinds of sandpipers, coots, water hens, and bitterns that he saw on the rivers and the ponds. All these descriptions are very interesting, especially since the Historian-Goose examined in detail these birds' customs, habits, and language.

The fish—the stinking crucian carp that inhabited the lake—having no means of resettlement, fell victim to the fishermen; the frogs, however, survive to this day, though in closer confines, in the canal that was constructed there.

69

Thus, having said everything about Kishinev—everything that is not too entertaining—I arouse a desire in the curious reader to visit Kishinev in person and see the former Supreme Court building, which needs repair; the ruins of Dibuglu's house; Krupensky's ancient castle with its storied past; the metropolitan church; the Field of Mars; Malina, etc.

70

While preparing for the journey, I must also inspect my imagination. A horse like this must be caressed, groomed, and tended, fed with the brain and watered with lifeblood. But then, as soon as your foot is in the stirrup . . . it spreads its wings . . . kicks the present with its hind legs . . . and look, it's already in the future or the past, at one pole or the other, in the sky or under the earth, everywhere and nowhere! A wondrous horse!

71

Let's go, my beloved people! Arm yourselves with patience for the long road through the Getic wilderness!

Godspeed! . . . The whip begins to crack
Upon the swift, intrepid horse . . .
But wait! The mistress calls me back;
She wants to say goodbye, of course!

"Farewell, my dear and honored guest!
You set out on a journey long!
This amulet put on your chest;
This talisman will make you strong,
By Calypsița you are blessed.
And don't forget me!" "I could never!"
"Remember me, or I will cry!
And if, dear lodger, you should ever
Have the occasion, please stop by!"
"I shall return!" "Well then, goodbye!"

As Mentor, in his wisdom, threw
Telemachus into the brine,
So now my Mentor flings me, too,
And plants me on this mount of mine!
And now I'm off . . .

72

From Kishinev down the Byk Valley, across the bridge by the village of Bulbok, up a high mountain, then following the ridge, then a long descent . . . and here for several versts the timeworn stone walls and towers of Tighina may be seen. The Dniester winds below, like the Tempter himself, through a broad valley, between gardens and woods, and beneath steep mountains. Beyond the river lie the village of Parcani and the quarantine station, then the city of Tiraspol, and still farther the walls of Kherson. What a picture this is! How far a man can see if his eyes are sharp and everything lies open before him!

73

Here, three versts up the Dniester from Bender, lies even now the village of Varnița. Here the son of the foremost *drabant* in the world, the great fugitive from the Battle of Poltava, who never drank strong drink and was never sober—here, I say, in 1713, if anyone remembers, the northern corporal, Charles XII, turned his *Exerzierhaus* into a fortress, and with a handful of Swedes opposed the entire Bender garrison. Here he fights *pro aris et focis*! In this unparalleled battle he loses part of his ear but none of his courage, nor his hope of defeating the twenty thousand Tatars and six thousand Turks besieging him. "Brave Swedes, my friends! Carry the stores of powder and bullets into our citadel—into the chancellery!" he cries and tries to extinguish his burning fortress with a barrel of brandy. Victory is almost within his grasp; Rosen has been promoted to colonel on the battlefield, but—O cursed jackboots with your long spurs! You have caused the fall of a hero!

74

I end my day, letting my followers reflect on the vicissitudes of fate and the oddities of man, and I lean back wearily on my couch.

"Here," says Byron, "here noisy joy subsides, here sorrow summons sleep, the sweet forgetfulness of life, the last refuge from adversity for the unfortunate man! Here lie the rebellious hopes of passions, the cares of treachery, and the calculations of restless ambition. Oblivion wraps everything in its wings, and existence seems buried alive in a tomb!"

Rest, rest, dreamer! Tomorrow new forces will lend wings to your pride; tomorrow you will cast your eye once more on nature and say, "It is all mine!"

Day 12

75

It is a sin to be so close to Tiraspol and not go to the town where I once learned to play twenty-five different kinds of solitaire; where the Dniester sterlet is so sweet and tender; where the sturgeon is so big, fat, and ruddy; where the beluga is huge; and where the freshly salted caviar is grainy! It would be a sin not to visit my dear friends, my dear hosts, and not to dine with them on Russian cabbage soup, amber fish soup, and pie, but the twenty-one days of quarantine restrain my readers and me from this innocent temptation.

76

Down the Dniester from Bender the views are charming, the landscape and its inhabitants are rich, the valley is covered with villages, and the entire stretch of the river is shaded with orchards and vineyards. How alive a person feels in a place where nature is beautiful, where the air is fresh and cannot be infected by the breath of oppressors and troublemakers!

77

We shall pause at one of these villages. Sit down, my guests, under an acacia, which will pour out its fragrance on us, and a hundred-year-old linden will protect us from the sun. The *mazil* host has already taken care to treat you. Zamfira and Zoiţa bring out their dowries, colorful carpets of their own handiwork, and lay them on the grass. They do not look at you, but their eyes are quick and fiery; their dark brown hair is braided; even time will not quench their blush; their breasts are plump; they are all freshness and health!

Now they bring you bunches of translucent grapes, walnuts, apples, plums, pears, muskmelons, watermelons, and freshly cut honeycomb as fragrant as that brought by the oread Melissa. The homemade wine is light and wholesome. Hark! The fiddle and *cobză* are heard; two gypsies have begun to sing the *mititică*, the elder daughters and brides are preparing to dance the *joc*; a crowd of young Moldavian men, dashing horsemen, have galloped up to them, dismounted, and now they all stand in a circle. Here you see how their lips are silent, their gazes are glued to the ground, and their arms, legs, and the whole circle are in motion. The *mititică* continues for a long time and is finally followed by *sârbești*, *bulgărești*, and *ciobănești*. These are merrier and livelier.

78

But everything long-lasting loses its worth. Ennui was born from uniformity; therefore, unable to share the enjoyment of the *joc* and weave myself into the ring of blushing Moldavian women, I tell my host, dear Zamfira, and lively Zoița, "*Mult prea mulțumesc!*" and with quiet steps I walk along the path through the hills and woods with my lovely female reader.

I

The country here is splendid, isn't it?
Is this your first time here?

SHE

It is indeed.

I

Do you like country life?

SHE

I do, I must admit.
Especially whenever . . .

I

I can read
Your mind! But you perhaps don't understand . . .

SHE

How painfully you press my hand!

I

Forgive me! I'm beside myself with love
For nature's beauty and the skies above!
Everything here is joyful, free, and sweet!
The spring fills me with liveliness and cheer!
So take this kiss of nature, I entreat;
In charm and goodness you are nature's peer!

79

Imperceptibly we have approached the place where the town of Tyras lay, according to tradition and *the map of the ancient history of Bessarabia.* Time has erased it from the face of the earth, and its remains are difficult to find. Perhaps the village of Palanka is the place where the immodest migrant from the island of Milo lived. She is beautiful and lively, like the imagination of fiery, amorous Anacreon. Her hair, like a shining stream of flowing lava, light sandals, and a thin covering as transparent as a cloud—these constitute her only clothes.

80

Reader, your gaze betrays your lust!
All right then, bless you, take your fill!
You see it all; e'en so, you must
Tell no one; be discreet and still.
This young Greek girl cannot surmise
Why you are looking at her frame;
And so she hides not from your eyes

Her riches, for she knows no shame!
Some evil fiend has you in thrall,
A feeling that you cannot sate.
You scoundrel! Nightfall you await;
You want to rob her of it all!

81

But perhaps Tyras was where the Slavs later founded Belgorod and where Akkerman is now; it is all the same to us. Did not Ovid, they will ask, live beyond the Dniester estuary? For there stands the town of Ovidiopol. No, I will reply, Ovidius Naso was exiled by Octavius Augustus to the town of Tomi in Moesia, where the town of Mankalya is now; it was there that the exiled poet lived for ten years. Perhaps some Genoese ship conveyed his tombstone as ballast to the site of present-day Ovidiopol and unintentionally sowed doubt regarding the legends in the minds of future generations.

Why seek the home of that forsaken bard,
and drag his dust to every burial ground?
He lived, he sang; remembrance stands on guard—
There, in the minds of man, his rest is found.

82

Now, my good friends! Before us lies the Black Sea. We can already imagine the formidable element itself with all its horrors; the ship that, as you remember, was being driven by the winds over the deep, and the terrible moment when the rigging broke, the water surged over, and the poor passengers cried, "We are lost!" Weeping and wailing drowned out the noise of the storm, hearts bled, and you . . . threw the book from your hands! Dear lovers of reading, who among you remembers Oberon and those charming stanzas ending with the words "*Sie hören nichts*"? That was also on the sea and at the most critical, sensitive moment.

83

I have never happened to see a storm at sea; it must be horrible! But I have read Captain Cook's voyages, and I have seen a storm in an open field. Here is how a stormy poet describes it:

Arising from the mountains grand,
And throwing on her gloomy shroud,
The storm-crone, in her somber cloud
Descends like war upon the land,
And stirs the elements to fight!
Her ally, known as Hurricane,
A hothead, rowdy and insane,
Whistles and blows with all his might!
Whate'er he meets, where'er he flies,
He breaks and tears and twists and cries,
Sending the country into fright.
Through wood and dale, across the land
Whirling up dirt and dust and sand,
He pushes clouds across the skies.
On all below him making war;
With dusty gloom he covers o'er
The sun's gold hair and shining eyes.
Her hood pulled down, behold her ride:
Knitting her brows o'er eyes of pitch,
The storm sweeps over like a witch;
Behind, in front, from every side
Swirl clouds, and Aquilo, with pride,
Gathering a windy choir from the north,
With mighty bellowing bursts forth,
The thunder clatters, roars again;
The lightning twists, a flattering snake,
Causing the hearts of men to shake.
Could I describe, with my weak pen . . .
Etc.

The clouds have prematurely extinguished the day, but that is not my fault, my kind, attentive readers!

Day 13

84

Now ended are the noise and thrills,
The clouds into the western hills
Depart, and nature's in a hush.
See in the East Aurora's blush;
With joyful sparkle flow the rills.
And Phoebus, leaving his sweet dreams
And lover, gives a frowning yawn;
With fiery cloak and sheaf of beams,
He mounts his phaeton; moving on
Through heaven to advance the dawn,
So let him go . . .

But how tedious, I think, it must be for him to ride every day along the same path! Just imagine, this same story has gone on for more than seven thousand years, without even mentioning beginninglessness and endlessness.

85

Whoever has rights must make use of them, or else he will lose them over time. Consequently, I shall retire from the field for a while and order all my readers to go immediately to the headquarters of Alexander the Great and be present in all his campaigns, according to this hero's record of service, which can be found in the historians Justin, Arrian, Quintus Curtius, Plutarch, Ptolemy, Diodorus of Sicily, Firdawsi ibn Farrukh, Muhammad ibn Mir-Khwandshah, Hamd-Allah ibn Abi Bakr, Yahya ibn 'Abd Allah, Dakhelui, 'Abd al-Rahman ibn Ahmad, and many other ancient Oriental historians and poets.

After returning to Babylon, after the death of Alexander—that is, upon reading the following translation of Jami's *Baharistan*—here it should be noted in advance that the following can only be found in the original manuscript of *Baharistan*—it is not altogether reliable and was questioned by 'Abd al-Rahman ibn Ahmad himself—upon reading the following translation, as I was saying, I shall reassume personal command of all those who are traveling with me.

Eskander

My child and my thought! Who created you? Was it not I? But you often don't heed me—I punish your rudeness with only my sorrow!

The air and the seas and the dry land may bind you in place, but no boundaries or fetters will ever deprive you of freedom; no weight can compress you!

All places, expanses, and times are accessible to you . . . How often I wish to cast off all my burdens, to fly freely after you, soar from one world to the next, from the deep to the heavens, from one age to another, to glide from the silence of death to the sweetness of life, and from tears to the raptures of infinite love!

Eskander was born with a soul made of granite, but whose scion was he? The legends are silent.

They came to him when he was still a proud youth and prepared for high thoughts and strong feelings.

For he, Philip's fosterling, thought his real father immortal and saw in the people his slaves.

His heart, full of pride, wished to know kindred love—and he chose as his father the lord of Olympus!

The gray rock bends over the deep like an old man stands over a coffin. And on it Eskander is seated.

The mountains stretch high to the west, like a pathway ascending to heaven.

And loud the sea roars: the Erythraean's huge billows rush on in their rows and attempt to subject the dry land to the ocean once more.

But no! The stout boulders of granite ward off the assault of the waves.

Now thoughtful, he looks to the distance and into the sea's murky depths, and he seems to perceive for the first time the charm and the bleakness of nature . . .

But how can those eyes remain curious, those eyes for which nothing is wondrous, those eyes to which all is familiar?

"What now do I want?" says he. "Whom do I search for by land and by sea?"

"I've seen the god Ammon . . . I've built a perpetual monument, down where the Nile meets the sea . . . The sands of Arabia can never devour my achievement . . . I have been to the Ganges and drunk from its waters divine!

"So what do the limits imposed by the world mean to me? Do I wish to impose my own self as a limit?

"Iran and the kingdoms of India are bound by my will, and four seas are encompassed by conquest and power!

"I've toppled the pride of those men who have flown up too high, who weren't able to breathe in the ether.

"The kings kneel before me—as Titans subjected to heaven!

"Is it rest that I seek? No, for rest is unbearable; it is a heaviness, pressing you down to the depths of the earth.

"Great wealth I despise; shiny stones and gold trinkets are nothing compared to the sun and the stars!

"The sun and the stars I would pluck from the sky; I would learn all their secrets and see the bright sea from which heaven's rays flow!

"I've tasted the substance of passion and the rapture of wholehearted feelings; I've seen how external despair can be envious of hidden regret.

"And what's more, I have scorned all the mortals!"

In the tent the sound of singing is heard.

"I cannot endure the gay songs of the bondswomen; they are like wailing to me!

"For who would sing gaily and feelingly simply to please other people but over the tomb of one's own satisfaction?

"And indeed, what is joy when true purpose is lacking? A moment of madness.

"The joy of great men is the smiling of nature emerging from chaos!

"But love . . . affection for dust . . . a feeling appropriate for weak men alone!

"It's possible, true, to forgive nature's absolute rule—be a slave to the wants it instills.

"But can one fulfill one's desires by exchanging one's feelings of shame?"

In the tent these words are heard:

My father, this sound I hear heightens my fears:
Your voice calling out, your dispiriting sigh!
But soon I will water the earth with my tears,
The place where your ashes uneasily lie!

ESKANDER

[*After a long silence*]

These sorrowful sounds! How they tear at my soul! But dear Zenda is beautiful! Bel would not ever forgive me for Zenda, if his priests could instill all their envy and wrath in cold marble!

The head priest was slain by the sword of my justice; the soul of the wicked disturber was worthy of punishment!

Return to the high walls of Babylon! Just to fulfill the desire of the maiden?

I offered her treasures of India, which she refused, for there's one thing alone that she wishes, named Babylon!

She told me she dreamed of the shade of her father, who asked her to come to his grave—to atone for his criminal soul with her innocent tears . . .

You may not believe it, but no one has ever so fervently prayed to the heavens as this maiden entreated me! . . .

If I had not noticed the passion with which she did pray, had not seen her desire to keep secret her love for Eskander,

Then I should have stifled my own innate feelings as well as my empty desire!

The sun cannot enter the dark and mysterious jungle of Zulmat;

And yet, in the forest of gloom there is hidden a fountain of brightness, whose waters regenerate life.

And Zenda possesses a heart just as bright—'tis the source of all bliss!

[*He exits into the tent.*]

**ALEXANDER'S CAMP ON THE BANKS OF THE TIGRIS.
IN THE DISTANCE IS BABYLON.**

[*A maiden in a white dress and veil walks out of the tent and up the hill. Black maidens follow her at a distance.*]

MAIDEN

Eskander! The earth is too small for you—rise to the heavenly thrones and topple the gods who hold sway in the world!

Climb up to the sky on the tomb of the peoples you've conquered!

The tomb that encloses the bones of my father! Will they serve as steps to your glory as well? No, proud ruler!

If only, my lord, you were kinder and closer in soul to poor Zenda . . .

If only, alas, you were free from this crime, in the eyes of the maiden who loves you . . .

Eskander, oh, then you'd be dearer to me than the reign of your will over all of the universe.

And dearer than all your inveterate visions, O heir to Olympus!

But now . . . your life's thread is still precious to me, but the Parcae have utmost control! . . .

Within my embrace you'll know bliss, but this bliss will lead straight to your end! . . .

I *will not* remain in a world where these frightening feelings are never at peace, ending only in death!

[*Sings*]

Procure me water from Ab-Hayt, that I may see
  My strength return and feel alive and whole!
Resentment was my father's sole bequest to me;
  My oath lies heavy on my soul!

Eskander! How can you resist this maiden's song?
Eskander, let us quickly fly to Babylon!

Yes, there without defense I'll fall into your arms,
You'll stir my spirit to enraptured bliss!
There love and vengeance, toxic charms,
Will join within our fervent kiss!

[*The black maidens stand in a circle and sing.*]

Maiden! Behold the stars Tair and 'Asad
Rise o'er the mountains, so stately and grand,
Sing to these guests, you who sorrows have had,
Sing them a prayer from an alien land!

Still are the winds, and the waters asleep.
Swans! Lend your feathers, as light as the air!
Would that into the night sky we could leap!
And in our friendship fly on to bright Tair!

Youths! Now where are you? Come over here,
Offer at Ka'ba a calf for the slaughter!
Youths! All your hearts are now trembling with fear;
Easier to steal from a father his daughter!

[*All exit.*]

BABYLONIAN COUNTRY PALACE NEAR THE TEMPLE OF SERAPIS

[*Eskander is in a frenzy of feeling; Zenda stands beside him, with tears in her eyes.*]

ESKANDER

O Zenda, embrace me again, I'm on fire! On my heart the vast ice of the Caucasus thaws, and my breath softens iron and stone!

Distressing, O Zenda? . . . No, sweet are the longings of love!

O Jupiter, father, be envious! Though you as a swan seduced Leda, still you must be envious!

O Zenda! The sun shines within you! The fire of desire . . . in your fervent embrace . . . I have doused it with flames!

And now I am drenched in them, just like the palace of Istakar: Years of hard labor were needed to build it, but one strong attacker destroyed it at once!

My blood is in turmoil! . . . 'Twas thus that great Pontus once raged . . . and then cast up his waves, to flood Lectonia and swallow it in the abyss!

The sky draws in close, and it hampers my breathing . . . I wish I could cast it all off, to breathe freely in infinite space!

[*Zenda rushes into his arms, but tearing away for a moment, hides behind the pillars of the palace.*]

Release me now, Zenda! And give me my sword! I will slash all the fetters with which you have chained Alexander to earth!

My sword! . . . But where are you, O maiden? Or are you a specter, a flame sent by Jove down from heaven to chastise me?

O Father, you tremble for fear that I'll steal all your will and your rule of the world!

Your thunder has struck me . . . Your lightning bolts wind round my body like snakes! . . .

And down you have cast me . . . to horrible Tartarus!

O Jupiter, you too can be envious . . . of a man who was lucky!

Immortal! . . . Eternity, though, is no gift!

[*He dies.*]

86

Oh tell me please, where have you been?
Where did you follow the phalanges?
Did you immerse your bodies in
The sacred water of the Ganges?
It helps you to forget with ease
All sins and shocks, and every grief;
No wonder guiltless Héloïse
So thirsted for this sweet relief.

87

I don't expect an answer, my companions! It's clear to me. Let's go! But what does this mean? A third of you are missing! O curiosity!

We were separated in the streets of Babylon! I'll follow you. What's the matter? Where are you going? . . . The tower of Babylon . . . of Babel . . . the airy gardens . . .

Hey, my friends! You're late! What, were you born after the Second Coming? Not everything leaves a trace of itself. Where are you looking for the tower? It should be outside the city, judging from an engraving of its construction, and according to the learned traveler Tavernier, the tower can be found in the province of Baghdad, midway between the Tigris and Euphrates.

Mount 'Aqarquf, or *Karkuf*, as Mr. Teixeira calls it, is its barely noticeable remnant. What news! . . .

I must frankly confess that it is as annoying for me as it is for you to jump from the province of Baghdad to Budzhak.

At the scene of the events of *One Thousand and One Nights* we could have gone into the palace of Caliph al-Mansur, but in time we shall be there again.

88

Where nature does not smile at me, I am indifferent to it. Only a genius can find something in utter emptiness.

Mickiewicz has already said all that that could be said about the Akkerman steppes, so I will not add a word and, like a *tumbleweed* driven by the east wind, I move from Akkerman and its vineyards to one of the German colonies of Budzhak. There I ask for a coffee and prematurely write an exclamation point at the sight of this hospitable and genial German woman, who says *gleich* before drawing a ladleful of coffee from a common pot stuck on the stove, where it is continually boiling and overcooking, like soldier's gruel! But I drink it up with the same relish as a knight on a campaign drinks old Rhine wine from a Johannisberger barrel.

89

From the German colony I head across the field of Kagul, where Rumyantsev routed the Turks, then on to Izmail. Here Suvorov in eleven hours did what the Egyptian Pharaoh Psammetichus with four hundred thousand troops barely managed to do in 254,040 hours at the Assyrian fortress of Azotus in Palestine.

A.D. 1790 and 670 B.C.—but what is time to a genius?

90

Hello there, Manechka, my pride!
My idol, shining like the day!
When only twelve you were a bride
And married off—too soon, I'd say!
Now you're a mother, full of bliss;
My feelings rush back in a whirl,
As here I sit and reminisce
Of how I loved to give a kiss
To you, O dear, delightful girl!

91

Having talked my fill about Budzhak and all the sights of former Bessarabian Tartary, I steal away unseen from the crowd of my readers, who are still boating with curiosity along the Vilkovo canals, imagining they are in Amsterdam. They examine the fortifications of Kiliya and Izmail; visit the port of Izmail; buy and eat oranges, *rahat lokum*, figs, plums, and *dulceață*; drink Greek wines and sherbet; smoke tobacco . . . I steal away from the crowd unseen and lost in thought, like Guarinos, I ride, "clip-clop, then at a trot," along the river Prut, the border of the former Turkish Empire, or in any case the former border of the Turkish Empire. This rearrangement of words means nothing, though Cromwell made great use of the comma . . .

So I ride and think:

If only there were no delays along the route;
By since there are, by God,
We'll make our way across the Prut,
Giving our horse a little prod.

92

I have suddenly grown tired of riding alone.

Oh, why is God chastising me?
I yawn; I suffer from ennui;
My strength is lost; I'm all forlorn!
If only I had not been born!

Ennui is a disease, said de Lévis; activity is the cure for it, and pleasure is a temporary relief.

Ennui was born of uniformity, La Motte says or writes, and La Bruyère preaches that laziness brought it into the world. And this is true:

I never knew despondence or despair
When I was busy with amours;
So why did I decide to swear
That women's wonderful allures
Would never more my interest claim? . . .

"Oh no," cried Cunegund's young knight,
"To go without love's heavenly flame
Is an intolerable plight!"

"The best thing is to marry!" said another knight.

I'd follow custom and enjoy
Having a castle and a spouse—
Until a irksome *domovoy*
Decides to drive me from the house!

"What's to be done?" he went on . . .

We harvest what we sow, that's right!
We all like to amuse and tease:
I've often been that selfsame sprite,
An imp, a *leshy* of the trees!

93

What a joy is there in riding, whether on the highway or the country lane of life! On the former you meet the poor in spirit, and on the latter the ordinary poor, such as this man who is begging for alms. Happiness! What is happiness? A foolish, improvident rich man who looks at poverty with disdain, squanders his money without need or measure, and probably, like me, will not take out a silver coin . . . nor say: "Take this, poor old man!"

94

In this manner I made my way little by little. Suddenly, ever-despondent ennui, languid melancholy, and wistful longing attacked my senses! Everything in me grew weary; my strength was exhausted; the cursed Charites squeezed my soul! But mighty sleep lay its saving aegis on me, and now my *armăsar*, an animal governed not only by reins but also by instinct, turns off the road, runs with disdain past a haystack, approaches a herd, carefully considers the mares, proudly goes up to one of them, greets her with his teeth and hind hooves, and—the villain!—interrupts my sweet trance. "You've lost your way, my dear!" I said, and turning him back to the road, I spurred him on and—fell asleep again . . .

Day 14

95

I do not remember whether my horse brought me back to Tulchin while I was asleep or whether my dream had conveyed me around Bessarabia; I only know that someone woke me up in the same apartment I had left several days ago to travel under the patronage of Adeona around the present and the past, the seen and the unseen, the near and the far, the physical and the moral world, senses and sensuality, and finally everywhere one can go around by land, sea, and the imagination, excluding only what one cannot go around, even on horseback.

96

After greeting the day with my usual dose of coffee, I glanced at the shelf. My gaze, like a sultan's, wandered long over the harem of books. Not a single one here, I thought, has not been in my hands. In *you* there is much fire, but no soul; *you* are old and therefore have become stupid; *you* are too delicate and sensitive; *you* are a dreamer, like a German philosopher; *you* are dry, *you* are too prolific; *you* . . . come here . . . my worn-out, beloved sultana, *World History*! Bear my son! And I shall name him Methuselah!

97

I had just lain down on the divan with my sultana when suddenly a visitor came in. Judging by his height he must have been from the race of the Rephaim!

"What are you doing?"

"Nothing."

"You're always tied to a book. What are you reading?"

"I'm rummaging through history; I want to learn about the origin of the Circassians."

"Ah! I lived among them. *Cherkez* is the Tatar name, which means pretty much the same as 'cutthroat'; the name of the people is *Khozry*. That's what they call themselves, and nothing else."

"What are you saying? . . . Aha! Let's look at an article about the Khazars: 'The Khazars . . . the White Ugrians . . . hold sway in the area between the Caspian and Maeotic Seas . . . Aha! Enemies of the Persians, and eventually of the Arabs . . . I understand!"

"Here are the Lezgins, and that's indeed what they call themselves—Lezgins. Near them live a very strong and distinctive people, the Avars, on the shores of the Caspian Sea. What's strange is that the Avar language is quite similar to Albanian."

"I'm not surprised; ancient Albania was on the shores of the Caspian Sea."

"Ah, I see! Now it's clear . . ."

"Where are you hurrying off to?"

"I'm going out into the garden."

"I'll catch up."

"Good!"

Then my guest left, and I headed out too, almost right after him.

98

The Podolian countryside is luxurious; the air is pure, fresh, and wholesome; the valleys are settled; the orchards are lush; the meadows are fragrant; the rows of poplars are majestic; nature blooms; and you, good Khokhly and Khokhlachki! Six days you labor by the sweat of your face for your masters, but the seventh day is for the Lord God and then off to the tavern. You are heading there, my wise men, as to Keramin . . . to judge and settle your affairs, drink, and dance. Fair maidens . . . no! There's not a single fair maiden among you! They're all plain, and all wearing flowers—poor flowers!

99

Tulchin is beautifully situated. The palace has a golden motto: May this always be the home of the free and virtuous. The vast Catholic church is full of Polish priests scolding their listeners. Rows of inns, where every traveler is bombarded by Jews and loaded with goods. That is Tulchin. But I forgot the extensive garden, which is called the *Good* Garden:

Yes, it was good, in days of yore,
When from the rocky Bosporan shore
A goddess traveled here to dwell.
'Twas better still, when she gave birth
To daughters full of charm and worth,
Who in all graces did excel!
Still it improved when day by day,
The maidens grew, as did their hearts,
At which a wing'd boy shot his darts,
Putting them under true love's sway!
How long ago did they grow bored
Of freedom and then tie the knot?
When did they cease to be adored,
When was their sovereign rule forgot?
But time can be both slow and fast;
I find this contrast to be true:
For happy people, all is past,
But for the wretched, all is new.

100

In the garden, I did not find my Rephaite, who is as full grown as the tall poplars. For a long time I walked around the ponds, looked at the swimming swans, and thought:

Once I, indifferent and daring,
Spent all my days in calm sublime;
Regretting never, never caring—
A swan upon the sea of time!

101

Approaching the house, up the hill to the right of the path leading to it stood an iron cage about the size of a gazebo, in which there lived a roller bird. After glancing curiously at this recluse, I rushed to jump over the bridge and quickly went down the path,

> Where once alone, to my surprise,
> I met . . . a lovely Polish lass!
> She gazed into my curious eyes;
> I into hers . . . That's all, alas!

102

As if tired from all the walking I have done in my life, I sat on a bench and recalled the past.

Almost from the very moment I made a loud speech in Sanskrit on my entry into the world, from that very moment to the age of five I was coddled and rocked to sleep; to the age of ten I was pampered and spoiled; to the age of fifteen I was taught and punished; at sixteen I rattled a saber in the tsar's service and twirled my silver sword knot; at seventeen the lower ranks stood before me and dared not utter a word without saying "your honor"; my sisters, brothers, and classmates marveled at my embroidered collar and aiguillette; my teachers viewed me with delight, as Alcamenes did his statue; and the beautiful girls . . . I shall not tell you how they looked at me; and at eighteen, nineteen, twenty, and so on, up to the present minute, many wonderful things occurred. My life in those years would fill three volumes with portraits and vignettes. But if I could relive all that time . . . what a wonderful edition it would be: *revue, corrigée, augmentée et illustrée . . .*

103

> Heavy with sadness, here I sigh;
> But languor wears down every part!
> I mourn my happiness gone by,
> And pity my dejected heart:
> 'Tis like a child whose nurse is gone,

He vainly taps the cradle wall,
But dear old nanny has withdrawn;
No one will comfort him at all!

Oh nanny, nanny, dear nurse of my heart! What would have happened to it without you? You are its deity! . . . It holds your temple and your altars! . . . Good, sweet nurse! Do not leave it!

104

I drown in musings dark and deep,
Away from all beloved things;
It seems that Saturn's fast asleep,
And time has hung its leaden wings.
But I too wish to find some rest;
There will be time to march ahead.
The raven on Prometheus fed:
So longing preys upon my chest!
I sleep. But this is quite surprising:
I dream that I am softly sneaking,
Like an adulterous elder, seeking
Susanna from her bath arising.

Such a dream would really be strange. What kind of idea was that? Where did it come from? But it was the result of a common accident. I had fallen asleep while sitting near the bathhouse; the noise of splashing water and the sound of a gentle voice must have suggested this dream to my imagination.

105

I soon awoke, jumped up, and set off with quick steps for home. At home, I noticed the unfolded map of Bessarabia and remembered that I was expected on the Prut. I flew there swiftly, like the sound of a word from a speaker to a listener, and then slowly, step by step, I traveled along the river, turned right, went through the valley to the village of Lapushna, past Chuchuleny, and arrived at the village of Lozovo. It is filled with gardens and situated between steep mountains covered with dense forest. I do not know why, but arriving at a place like this after a long journey is as pleasurable as coming home. Stopping next to a *casă*, I went in. How tidy! The walls are as white as snow; opposite the door, on the wallpaper, are icons adorned with flowers; the shelves and beams are covered with large apples and little star-shaped pumpkins. A wide, soft divan stretches along the entire wall under the icons; a neat little table stands in front of it; next to the walls, on top of the divan, are chests with the dowry of the host's daughters and colorful carpets they have woven.

106

While they were preparing my dinner and roasting the partridge and woodcock I had shot on the road, I examined the paintings and the significance of the icons. Suddenly, a sheet of paper stuck behind the wallpaper drew my attention. It was written in Russian, and the uniform rhymes seemed to light up. "It's poetry!" I cried. Let's read it:

107

In a Moldavian village, I
Was taken ill, for God ordained
That hardship. I was drained
And like an ancient corpse, turned dry.
My batman saw I was a shade;
There was no journey to prepare;
And therefore night and day he stayed
In bed. The hostess, young and fair,
Attentive, but remaining chaste,
Softly around my bedroom paced.
At times, in boredom, I would hear
Immodest stories from this dear;
Măriucă's tales of her affairs
Alleviated all my cares.

"An army regiment sojourned here"
(She'd often tell me and recall);
"A sergeant major, tall, sincere,
Loved me, and drew me on the wall,

Dancing the joc. Take a peek!
'This is me,' he said, 'and you,
My *Mărioliţa mititică*,
My soulmate, and my darling true!'
Two years with me did he remain,
We got *Părinte* to agree
To bless us; so till his campaign
Ilya Yevseich lived with me.
How can I let his memory go?
He sewed me frocks of calico!
Many a tear for him I've cried,
Of grief I almost would have died,
But then I thought, he's gone or dead,
Just six months after I was wed!
Of the Moldavian land I tire,
Although I've always lived right here.
Now a *muscal* do I admire:
A young lieutenant; for a year
He's lived here with his whole platoon.
He gave mama a hundred *lei*,
A ring with jewels finely hewn . . ."
. . . .

108

Here a woman entering interrupted my reading of the poem.

"Mărioliţa!"

"What?" she answered suddenly.

"Ilya Yevseich sends his regards!"

Mărioliţa blushed, hid, and then there was no trace of her.

After dinner I continued to read the poem I found . . . You probably want to know its continuation and ending, but can I print somebody else's work? I'm sure you'll agree.

In the evening Mărioliţa appeared again. For a long time she looked for something around the room; it seems the desire to know about the health of Ilya Yevseich was bothering her; but I pretended to be asleep, and soon I actually fell asleep.

Day 15

109

When I turn fifty, I shall recount or describe my campaigns in much more detail. After traveling with *post*-horses, then with *long-distance* horses, I shall retire to a settled life, imitating nature, in which everything is constant except the weather and people—excluding from the latter all the dear women known to me and my readers.

110

This is the last hand I deal in the first volume of my travels; it will decide who walks away the loser: I or the reader.

Nothing keeps a gambler at the table like a loss; let an author see a few thousand copies of his book fly off the shelves, and he will gladly stake a fresh bank, while the enterprising bookseller will go *va banque*.

111

But I've begun to ramble. Several days have already passed since the manifesto declaring war on the sultan was issued. From Lozovo my eyes again turn to Tulchin. Meanwhile, my travel packs are being prepared, and the mail coach is waiting at the porch. Farewell, my dear friends! Pray for me! When shall we see each other again? Farewell! But we still must listen to the whole prayer. It's finished! The cross is kissed; the holy water is sprinkled; farewell!

Thus I said goodbye to Tulchin on the twentieth of April, 1828; on the twenty-second I was already in Kishinev, and on the twenty-fifth I crossed the river Prut with the troops at the town of Fălciu.

In an officer's campaign notes published in the *Northern Bee*, Fălciu was made into a fortress of the third rank.

Let Fălciu be a fort, forsooth,
Although it has no moat or wall,
And likewise I'm prepared to call
Absurdity the honest truth.

112

"Here is the end of the first part of my journey!" I shouted, and struck the table with my fist. Everything on it fell to the floor, the inkstand bounced, the ink splattered, and a black drop drowned Iași.

113

If man, during the creation of the universe, had been given the freedom to choose a home for himself, he would have hovered in indecision to this day, like the ether between worlds. Likewise, I know not where to settle . . .

114

Young Cytherea's son I now implore:
Give me swift wings to fly away!
For on the heavenly Tauric shore
I wish to greet the shining day.
There I, tired traveler, off will throw
The heavy burden of my woe.

There I shall feel both free and light:
There up to Chatyr-Dag's great height
I'll gaze, and skipping o'er the rills,
Like a chamois, I'll climb the hills.
Then like a river in its race,
I'll rush down to a friend's embrace!

"Who is this friend?" you will ask me. Sigh deeply for something you once loved more than anything in the world; gaze at what is dearest to you now; merge these two feelings. If a being is born out of this merger, it will be like my friend.

115

All things befit her, so it seems;
The tricks she plays are always fitting,
And in the heat of childish schemes,
She's swifter than that boy who flitting
Round with his arrows of desire
Conquered the universe entire.

Her features beckon and bespeak
A spirit passionate and wise,
When bashful, she casts down her eyes;
A rosy blush spreads o'er her cheek.
But suddenly she bends her head,
And pensively she folds her arms,
And then this thought my soul alarms:
The lady is already wed.

Her heart desires freedom pure,
By inexperience 'tis worn thin;
How patiently does she endure
The illness of the soul! She's akin
To a sick crone, in fretful rest.
She's charming in her feeble state.
But tell me, O perfidious fate!
Why is her pillow not my chest!

My heart would beat, with feelings deep,
Under that sweet, angelic head!
And by such tender guile led,
My heart would rock it right to sleep!

116

Like Cincinnatus, who performed a great feat in fifteen days, I humbly retire from the writing desk to the divan to indulge in sweet repose.

Before his expedition into Asia, Alexander gave up everything he had. "But what have you left for yourself?" he was asked. "Hope," he replied.

Thirty-five thousand brave Macedonians were ready to support his hope.

Thus concluding what is nothing less than my entry onto the field of travel, I solemnly and publicly declare that until thirty-five thousand readers are counted under my banners, and until I treat their imagination, on the fields of the manuscript of the second volume, to a wonderful dinner, compared with which all the dinners given by Julius Caesar to the Roman people were nothing more than a light snack after a glass of vodka—until then, I say, I will not take another step toward new conquests in the field of Russian literature!

Part 2

Lorsque *quelque* est placé devant le substantif *chose,* ces deux mots s'emploient souvent comme un seul . . . par ex.: *avez-vous lu ce livre?—Non, j'en ai lu* quelque chose *qui m'a paru bon.*

—*Grammaire françoise de Lhomond,* revue, corrigée et augmentée par Letellier, douzième edition, page 128

Day 16

117

Out of the weakness inherent in the human race, putting aside my worries about all the old beginnings, I now proceed to a new beginning. Can I look on my newborn idea with indifference? No. Skillfully, gently, I take this infant from the depths of my head, give her a name, bless her, and lower her into the baptismal font . . . A baby, a baby! What a delight for a sentimental father!

In holy faith do I baptize
This child. I kiss her and am kind;
I cherish her and form her mind.
Live and grow up, as I devise,
Beloved, gentle girl, my dear!
Be never bound in clothes severe,
And know no tears! For weeping long
Will merely make your close ones sad.
Mamunya now will sing a song;
Hear Vaska purring—he is glad;
So goo-goo, baby—have a laugh!

118

Now I set off calmly on my way . . .

Sit in this carriage, wing'd and light,
And let us fly, my reader-friend!
Thou northern resident, turn your sight
South, east, and west—where shall we tend?
To where we've been or where we'll be?

To wondrous, heavenly dwelling places,
The enlightened world or savagery,
To distant stars and unknown races?
I care not, if my cherished flock
Flies after me through every shock,
From world to world, within, without,
But if you tire, then give a shout!

119

So let us stuff our imagination and thoughts into our knapsack, and—good luck! We need no passports or traveling papers; we are free people. Nor do we need post-horses; we have our own, and what horses they are! There is nowhere they cannot take you. Just hold on, and they will carry you forever and ever upward! Up there is the temple of glory. "Glory cannot be based on truth alone!" said Quintus Curtius one cloudy day.

The mind, courage, imagination, and all intellectual wealth in general are good only when they are active. Without movement they are all dead capital, and therefore:

Now flit and fly ahead, my horse,
You have no need of spurs or crop:
Through fire and water make your course,
Through wilds and o'er each mountaintop.
Rear up, ride freely, never tire,
With every bound you're more alive!
Fly into heaven, ever higher,
Or down to Pluto's kingdom dive,
Where all is dark . . .

120

Give me some candles! And yet our path is clear everywhere. It is lit not by the ordinary sun that is so familiar to us and that we would sometimes willingly trade for a May moon, not by the sun that fell to the earth along with the sky and was shattered, not by the sun that perished in the universal fire, not by the sun that was carried away by the wind, not by the sun that rose to heaven after the death of the first four ages of the world and that illuminates new prejudices and the fifth age, but by hope, the spiritual sun! . . . hope! . . . God, what a wealth of rays! . . . And so many eclipses! . . . Brilliant, deceptive star! . . . It shines and shines, and nothing is visible. . . . It's dark . . . give me a candle!

121

Here . . . the face of the earth is before us . . . Have a pleasant journey! . . . A hare will not cross our path, an axle will not break, a wheel will not be smashed to pieces, and we shall not break our necks . . . Hey, *ciubucci-pașa*! A pipe! And so . . . we're already on the divan. Our gazes travel across the wide map. Look, I'm running my index finger over it. My finger is powerful, like the finger of Time. Do you want me, like him, to erase cities, mountains, and the borders of kingdoms from the face of the earth? . . . Do you want me to set fire to the Arctic Ocean and turn the White Sea into the Black? But you believe without proof both my power and the power of time, though not in the same way. To create is glory; to destroy is sin; destruction, however, makes way for creation. Everything is built on ruins.

122

"Where is that marvelous dinner promised to us?" I am asked by a curious person, a miserable creature who wants to be omniscient. Tomorrow I shall satisfy your curiosity, hunger, and thirst, but now it is evening, and the morning is wiser than the evening. Just imagine: one evening, touched to the depths of my heart, I said to another earthly creature, "Listen!" grabbing that creature's arm and jumping up. "Listen!" I repeated and then said slowly, "It's time to sleep!" and then I lay back down on the divan. Why do you think this happened? Because my fiery words had illuminated reason and rejected thoughtless delight. Waking up the next day, I thought about it and said emphatically, "The evening is stupid!"

123

What's next? Next is the fact that until this hundred and twenty-third chapter, I have retained my freedom of heart, so now I change the dedication of *The Wanderer.* "To you!" What thousand-mindedness! How laconic! This is like when the Indian Lord Izuara said to his wife, "*Gum*"—she answered, "*Om,*" and Izuara created the world in the form in which it appears to the Indians; for we see it from a completely different perspective.

The word *Gum!* encompasses the whole project, or the intention of creation and the question of agreement. The word *Om!* comprises praise, amendments, supplements (especially regarding the existence of the female sex), and finally agreement, confirmation, and so on.

This is how the meaning of these words is explained by the interpreters of Sanskrit, the wise Father Paolino di Santo Bartolomeo and Langlès, who repudiate the work of the philologists William Jones, Wilkins, etc., who say that the mysterious word *Om!* is an image of the deity and is composed of three Devanagari letters: *a* and *u*, which merge to produce *o*, or with the addition of *m*: *Om!*—that is, the creator, preserver, and destroyer.

This is understandable. The Sanskrit language is the *nothing* from which all other languages of the earth were formed, or the sea from which all the rivers of the Word flow.

124

"Let the weak, who are drowned in bliss and luxury, call travel foolish; let them be amazed by the courage of those who, quitting the feather bed, overcome all the hardships, all the difficulties of a long journey. The mountain air is full of fragrance and sweet, life-giving vigor, which jaded idleness has never felt!"

This, or something similar, was said by my dear, ever-thoughtful—no!—an ever-smoking, flaming volcano, spewing lava on all things: Byron/Beyron/Biron.

With a deep sigh, I set out across the vast map of the perennially disputed areas of the globe to seek this mountain air and beautiful scenery. Nature is good only where it is sanctified by the contentment of man, where he himself is equal to its beauty and splendor.

"Oh, that's the plain truth!" someone will say who takes no part in the buying up of nature and whose property is limited to the surface of his clothes.

125

"Attention! Fall in! March, march!" could be heard in the south of Russia. As quick as time, the troops were approaching the border.

Here is what lay before my eyes: a lengthy valley, green reeds, marshes, lakes, the river Prut. The town of Fălciu on a hill on the opposite shore. Regiments and wagon trains stretching along a winding road. . . . A pontoon bridge! Goodbye, Russia!

Now childlike tears begin to swell
And flow down in a stream of heat,
Adieu, my native land! Farewell
To all on earth that's good and sweet!
Farewell, you lovely maidens dear!
The final crossing looms ahead!
The Russian Tsardom's edge is here:
Farther my soul is loath to tread;
My body's well, my heart's in pain!
Though I'm a soldier, as you see,
In Sultan Mahmud's strange domain,
My nights will ever sleepless be!

Here angelic sensibility will perhaps make her (but who is she?) cry unintentionally:

"My God, how awful! What a shame!
From lack of sleep he'll surely die!"
"Fear not, my dear! For sleep will claim
Him soon—away his grief will fly."

Day 17

126

Ezopka! Sunk in sleep! Come chase
Penelope now out of bed,
Set up the globe upon its base,
And Europe on the table spread!
Well done!— Now from the chest
Bring me that picture book, just so;
Good man! . . . Now to the market go:
Some cabbage soup, a roast—your best—
Some waffles, cream on top to twirl . . .
Go!
        For the rhyme: "So is an *earl*
Coming to dinner?"
                        "Maybe so."

127

I cannot imagine—and thus neither can you, my kind visitors—that my Ezopka could prepare a magnificent dinner for several thousand persons. No, he is still so innocent of culinary knowledge that often my soup is as appetizing as the water of the Asphaltic Sea, and the roast resembles a piece of ebony from which you might carve anything you want. And yet, O gentlemen gastronomers, how he roasts game! . . . If all the snipes, jacksnipes, great snipes, woodcocks, curlews, partridges, quails, little bustards, great bustards—which I did not fail to shoot, thanks to Kühlenz's art and my own—if this game could feel with what solicitude and tenderness Ezopka treated it, as he browned it on the spit, in the frying pan, and in the stewpot, and then brought it to the table, if this game could feel how it delighted my tastebuds as my tongue caressed and kissed its every joint, then it would shudder with spiritual pleasure and let out a cry of joy, for what is sweeter than the moment when you give delight to others by sacrificing some earthly possession?

"Ezopka, you're a genius!" I said to him one day; "Am I mistaken?" "No," he muttered and rubbed his nose with his fist.

How then can Ezopka, who is like a creature endowed with only the sense of touch, roast game so ingeniously? If mental abilities do not suffice, neither can animal instinct dictate the steps and time required to cook it perfectly.

Perhaps for this you need an excellent sense of taste? But my Ezopka cannot tell the difference between salt and pepper if his eyes are closed.

Perhaps you need perfect vision, to penetrate into the birds lying in the pot or pan? But my Ezopka did not roast the game for Vaska the cat, yet Vaska ate it up before his eyes without him noticing.

Perhaps you need the kind of hearing that can understand the language of inanimate creatures, which only squeak and chirr? But my Ezopka is as deaf as a post or whatever solid object you may choose.

Perhaps you need a subtle sense of smell, to recognize the vapor coming from underdone, done, and overdone meat? But Ezopka cannot even distinguish incense from any other smell.

What then is genius?

Genius of the mind will tell no one "You are stupid!" but will say: "You don't know this; you don't understand; this doesn't relate to your feelings or your understanding; move on; this is not your sphere, not your place, not air you can breathe, not a language you can understand; you have neither friends, nor colleagues, nor rivals here." But keep going, Ezopka! Keep going! You are a genius in the area where the only thing demanded of genius is the ability to roast game perfectly.

128

Vertumnus grants a gift divine,
But hold this thought within your brain:
What now seems sound and rather fine
Tomorrow will seem quite insane.

Day 18

129

My dear gentlemen readers and traveling companions! I welcome your happy entrance into the abode of the wandering son!

My dear lady readers and traveling companions, as lovely as the chaste virgin who dwelled before the founding of the Manchurian kingdom at the foot of *Golmin Šanggiyan Alin*. Your presence invigorates me like the pool of Siloam and revives my soul like confidence.

Peace and pleasure to those who enter my dwelling . . . Please feel at home . . . All the unimaginable wealth and beauty of nature is at your service . . . The abode of my imagination is vast. Are you tired? Sit down on the comfortable, luxurious throne from which Xerxes beheld the immense fleet of Persia. Do you want to cool down? Here is a fountain, like a waterspout in the Atlantic Ocean touching the sky. Do you want solitude? Here is the world before the creation of the first human. Do you want a refuge from unhappiness? Here is the sky.

Everything is here, everything except the beginning and the end.

130

Blessed contemporaries of the infancy of the world! You who dwell on enchanted islands, in sunny gardens, near the vaults of heaven, by the sources of light! . . . You, the fruits of the Fall, the children of love, the first families of nations! . . . Look, here are seeds saved from the Flood and scattered across the earth; here is your offspring! Do you rejoice when you look at our sumptuous feast? You fed on juicy fruits, but we—we feed on imagination.

131

But the dinner hour draws near. Let us make ourselves comfortable in this field. Help me bring hither all the beauty of nature.

For surroundings, we will choose the best of all the mountains known and unknown to geography. Our seclusion must be majestic. In the blue sky shall stand Chimborazo, a monument to the creation of the world. Behind it, like a bright crown with seven golden domes, shall be Mount Sumeru—the center of the universe. Beside it, Karkuf, crowned with the tower of Babel. Amid the ridges shall be the falls of Niagara. The plain stretching from here into the distance, shall be dotted with hills from Cythera, palms from Salem, cedars from Lebanon, poplars from Jericho, dates from Mecca, oranges from Malta, chestnuts from India, pomegranates from Algiers, pistachios from Aleppo, and a vineyard from Corinth.

A natural arbor formed by a fig tree from paradise and a tamarisk from the banks of the Nile shields us from the sun. Acacias and Syrian roses caress our noses. Here is an Andean wax palm, two hundred feet tall. Here is a baobab from the shores of Cape Verde, fifteen sazhens around. Here is a balsam poplar from North America, a Dalecarlian oak, a Tauric laurel, and an evergreen holm oak.

132

We should have a diversity of nature, tastes, and climate within reach. And what could be more diverse than the climate of Sannin? "The head of Sannin," say the Arab poets, "is clothed in winter; spring adorns his shoulders; autumn lies upon his breast; and summer rests at his feet!"

For someone used to Oriental luxury and languor, to Asiatic idleness, the valley of Syria stretches out below. Yonder rises a high hill, and all around it nature smiles. Upon this hill I convey from Delhi the sumptuous, bright halls of Quli Khan. They are as splendid as the orb of day; the walls are covered with golden scales; the ceiling is studded with radiant gems, on which one's gaze lingers involuntarily, as on a midnight sky strewn with constellations. On one side twelve massive golden columns uphold the vaulting above a broad, spacious divan. A canopy overhangs it, like the rosy clouds that gather round the western sun. The marble floor is as slippery as the path to greatness. Amid the halls a tall fountain falls into a jasper basin, its coolness soothing weariness and slaking thirst. Through the clear gleams of tumbling water one sees the image of divine Allatallah.* It is a pink marble statue, but she seems bent on quenching in the waves the fire of her own voluptuous desire. But what are Arabian Allatallah, Persian Anaya, Greek Venus, and Slavic Lada next to that charming female reader of mine, whom love has immersed in thought and fatigue lowered onto the divan, soft as the waves of the Euphrates when it flowed through the earthly paradise. My indiscreet gaze rested on her forever . . . She noticed, blushed, lowered her eyes—and all the diamonds in the palace of Quli Khan lost their glow. Oh, without those eyes there is no light anywhere in nature! . . . So, here and no farther . . .

133

I would expose your traits to view,
And trace the beauty that I see,
So as to find . . . create . . . to be
With you! But who and where are you?
Upon the earth do you reside;
In mortal life do you take part?
Or from the shadows do you glide,
You unseen temptress of the heart,
With some great lump of golden fire,
To set aflame my soul entire?

Follow the wonders of the past,
And having reached your sixteenth year,
Come down, upon the earth appear,
Be baptized; take the faith at last!

Above the font, in ardent praise,
The angels intertwined would sing,
And I, as godfather, would raise
The maiden from the holy spring.

---

* Arabian Venus.

134

But for someone who, like a simple son and friend of nature, loves to look at her beauty, a Turkestani carpet speckled with multicolored hieroglyphics like the Egyptian Dendera zodiac, has been laid on the ground. Sit down, my guests! While I am taking the trouble to put nature and climate in their places, I invite you to have a snack. I offer you neither the anointing oil of Venus, nor the nectar of Olympus, but a vial filled with the breath of the woman you worship; this drink revives hunger and thirst. I offer neither a marinated palate, nor marrow, nor a heart with truffles and anchovies, but a sweet kiss of meeting.

135

Then chaos filled infinite space, and the elements knew neither union nor enmity.

And all was filled up—so it seemed—with no space for the smallest, dimensionless atom.

But space was abundant for thought and free will.

And lo! without splitting the chaos asunder, these two entities delved deep within and found freedom—no obstacles anywhere.

And soon they flowed out of there, one from another, then one on another collapsed.

And then they were rushing all over, reflecting all over a radiant and beautiful notion about the creation.

They stopped in their course; then without a loud crash, all began to divide into parts, and each part was assembled in line with the greatness and form of the thought that infused it.

And all of those parts became worlds.

The burst of division fragmented their physical bonds; even so, their close kinship attracted them all to each other . . .

136

"What's this?"

"I'm composing the system of the world; listen! 'Then chaos filled infinite space, and the elements . . .'"

"Enough, my dear! You're raving."

"What do you mean, raving? . . . Showing the true number of elements! . . . Discovering the bonds of the universe! . . . Is that raving?"

"Raving, my dear! Look . . . they're expecting you."

"Ah! . . ."

137

All but forgot! How very tough
To keep the oaths that one has made!
One simple oath is quite enough,
A second one is reckless stuff;
A third is better to evade.
But now on promises alone
The social world must onward roll,
People, like skeletons, have grown
To be devoid of heart and soul.

I wanted to talk about *oats,* not *oaths,* and made a mistake, but I'm sure you won't punish me for it. Who doesn't know that oaths are easier to take than oats?

I am confident, however, that even if you came to my house oversaturated with the external luxury of ordinary society dinners, I should still find new food for you, light and digestible.

138

Venerable elders! Yours is the first step, the first place, the first word, and primacy in everything. Neither lineage, nor wealth, nor rank, nor merits release us from the honors due to you. "Experience and time have made you keepers of wisdom," say the Chinese. I glorify the year 2967 before Christ, which saw the founding of the Chinese kingdom! I glorify Emperor Taihao Fuxi, the founder thereof! I glorify the people for whom old age means a sacred right to be respected!

Sit on this rock, whence you can see the entire expanse of each person's life. Sit under these lindens, from which diligence has gathered honeycombs. I can already see the question in your eyes:

"What could you serve us, young man? We've tried everything . . . tasted every dish that existence offers to man . . . we're full . . . What remains for us?" What remains is to bite into these sugarplums, which contain hidden slips of paper with questions:

"Were you a human in the course of your life?"

"How many fables did Pilpai, Aesop, and Krylov write about you?"

"Did at least one person ever say to you from the heart: *You are good!*? . . ."

"Will you live in posterity or in the memory of all who knew you, not like the man who burned the temple at Ephesus, but like . . . like the one who, for the benefit of his neighbors, gained one talent for the two given to him? . . ."

"That is what remains for us as food, and for comfort we must stand on the highway of life as road signs to kind passersby."

Honor and glory to you, venerable elders! May heaven send you the blessed longevity of Yandi Shennong!

139

Now to you, my female readers . . . honored guests . . . grannies! . . . But you have already taken matters into your own hands. Words are brimming on your lips. You have hauled the present before the bar of the past. . . . You are already condemning it for the corrupt character of the people of the new century, its strange fashions, its ugly clothing, its odd customs, its bad habits, its rejection of all that is old and decrepit. You are right! Who can contradict you? . . . The past and the future are always better than the present.

> The past and I have seldom been apart,
> We've lived together, though by discord split,
> Oh grannies, both my soul and heart
> Have long and deeply grieved for it!

140

A good host should be moved to express his hospitality in all directions—the epitome of fickleness; like the sun, he should shine the same for everyone; he should be a slave to the whims of his guests; he should be as polite as flattery itself; he should speak like hundred-mouthed rumor, be as friendly as a lover and as patient as a husband.

Can I fulfill all these conditions? I, the lone Wanderer! Oh, if only . . .

How a certain creature's help can increase one's strength, lighten one's labor, and clear one's eyes and soul! . . . If only this dash —— could be replaced with a name, then I myself would not glance at the next chapter.

But ——— may be there among my guests . . .

Where'er I turn my gaze or stare,
I fall into a daydream sweet!
I look for someone everywhere,
And in my mind with someone meet.

This secret sprite, to my surprise,
Has conquered my imagination
And clothed my heart and ears and eyes
In wonderful hallucination!

Her unseen form is passing fair,
Her unheard voice is clear and mild;
With her, I would forget all care
And be as joyful as a child.

But where then is this unknown sprite,
This angel, maiden of my mind,
With whom I'm eager to unite,
To be like lyre and song entwined?

O maiden, weave your thoughts o'er me,
With future visions I am humming,
Your apparition may well be
A thrilling portent of your coming!

141

She is not here.

142

Gather round, dear friends! Lively, fiery young men! What shall I bring as food for your feelings, minds, and hearts?

The food for your mind is the whole universe. The food for the heart is sacred duties and—even more—reciprocated love from the woman about whom you are now dreaming, to whom you are listening, with whom life is everything and everything is life.

The food for your feelings is the present!

143

Nature's creation now is crowned complete!
Beneath the palms the flowers stir!
Where did the maiden spend her youth discreet?
Who fostered all that beauty intermixed in her?

May she have lovely offspring, she who knew neither cradle nor the embrace of parents, she in whom the first feeling was love and the second, repentance!

You, to whom I am chained, like Prometheus to the Caucasian rock! . . . You, charming *nothing and everything*! . . . My gold and diamond ones! As weak as the heart, as light as thought, as tender as feeling, as proud as the mind!

I meet you with the Mongolian greeting: *Amur!*

The shackles from you mortal men
I take with arms unfurled.
For you I will return Eiren
Unto the world!

On this dish before you are the gardens of Alcinous, sung by the blind Amur . . . the blind Homer, I meant to say.

Listen to what he says about these gardens:

"The gardens of Alcinous are always covered with fruits; a tender zephyr preserves their life, strength, and juices; some ripen, others are born; behind the ripe pomegranate and orange hide new ones, still forming; one ripe fig gives way to another; a ready olive is replaced by one newly born . . ."

Are not your attachments also like the trees in the gardens of Alcinous? One feeling has ripened, another is being born . . . the old one gives way to the new.

Tell me, ever-loving beings! Do you remember the past? Are you entrusting yourselves fully to the present? Are your thoughts not overtaking time? Are you not always traveling into the future? Does what you see not disappoint you? "That's not it!" you think and—again you take flight! But . . .

Blessed are they whose feelings tend
To mutual affection true,
They whisper to their tender friend:
I am not one and we're not two!
I am not one and we're not two!

144

I now address you sufferers and laborers of the world. You to whom neither sweet food nor songs of love and the nightingale will restore calm and sleep! . . . You who through illnesses or circumstances, willingly or unwillingly, are excluded from life but still exist! You who are deprived of all but the mantle of heaven! . . . For you a cup filled with bitter patience! . . . Drink it to the dregs! . . . And you will see that a smile still exists even for your lips.

As for you, wretched people, and yet surrounded by all the means and resources of life! Here is a source of living water! Read the inscription nailed over it, and follow it:

"For six weeks turn day into night and night into day; that is, sleep during the day and stay awake and toil at night; eat dinner at midnight; and observe the strict diet prescribed by medicine for patients suffering from disorders of the circulatory, nervous, or digestive systems. Your body will strengthen, your soul will live, and you will begin to crave life!"

145

Here, here in a fragrant meadow under a spreading linden, I shall sit down with you, fat, well-fed calf-gastronomes! The best time of day is the transition from hunger and thirst to ecstasy and satiety. I love your conversation! You are always joyful, like dreamy creatures on whom heaven has bestowed endless life, indefatigable strength, inexhaustible wealth, unchangeable love, true friendship, eternal health, and unfading beauty!

Your words are sonorous, like popping corks! Your meaning foams like champagne!

I love these glasses effervescent,
The feasts where muddled clamor thrives,
The mind is wing'd and incandescent,
The speeches there are sharp as knives!

Here, my friends, are dishes that stimulate the tastebuds with their causticity and sharpness.

Oh! On the Japanese Zang porcelain lies a curlew stuffed with truffles, anchovies, and oysters! As stuffed as the age is with events!

This rich pashtet before you lies;
'Tis full of fat, as you like best,
As rosy as Aisha's breast,
As puffy as Muhammad's eyes!
But gentle friends, I now must go,
And leave this feast with pleasures deep;
My evening clothing off I throw;
To greet with honor quiet sleep.

Day 19

146

If a singer's soul, feelings, and words have a relation to time and carry seeds for the soul, feelings, and words of posterity, then envious ignorance will fall like Goliath at the hand of David and harmony will subdue thunder.

If a singer's thoughts are the rays of the rising sun, then they will awaken, warm, and ignite the understanding soul.

But if the singer is an echo of sounds already pronounced, if he is a ray of the setting sun, then let him not wonder at the indifference and inattention of others to his cold enthusiasm.

Akbah, one of Omar's generals, subjected the Berbers and many other peoples to the rule of his caliph; he rode on victoriously to the very limits of Africa; and when the ocean stopped him, he plunged on horseback into the sea, drew his sword, and cried: "God of Mahomet! Thou seest it! If it were not for this element, I should go further; I should find new peoples and force them to worship your name!"

And so the poet—I was going to continue, but circumstances have dragged me on to the next chapter.

147

I will not describe my strange situation; people care about the situation of others only when it concerns them physically or morally. But from the following words that I felt obliged to put here, my situation will be clear:

> You're full of feelings burning free,
> You're very tender, very dear;
> But in comparison with me,

You're quite the opposite, I fear.
For you are light and I'm obscurity;
You're joyful; I'm dejected;
You're horizontal in your purity,
And I am vertically directed.

Perfection of thoughts and works depends on a happy frame of mind . . . Can a man always be happy? . . . And yet . . .

148

And yet, the army has already crossed the border. Lt. Gen. Kreutz's detachment has marched into Iași. The *bim beşli ağa* has disappeared, and the *divan efendi* and sovereign prince have surrendered to the protectorship of Russia.

The people gathered around the lancers' regiments, blessing the banners of the Russian tsar. An enthusiastic Hetairist in black clothes and a hood shouted, "Long live Emperor Nicholas!"; his hands were raised toward heaven, and in his right hand was an open book of prophecies. "Fly, bright angel of Russia!" he cried in Greek.

"Fly to us, Russian angel, fly!
You've brought your torch to us afflicted,
This Agathangelus predicted,
And holy John did prophesy!"

"*Venit, venit Muscal! Venit cavalerie de Împărat! Slavă lui Dumnezeu! Καλά είναι!* Good, good! *Și eu* sherved the tshar!" shouted one Greek creature, skinny as a human skeleton, who had served under six Moldavian princes and seen many wonders in his time—including a Hebrew sorcerer who once cast spells to call an evil spirit into a glass full of water . . . a mountainous feast in the glass . . . noise, screeching, screaming . . . but here the elder one appears! . . . the evil spirit sits at the embroidery-covered table . . . they discuss and argue . . . about the fate of fortune tellers, buried treasures, a lost object, a guilty man, a thief . . . the Hebrew sorcerer stands over the glass with a huge Talmud, reads prayers and spells, repeats the words of the evil spirit, predicts the future, and—it all comes true! . . .

"You saw this?" "I shaw it, I shaw it myself!" the *Graikos* repeats. "I'm very glad, but goodbye, my friend; we'll see each other again."

149

Everyone knows that on the twenty-fifth of April, 1828, there was a border crossing at the town of Skulyany, the town of Fălciu, and the village of Vadului Isakchi, but not everyone knows the difficulties of crossing in the spring, during the flooding of the rivers. At Vadului-Isakchi the Prut Valley is four versts wide. The whole space is flooded, but anything can be overcome. In one night a bridge and dam across the flood were made ready. This village was formerly called Traian, probably because on the mountain above it is the end of the old border also called *Traian—via Trajani—Trajan's Wall.*

In addition to everything I once said about Trajan's Wall, I should conclude all my investigations and contemplations with the following:

Bessarabia, Moldavia, Wallachia, Bulgaria, Transylvania, etc., etc., are broken up in all directions by walls. These walls are none other than dry, fortified, borders.

In Bessarabia, the lower part of Trajan's Wall separated the land belonging to the Greek colonies on the shore of the Black Sea from the nomadic peoples of the Budzhak wilderness.

The upper part served as a border between the steppes and the rich, settled uplands of Bessarabia.

The town of Galați, a former Greek and then Roman colony, is separated from the Getic wilderness by a similar high wall.

It is the same story everywhere else.

150

So then, opposite the village of Traian, almost in the same spot where there was once a permanent ford and a stone bridge, the Russians built a dam and marched into Moldavia.

By the way, about the river Prut: its waves are born in the Carpathian Mountains and die in the Danube. The width of the river is generally between five and ten sazhens. The water is turbid on account of its speed but healthy, with the usual properties of strengthening mineral waters.

From the very border with Austria to the town of Lipkany it sneaks along the steep, wooded bank of Moldavia. On our side the valley is open, and settlements are frequent. I remember that, while traveling around the border mountains, I stopped overnight in the village of Mamalyga at the house of a venerable old *yesaul.* He prodded his Kalmyk servant vigorously, and the kettle was boiling in an instant. I offered him tea with Jamaican rum. "Oh, no!" he exclaimed.

Now may the Lord God strike me dumb,
No Cossack of the Don I'd be
If I should spoil my tea with rum
Or, God forbid, my rum with tea!
Just add hot water; that's for me!
Punsht—what the nobles guzzle down!
And brandy! Knock you off your horse!
Speaking of which, mine's great, of course!
Throughout our ataman's great town,
And in the stable of the count,
Old boy, you can't find such a mount!
Aha! It must be time for bed:
I see that you've begun to snore!
Myself, I rose today before
The dawn; a hundred miles I sped
Along the cordon line, that's right!
Well then, dear sir, good night, good night!

151

Since the preceding chapter began with a river crossing, I wanted to end it with a discussion of the difficulties of carrying a thought from one chapter to another, from one verse to another, and so on, but I must, against my will, defer this endeavor until my article about the Archipelago.

Day 20

152

Sometimes, when stepping out onto the field of day, I have thought about the universe, man, and life.

The universe is . . . . ; man is . . . . ; life is . . . . These definitions are not entirely clear; time, however, will complete and explain them.

Considered mathematically, the universe is x, man is y, and life is z. If we give the most enormous value to x (because what can be larger than the universe in the physical world?), we immediately determine both y and z; but since the value of x is arbitrary, the concepts y and z, because of the different bases of these systems, are as different as $-\infty$ and $+\infty$. Owing to circumstances unrelated to the scholarship and discoveries of past and future centuries, and although the present lives at the expense of the past, I must now define the magnetic force.

Since everything necessarily leaves a trace, the magnetic force is none other than the trace of the globe's flight . . . The globe rushes along with the South Pole in front, and therefore its trace is left on the North. Streams of ignited ether, emanating from the continuous constant cleaving of that ether by the earth's motion, form the direction of the magnetic force from south to north . . . From this we can conclude that the aurora borealis is a visible glow left in the wake of the globe's rapid flight.

The relation of a magnet to iron is also clear: iron is none other than the stream of boiling terrestrial matter at the South Pole caused by the constriction and ignition of the ether . . . and the direction of the streams of this metal in the earth must be from south to north.

There you have it! Truth is needed everywhere.

153

From the town of Lipkany to the village of Kosteshty, the river Prut flows for the most part between rocky banks. At Kosteshty, on its first day of flowing, it met an irresistible crenelated granite wall, but the wall parted before the waves of Hierasus, like the sea before the people of Israel.

Beyond the Kosteshty cliffs, the high left bank stretches for about five versts, steep and precarious. The whole slope for several versts is covered with burial mounds. This place is called *Suta de Movile* (a hundred tombs, or mounds). The unevenness of the place calls to mind a strong earthquake or terrible battle, but those who witnessed these events have lain a few thousand years under a layer of earth, not caring that a living man would give a great deal to an ancient dead man for stories of the events of his time.

Farther on, the river Prut flows through a marshier and reedier plain. From Skulyany the road to Iași snakes to the right and the one to Kishinev to the left.

On the latter road, Providence took away Prince Potyomkin's brilliance, honors, and cares and sent him to the source of strength along the path of no return.

Below Skulyany and Țuțora, where Peter the Great once camped, the river Prut sinks deeper and deeper into the reeds. The marshy, lake-covered valley widens here.

During floods the shores are muddy and impassable. But you, Wanderer, who were sent to reinforce the border line along this elemental snake, 740 versts long, rode across safely on horseback.

Over the course of four months, two hundred and fifty Don border horses carried you across these waters as bravely as Jupiter carried the daughter of King Agenor from the shores of Phoenicia to the island of Crete.

Europa on the hornèd thief
Rides o'er the sea—no time to weep;
She prays that Zeus will grant relief
And watch her safely o'er the deep.
O maid, fear not the briny blue!
'Tis Zeus himself who carries you!

154

I appear to have strayed from the road! . . . In what chapter did I turn right or left? . . . It seems to have happened at the beginning of the previous one . . . Such blunders are often made by enthusiastic, loving, careless, and distracted people . . . All these virtues reside in me at the same time: enthusiasm in my soul, love in my heart, carelessness in my disposition, and distraction in my thoughts.

But can one keep on going straight?
A church on one side, then a wall,
A river, marsh, and garden gate.
A thousand barriers long and tall!
Well just go back again, that's all!
Go back? But what if I have springs,
Machines to take me to the sky?
A little effort—on my wings
I flutter up and forward fly!

155

Onward! . . . Let us follow Lt. Gen. Baron Geismar's detachment, the flying vanguard of the Sixth Corps . . . Over five days, he rushes across the plains of Wallachia for 228 versts and arrives in Bucharest on the thirtieth of April. The metropolitan, clergy, boyars, and people greet him as the savior who has warned them about the destructive advance of the Turks across the Danube.

The flat land around Bucharest does not reward curious eyes with views of the city or the surrounding area. When you approach the Wallachian capital through the small bushes and young forests, you enter it almost imperceptibly . . .

156

Upon a long and crooked street,
I rode and rode—and soon grew weary,
And just my luck—I chanced to meet
A crowd of faces dull and dreary:
Each grizzly boyar with his mate,

Their fox-fur jackets—they are not
Of any interest . . . March on straight
To Antonache's! Walk . . . or trot . . .
Or gallop! . . . Stop! . . . What is this place?
A naiad in the window there!
Aha! She seems to know my face.
Look how she smiles, without a care! . . .
She's fifteen! . . . What a wondrous turn!
With ardent blush and tresses black,
A buxom breast and eyes that burn!
She's all aglow! But she's stepped back.
Though she is hidden from my sight,
My blood is in a sorry plight!

157

I'm weary from the road! . . . Eat, drink, sleep! . . . *Ei, măi! țigănești, moldovenești, românești, grecești, frumușică! Degrabă, mâncat!*

"Do hurry up!"

FRENCH SERVANT

"Plait-il, monsieur?"
"Manger, monsieur!"

GERMAN MAID

"Gleich, was Sie wollen."

JEWISH SERVANT

"A snack?"
"Of course, and I'd prefer
It soon! I'm famished—bring it all in!"

GERMAN GIRL

"Wir haben Schnepfen."
"Well, *sehr gut!*"

MOLDAVIAN SERVANT

"Lichior poftești?"
  "Yes, just so . . ."

JEW WITH GOODS

"Some signets, rings!"
  "You Judas, go!"

ANOTHER JEW

"And lining, cloth!"

ARMENIAN WITH GOODS

"And ghermesut! . . ."

HEBREW CONJURER

"Ekh verde enen etvas tsáen!"
"Enough! From whence did they all fly in?
Chase them away!"

HOST [*driving them away*]

"Poftim, poftim!"

ARMENIANS

"Mazur buyurun sultanım!"

[*They exit.*]

GREEK SERVANT

"Idou kaponi kai salatan!"
"A sultan or a eunuch chicken,
I do not care . . . but what's in that one?
Its unclean spirit makes me sicken!"

HOST

"Anasına . . ." etc.

158

Thus all the abovementioned persons, merchants and hawkers, importunate Jews and bothersome Armenians, laden Tyrolese, restaurant *slujitori* of various nations, and Lottchen, who forced me to say, in German, "Well, *sehr gut!*"—each of these in turn, with his own unit, took the measure of my patience and hunger. But finally the hucksters were expelled with a Turkish curse, and the waiters gave me a cup of broth, a brace of snipe with salad, and a sponge cake baked back in 1820 for Prince Callimachi's expected accession to the divan of Wallachia. Then I drank, as usual, some Râmnic wine and a cup of *'fee*, since the *coffee* they gave me did not deserve even the name *'offee*.

As someone quite experienced in satisfying my hunger and quenching my thirst, I polished it off in five minutes: I scolded the maidservant for her excessive speed and intolerable slowness, said a few more words in German, and went to my room.

DERZHAVIN

Upon a velvet couch I lie . . .

I

Hold on, I'll finish, let me try,
This picture fits me to a T,
I'm lying just like this, you see . . .
But now . . . it's time to sleep . . .

Day 21

159

What, why should I chase after you?
The shadow of a woman sly?
No, friend! 'Tis I you should pursue;
To strive for glory I won't try!
For that is but a foolish story,
When I am not in love with glory!

This morning thus I loudly cried
And forward like a whirlwind flew,
Just like the dove Xisuthrus spied,
To seek a refuge in the blue.

160

Tell me, good readers, is it not criminal to think that, for the perfection of existence, people and all their relationships must be cast in the same mold? Where have I come across such ideas? "How very wise!" says a dissatisfied man. "Why is life a reward for some and a punishment for others?" If I had lived a life before this one, I would answer him, but it seems I have not.

Poor piece of beautiful marble! You did not fall into the hands of Phidias! How people would have marveled at you! . . . You ended up in a wall, a column, a staircase! . . . No one sees you, and everyone tramples you underfoot! . . . Poor piece of beautiful marble! But it cannot be helped; be comforted; it is merely for variety. And what is variety for? For perpetual motion. And perpetual motion? For existence. And existence? For destruction. And destruction? For a beginning. And a beginning? For an end! And an end? For a connection; and a connection? For a union; and a union? For a birth . . . etc. A wise man says this and is very pleased with himself . . . Trust me, you only need patience: over time you will end up in a museum as an ancient stone, and then your appearance will shine forth again.

161

I included chapter 160 because it was meant to exist and precisely in the form in which I included it. All its flaws and imperfections are not on my account . . . A beautiful thought is like marble, and if it falls into the hands not of Phidias but of a simple stonemason, then he will carve it against all rules of sculpture.

Here someone crept up behind me and covered my eyes with her hands . . .

162

My friend, please let me be, you pest!
You irritate me more and more.
You really want to be caressed
Today, with all my work in store?
I'm busy; there are better times
For tender love! . . . Oh, what a pain!
Leave me alone! Don't tear my rhymes!
You're whining? . . . Not again! . . .
Oh, you! . . . Where have my verses gone?
My tongue is mute; my thoughts are dire!
Chapter one hundred forty-one—
Behold—is burning in the fire!
What perished was no daydream airy,
But fair in aspect, like a Peri!
O reader, do you feel the cost
Of what we in the fire have lost?

Yes, a loss, a loss to both of us! If I had the time and if the fountain of Bakhchisaray were in my heart, I would surely build a basin on this place and fill it with my tears! But . . .

163

Here it is not fashionable to walk; it is in fact impossible to go on foot on account of the narrow streets, the unevenness of the wooden pavement, the suffocating dust, the dirt, the splashes from passing carriages . . . For those reasons, it is fashionable here to go about in *butci.*

In the evening, the beauties of Bucharest in their dressing rooms, in front of alluring pier glasses, remove the curling irons from their hair; they wash their faces with virgin's milk; a blush of artificial bashfulness begins to glow on their cheeks; their eyebrows are darkened; languorous lines appear under their eyelashes; corsets bind their waists . . .

O fruits of the Hesperides!
Though you be pressed in plate and mail,
Your modest works do not avail,
A sly gaze through the armor sees!
My life would be too hard to bear,
The *nec plus ultra,* far too much!
Were I, my friends, to lose fore'er . . .
Were I to lose . . . my sense of touch!

164

What next? Next . . . The beauties apply transparent streams to their heads; strings of pearls, like snakes, are woven into their hair; gold chains are placed on their necks; rainbow butterflies on their bosoms; keys on their belts; *sotteuse* watches on their belts; Gothic bracelets on their hands; elastic gloves; eyeglasses; and dresses . . . and their ornaments . . . and sleeves *à l'ange qui vole.* Everything is so colorful, so newfangled, so made-up!

Madame la marchande de modes, like a picture from the *Journal des dames* brought to life, is fussing about the beauties of the South, pinning one thing, tying another, tightening a third, pouring taste, true corporeal elegance, and sartorial harmony into their souls . . .

Finally the toilet is completed. The Arnaut enters. "Butca gata!" he says, and now the small feet in satin slippers carry the light Romanian woman into the Viennese carriage. The coachman, wearing a Hungarian costume speckled with lace and a Hetairist cap, pulls the rains and cracks the whip; the stallions toss their manes and rear up; the harness rattles; the carriage begins to sway; it flies through the gate and moves smoothly down the street in a row with all the others . . . The charming Romanian woman is satisfied and happy.

Thus, hundreds of carriages stretch through Bucharest like moving greenhouses. The sounds: "Kali imera sas! Hoş geldin! Seara buna! Vecher dobry! Bon soir! Guten Abend! Wie befinden Sie . . . Sie . . . Sie . . . Sie . . . sich?" merge with the clatter of the wheels and continue until they are exhausted.

This is evidently one of the enjoyments of the fairer sex here.

165

Night has long since come, my dear readers! I would wish you sweet dreams; but my imagination is still so vivid and active . . . and has carried me to the house of a Wallachian boyar.

Am I really—you think—going to describe how I drove up to the entrance, how I climbed the grand staircase, how in the antechamber several Arnauts ran up to me and only one managed to take off my overcoat, how I paused outside the hall, how I entered it, how I attracted the attention of the beau monde of Bucharest, how my gaze flew over everyone's faces, how my attention was riveted, how propriety diverted it, and how I approached the hostess? . . . Not at all! I shall just tell you that Montesquieu measured people's activity with Réaumur's thermometer, but Volney silenced him. A man's needs and necessities are the reasons for his fast or slow activity. Both in society and in a wild state, people are inactive, slow, and pampered if the land they inhabit is luxurious and rich in all that is necessary for existence . . . On the other hand, deficiencies, stinginess, and infertility in nature compel men to labor, action, ingenuity, and perpetual motion.

Would someone like me sow an open field lying beneath his hand with thoughts, dreams, events, and all his notions of things if he were satisfied with the present? . . . But now I turn to the master of the house.

166

Imagine a Wallachian boyar sitting on a large divan. Here he is . . . His clothes are magnificent, colorful, and sumptuous, like a picture in a book depicting the costumes of different nations . . . His position is as still as a sculpted image of the Mongol deity Shakyamuni . . . He crosses and hides his legs, like vulgar things, under the health and prosperity of his large frame. His appearance is copied from the self-importance of the last pasha, at whom he once dared to look, approaching him with fear and trembling.

He is important, yes indeed!
Three inches long is his mustache;
His beard two cubits, gray as ash.
A yard of amber—have a look—
And a six-fathom-long chibouk!
He is important, yes indeed!

Day 22

167

Leaving you, my companions, to enjoy all the pleasures of life in Bucharest, I must excuse myself and go to observe the movement of our troops.

What can be more interesting than the first skirmish with an enemy! . . . Man is naturally good and is not disposed—especially in moments of reason—to turn himself and others prematurely into dirt and to deprive a humble soul of its covering, but one must see how quickly he is filled with fury against the enemy, with what pleasure he destroys the other's ability to live! I say nothing of the barbaric military customs and pleasures: of the Pecheneg who prefers the skull of his enemy to a precious chalice; of the Janissary who cuts pockets in the sides of a corpse and stuffs his dead enemy's hands into them.

168

On the twenty-seventh of April the vanguard of the Seventh Corps reached the village of Baldogineşti, eight versts from the fortress of İbrail. Here was the first meeting with the enemy. A party from His Imperial Highness the heir's ataman regiment, under the command of the brave Katasonov, overtook a detachment of Turks, who had left the fortress to forage . . . Thirty Turks were killed; eighteen were captured.

On the first of May, the Seventh Corps besieged the fortress. On the seventh of May, His Imperial Highness the Grand Duke Mikhail Petrovich took command of the siege corps.

The next day, the presence of Emperor Nicholas himself shone forth on the walls of İbrail.

169

The first brilliant exploit of the Turkish campaign belonged to the Danube flotilla under the command of Captain of the First Rank Zavadovsky.

Like a cloud, the reckless Zavadovsky swept past the fortress and burst with thunder amid the Turkish flotilla . . . The deed was done! . . . The enemy admiral's boat and eleven vessels with their artillery were captured, and eight were burned, wrecked, or run aground.

Success in an enterprise, in my opinion, is the best reward.

170

My friends! Future generations, future heroes! . . . Someday you too will have seen your fill of courage, bravery, great deeds, and human frailty! . . . And you will look respectfully at a five-pood mortar, which sits grandly in a large armchair like an old lady, coughing and spitting on everyone . . . And you will see how a bomb flies through the sky, by day like a black raven, by night like a meteor.

It has fallen onto the city and burst through a roof; it is within the house but is suffocating there . . . Now it has broken into the open air . . . and the whole house is blown apart . . . But now another bomb is flying right behind it . . . and so on.

171

What can be more disagreeable than stops on the road! The horses wear themselves out, a wheel breaks, an axle fractures, there is a difficult crossing, a devilish bridge, a mountain, a river crossing, and everything that is annoying, obnoxious, wearisome, and unbearable!

These very feelings kill me whenever my imagination ceases. Whipping and prodding are of no use . . . Raising hell on earth, I walk across the open field to the next chapter and seek in vain for places to unload all the emptiness that sometimes floods my mind.

In these foolish moments of life, it seems that everything has already been invented, said, and written.

For a long, long time you wait for your soul to repeat, louder than before: little, little has yet been thought, said, or written! . . . In those moments it is so easy to write.

So I take up my pen and, fulfilling the promise of chapter 45, I write:

The harmony emitted by the mouth of a lovely woman consists of consonant sounds, like the flow of the universe . . .

But before I continue, look at this sweet, angelic reader! If Prometheus lived in our times, he would steal the miraculous fire not from heaven, but from her eyes . . . See how she blushes! Thus a rose bloomed for an instant at the creation of the world! . . . Her bosom heaves . . . Are these not waves clothed in foam?

> Now to compare is my design:
> It's not a *that* that makes you glow;
> It's not a darling *I don't know*;
> But it's a *something* quite divine!

So then, the best sounds are those heard in the moment when the earth turns into heaven, when one moment of eternal bliss dissolves, according to Hahnemann's system, in the infinite ocean of time, and one drop of that spiritual balm is poured into the soul of man.

But cast a glance at her again!

> What liveliness, eyes clear and bright!
> Those lips, that blush, that graceful frame!
> Her soul's as pristine as a flame!
> Her husband is . . . an Abelite!
> Villain! You've taken life away
> From those could have lived in truth!
> With their own blood, full many a youth
> Would try to blot your sin away.

She is a virtuous, innocent angel! . . .

172

Here I must say something about the harmony of genii.

Their voices and the words they sing are sweet;
I could attempt to sing them out for you.
But I'm afraid my listeners would meet
My song with nervous fits, not quite undue.
And so, according to my right innate,
Which you too are obliged now to admit,
I have, dear readers, opened wide the gate,

This boring chapter finally to quit.

Day 23

173

One fine morning in May 1828, according to the dispositions for the movement of the Second Army headquarters, I rose before the sun; . . . a Cossack brought me my horse; I mounted, girded his sides with my whip, and set off on the road to Galați.

Farewell, modest hut of Hacı Kaptan, in which I tasted my first sweet dreams under the roar of siege weapons! . . . Farewell, İbrail! I would recount how your walls and mosques fell under the Russian thunder; I would describe your siege by all the rules set out in Vauban, Saint-Paul, Folard, Bélidor, Coehoorn, and Cormontaigne . . . but duty and imagination draw me across the Danube.

174

Hurrah, delights sublime and bold!
Temptations that green youth begets!
What man has never been consoled
By George and two thick epaulets?

Sing the song "A Cossack Rides Across the Danube . . ." etc., i.e., across the Balkans, but how long he must ride only the top brass know.

Still, what a sad road for the Cossack! . . . First, because he bid farewell to his girl, and second . . . but all other reasons are nothing compared with the first!

Ten days before the Russian centurion on the İbrail bastion first cried, "Who goes there?" the Third Corps, inspired by the presence of the brave and generous Russian tsar, built a dike five versts long through the marshes and reeds of the Danube, erected a bridge over the river, and like a giant bogatyr, stepped over all obstacles and went on to build wonders in the Balkans.

Here Darius once marched in the opposite direction against the nomadic Scythians, but then the earth was 2,336 years younger, and the river Danube was called the Ister, which flowed from distant lands where the sun rests.

Great events are the keys that wind the mechanism of perpetual motion.

175

See how our battery of twenty-four guns bombards the Turkish coast and the enemy fortifications! The Danube flotilla rushes past under Muhammadan fire right under the İshakçı fortress; the boats of the Zaporozhian Cossacks and barges arrive like a flock of swans; the jäger regiments are loaded up and carried to the other side . . . But then the fire intensifies; a cloud of smoke lies over the broad Danube; everything vanishes from view; only the thunder of the guns rolls in the immense distance, in the convolutions of the Danube, between the rocks, on the lakes, in the reeds . . . But suddenly the thunderclaps subside . . . and are replaced by the crackle of rapid rifle fire . . . Everything clears up . . . On the Danube there is already a pontoon bridge, across which troops and guns are rushing . . . The sun is blazing; rows of bayonets are shining; the Danube is calm; the Russians are in Bulgaria; crowds of Turks scatter in fear and flee into the fortress. İshakçı is besieged.

Warrior! If you were at the crossing of the Danube, then remember how you ran across the pontoon bridge, looked to your left into the Turkish trench, to your right into the redoubt abandoned by the enemy with its hideous weapons, how you hurried uphill, climbed breathlessly onto the terrible Vizier's Mound, sat down, caught your breath, then looked around you . . . Do you remember how wonderful nature seemed to you? . . . Directly to the north you saw the whole setup of the crossing, behind it the marshy, reedy shore and the newly laid road, farther on the village of Satunovo, then the Budzhak steppes and the hills stretching out . . . On the right were distant Izmail, the meandering Danube, bright lakes, green reeds, blue fog above a band of sea . . . On the left was the wild fortress of İshakçı, then the mouths of the Prut and the Siret, the town of Galați, and, barely noticeable in the smoke, İbrail . . . Behind you is the shore of Babadağ, the wooded mountains, and the road leading to the capital of the sultan . . . You were spellbound, warrior! Your eyes grew weary, you heaved a sigh for the past, and you crossed once more into the enticing future! . . .

Having finished my day with an exclamation point, I was pleased with myself and slept so soundly that if the fiery kiss of love had scorched my lips, I should not have felt the slightest pain.

Day 24

176

When the natural mind and unspoiled heart had inseparable and amicable dominion over mankind, that was the golden age.

Then came the ardent summers of the world: the mind gave free rein to the heart; that was the silver age.

Finally, the heart was exhausted; the mind took over; the iron age had arrived.

See how the cold mind reigns! . . . It shines in the eyes of mankind . . . and in the chest there is a lump of iron! . . . Now it is neither wisdom nor feelings that put everything in motion, but the calculations of the mind and the magnetic force!

Ye heavenly host, revive the heart!

177

The previous chapter described humanity in general; as for my own heart, I still live in the silver age.

> I know not what to do with this poor heart of mine:
> When you are far away, it aches, it pines, it mourns!
> So take it for yourself! To me it is unfaithful;
> It now loves only you, my tender, loving friend!
>
> Receive it, for to you alone do I bequeath it;
> Before we lived as friends; we were inseparable;
> But now it chooses love and scorns my friendship;
> So may it find in you the feelings that it seeks!
>
> I know not why it grew so lonely and so cold
> Within its native breast, which gave it such affection;

I hope that it may find in you the sweeter flame
That I myself had not the strength to feed to it.

But if you do not bear that flame of loving passion,
Take not my heart, for from the touch of frigid feelings
It will soon fade away, and I will be as nothing,
A shrine without an idol, life deprived of hope!

Everything seeks true love; but just yesterday I met a lovely romantic creature who sought it, found it, and—like the cock in Aesop's fable—spurned the diamond it had found!

178

179

After yesterday's meeting, filled with chagrin, I knew not what to put in chapter 178; but you cannot call it empty, for nature abhors a vacuum.

180

Once, feeling dejected, I was lying in a dark corner, on my divan . . . I would have drowned in meditation if two eccentrics had not saved me against my will, their loud dispute taking place in the adjoining room.

FIRST VOICE

Don't keep on talking and explaining! . . . Sublime love! I know it, I know it! . . . This, my friend, is the same as common, earthly love, but in chains, you understand? . . . . . . It consists of two . . . . . . but the spiritual part is eternally free . . . . . . the goal of desires . . . obstacles . . . . . . impossibility . . . . . . the poor heart begins to suffer; the compassionate soul grieves along with the heart; offended, unfulfilled desire drives at least the thoughts to the elusive goal . . . but imagination is villainy! O people, people! . . . But of all people, lovers are the most amusing!

SECOND VOICE

Intolerable words! And to think I listened to them! Do you really not understand that love is the union of the universe, the involuntary attraction of homogeneous, uniform beings to each other . . . Can this inscrutable feeling be considered the pursuit of satisfaction by wanton desires? . . . Is love really an arbitrary goal and a game of willful pride? . . . I've seen beautiful, lovely women; the conquest of their feelings would flatter the vanity even of La Rochefoucauld; but I looked on them as creatures from a foreign land, whose language was incomprehensible and whose customs were strange . . . I've seen charming, dear women; brought close to them by circumstances, I grew accustomed to them, and I might have mistaken habit for love; I might have loved them, but I would not sacrifice myself for them! . . .

FIRST VOICE

It's clear; you needn't finish . . . What follows is ethereal love, or the anguish of two creatures that have one soul, but two hearts! . . . It's quite clear! The soul they share strives to bring them impossibly together, to merge them into a mathematical line.

SECOND VOICE

No, it's not clear for people on earth!

FIRST VICE

How? To what extent should we love a woman, for instance?

SECOND VOICE

If I allowed for madness in true love, I'd say that one ought to love another more than life itself; but according to the reasoning of the heart, we ought to love our chosen object as our own life! . . . Is that clear?

FIRST VOICE

Not really! For me only one thing is clear: he who knights himself must choose a helmet that fits his head, because if it is too small, it will fall off, and if it is too large, it will cover his eyes and ears and sometimes even sit on his neck. But enough about sublime love. My main advice to you, young enthusiast, is, don't trust women!

SECOND VOICE

Much obliged! All you have to do now is say to all women, "Don't trust men!" . . . Oh, then people would be happy and calm! . . . No! . . . I would sooner not trust my own feelings; they are our real flatterers, which our pride alone makes us trust! . . . There is as much good and evil in women as in us; their character . . .

FIRST VOICE

Their character's unknown to me.
Can I, not very wise or smart—
I still count on my fingers—see
The worth of lodgers in the heart?
Women forgive all earthly flaws;
Their character's an unmatched gem;
I love them, but by nature pause
Before I put my trust in them.
It's normal from love's bonds to try
To flee and gain a freer state.
Moreover, nature did create
For every moth and butterfly,
Sweet flowers in immense supply.
Why should we fear abundant things?
Drink honey, fly from flower to flower,
Till time with all its wicked power
Cuts off your iridescent wings!
Let life's brief river flow on fast,
Let no love bind you to the past!
So seize your joys and live with glee,
From chains of passion be set free;
And laugh that any love can last!

SECOND VOICE

Enough! I won't talk to you! . . . Those are rules of a depraved heart! . . . Farewell, you disturber of faith and trust! . . .

FIRST VOICE

Till we meet again!

Tired of listening to this dispute, I jumped off the divan, grabbed my peaked cap, and set off on my campaign. A few moments later, I was again on the Danube.

181

Without describing in detail the road from the fortress of İshakçı to the town of Babadağ, I will only say that the isolated mountains, the hills, the shrub-covered valleys, on the right the rocks of Denistepe and the woods, and on the left silver Lake Razim and beyond it the blue sea, and, finally, blossoming May, the clear sky, and the fragrant air—all of this charmed the feelings of the Turkish visitors: their campaign felt like a stroll, and the region of Babadağ seemed like Eden—though without houris.

During the movement of the main forces from İshakçı to Babadağ, detachments were sent to Tulça, Maçin, and Hırsova. While they fulfill their purpose, we shall follow the emperor's quarters and the headquarters of the Second Army via Bey Davud and Satışköy to Karasu.

182

After the Babadağ region was occupied, Karasu was designated as the place to wait for the army's initial successes in besieging the fortresses.

Here, in front of Trajan's Wall, on the gently sloping left bank of the Karasu, the emperor's field capital was set up in all its brilliance.

The city of tents with golden tops was surrounded by hedges. The sky was clear; the clouds were afraid to prevent the sun from playing on the bright Russian guns and bayonets.

For several days, it was a camp of silence, like the space between lightning and thunder, as Byron says. But suddenly several hundred guns rang out in honor of the capture of the fortresses of İbrail and Maçin . . . Süleyman Paşa and Cafer Paşa first felt that the time was long past when devout Muslims under the command of Omar subdued thirty thousand cities and castles, destroyed four thousand churches, and built fourteen hundred mosques.

183

Soon a single, sonorous bell in the camp announced a public prayer service for the conquest of the fortresses of Hırsova, Tulça, and finally Köstence. In the first, İşim Paşa, in the second İbrahim Paşa, and in the third Abdullah Bey bowed their horsetails to the Russian flag, handed them to the victors, and set off to offer excuses for their failures before the Sublime Porte.

184

In front of the Russian tsar's quarters, colored banners are waving . . . The Russian tsar is radiant, surrounded by his sons and the eyes of Europe.

Only victorious, powdery clouds float in the sky.

The military tradespeople have gathered in crowds; they watch in awe, murmuring in different languages: Russian, Moldavian, Bulgarian, Turkish, Serbian, German, French, Italian, and Greek.

Imagine, dear readers, with what pleasure I shall remember this venerable picture in my old age! In the crowd of staff officers, in a scene drawn from Bouilly, one can see the physiognomy of the Wanderer, on which these words seem to be inscribed: "How soon shall I awake?"

With what pride, laying aside the pen that is toiling over a description of the *future*, shall I sit in state among my good friends and relate the events of the *past* in the following way:

185

"Back when . . ." At the beginning of the story, without a doubt, I shall take a pinch of snuff, wheeze like a wall clock, and sneeze loudly; the attentive guests will say, "God bless you!" and then fall silent; I shall thank them and then continue my story in the following way:

"Back when I galloped along the ridge of Trajan's Wall that runs through Bulgaria, along the bank of the Karasu to the Köstence fortress, which was once called Ister, and then Constantiana . . .

"It seems that was on the eighth of June, 1828, as history tells us," one of my friends will say. "Oh no!" another will interrupt, "it was on the twentieth of June; I remember; I've read Valentini!" This will flare up into a chronico-chronological debate, which will be interrupted by the arrival of new guests and perhaps even ladies. Therefore, forgetting the past, I shall surrender entirely to the present.

186

For reasons that are known—though not to me, as I have delved into the strategy only of my own movements—the imperial quarters and Second Army headquarters moved from their initial position on the Karasu to a second position, about ten versts up, by the lakes . . . There a camp was pitched according to all the rules of castrametation.

But night has already arrived—a quiet night . . . What a picture! . . . Camp and bivouac fires, scattered in the darkness, flicker around you; they stretch up to the very sky, and the stars on the horizon look like a continuation of the fires of the Russian camp.

For a long time Russian sounds have not echoed in the lands beyond the Danube! . . . Call to each other, you unsleeping ones! And I . . . Montaigne said: "Notre veillée est plus endormie que le dormir; notre sagesse moins sage que la folie; nos songes valent mieux que nos discours."

Day 25

187

The clock struck seven . . . The morning rays were awaiting my return from the realm of Erebus's grandson . . . and their expectation was soon fulfilled. A ghost-drawn chariot stopped at the porch, and I arose in all my beauty like a dolphin from the waves . . . the feathery waves.

Where do you think I was?

> Beside the snowy Alps, where Leman
> Roars up against the cliffs, and sighs,
> Where Julie's love by some foul demon
> Was tempted once to his demise;
> Yes, I was there . . .

188

Once upon a time, far from the places where mankind is plagued by insatiable desires and unbridled passions, people enjoyed the beauty of nature, the silence of life, and the tranquility of the soul. Pure was their breath, like the air of Helvetia. There was no animosity among them. Their hearts were not like islands scattered across the sea; rather, they formed one land, one chain of customs, habits, friendship, and love.

Maidens! You maidens whom I see and meet! If you could see the dress and adornments of those maidens about whom I am thinking now! . . . What luxury! So much gold, so many jewels! What a dazzling glow! And nothing obscures their natural beauty! . . . Will their modesty conceal it? . . . What adornments are more luxurious than innocence and virtue!

Laugh, laugh, you winged ones whom I see and meet! Oh, may divine Providence call forth in your souls, at least for a moment, that feeling called *nature*!

What pleasure now remains for a person? Only the momentary forgetting of eternal grief.

The mind has swallowed up the heart . . . and earthly happiness is the heart's domain!

189

If somebody were to claim the right to reproach me by saying that my heart is as cold as ice, I would not swear that he is wrong—no indeed! . . . Let my heart be like a piece of ice brought from the Arctic Ocean, from the northern point where all imagined meridians run together! . . . Let my heart be like that! . . . Perhaps the polar ice is as hard as flint, and striking one piece with another would produce sparks . . . but what sparks? The sparks of love! . . . If someone gives me even one such spark, I shall be content, for what is better than *sincere love*?

190

Love! . . . I believe the legends of charming Hesiod and passionate Sappho . . . Their hearts knew you . . . I trust them: you, Love, are the daughter of heaven and earth! . . . You are deity and demon, clairvoyant and blind, heaven and hell, bliss and suffering!

> You tempter, you seductive liar,
> Inconstant dweller of my heart,
> You source of the mysterious fire,
> Treacherous spirit, now depart!
> I need you not, you fleeting friend!
> As joy and fate are wont to do,
> You only to yourself are true,
> Can only on yourself depend.
> So take the treasures of your dream
> To some new victim of your lie!
> Change hearts, for all these feelings seem
> Like flowers—they quickly fade and die!

191

Often, and how often . . . after a monologue like the one above, uttered in distress, there is suddenly a sharp transition to the following:

Too long has she my soul misled,
She pulls me to the whirlpool's brink!
Watch her rise up and downward sink
To the enchanted riverbed!
Will all my senses melt away?
She floats up and the waters play! . . .
The dark waves rock her form about! . . .
Now in a diamond tent of spray,
She lies in languor, all stretched out,
She tempts me, fills me with dismay!
I'll dive in, that the water's chill
May quell my heart's incessant fire!
But I'm afraid Rusalka will
Now smother me with her desire!

192

Just as I am carried away by my vivid imagination, most people are carried away by ardent passions and forget their responsibilities . . . but I . . . I am not led astray for long by the tyranny of unbridled thoughts! . . . So I turned them back to the highway once again. But I do not want to come back down to earth completely . . . I will fly on the seventh layer of air . . . Passing by Magura, I cannot help but stop on the summit of this familiar mountain . . . I see clearly before me the Carpathian range, and its branches that run through Hungary, Galicia, Transylvania, and Moldavia, like the petrified waves of a furious ocean, illuminated by Zoroaster's bright divinity; but instead of exclaiming "What a majestic picture!" I gaze with indifference at the boundless space. Below me all is quiet. Where are the people? Where is their noisy, perpetual motion; where are their endless worries? I cannot see or hear them! How peaceful they are! They do not disturb the calm of nature! . . . Oh, if I had time, I would climb the airy steps to the first gold-lined cloud; like Jupiter I would look down at the earth and inscribe my thoughts about mankind with a thunderbolt in the blue air!

193

Its infancy . . . Here everyone will inadvertently recall how his mommy cherished him . . .

> It's true! And if you, joking maybe,
> Sang him a song about a kitten;
> A grown-up, thirty-year-old baby
> Would lie down in the cradle, smitten . . .
> I love you, mamenka, a lot!
> I'm joyful and I aim to please!
> You say that I'm a naughty tot?
> Well then, just put me on your knees,
> Your babe's so lovable, so nice,
> You must be merciful and mild,
> Do not interpret as a vice
> The silly mischief of this child . . .

194

How pleasant the twilight is at times! . . . But, by God, today my readers and I didn't even fly the distance between the convergence of two mathematical lines!

Day 26

195

How pleasant it will be, my dear, good friend, when you meet me—or if not me, then at least my thoughts about everything and everyone and my memories of those whom I loved and love! . . . Tell me, on which step of the stairway to happiness are you now? . . . Which way are you looking: north, west, south, east, at the sky, or at the earth? . . . Have you experienced what life is? . . . Once I dreamed of life and started to write chapter 152 . . . Every beginning ought to have a continuation; therefore:

Existence is a sphere; life is the set of circles that go around it in all directions; people are the points along these curves.

"Good!" said one of the greatest minds of some indeterminate century, as he took a piece of chalk and drew a circle on the wall, representing a sphere, drew a diameter *AB*, then perpendicular to that, at equal distance from the extremities *A* and *B*, the circumference *C*, and he began to speak in the following way:

Points *A* and *B* are the extremities of our feelings and emotions. *A* is the extremity of good . . . *B* is the extremity of evil . . . The circle *CD*, equidistant from the extremities, is the only way to possible longevity.

Man is born into the world on one of the points of this circle. If he is well directed and constantly travels along *CD*, then from the *zenith*, or his point of birth, to the *nadir*, he travels by moving away, strengthening and encouraging himself more and more. From the *nadir*, the next part of his path is a return . . . While still imagining that he is moving away from the point of the *beginning of his life's path*, he in fact is approaching it. If he reaches it, then this emaciated, withered creature will be the same infant but stretched out by time and filled . . . with earth!

Oh, how blessed is he who has passed through all the *pluses* from 0 to 1 and all the *minuses* from 1 to 0!

If someone's life has deviated from the circle *CD* to one of the poles or extremities, then it is very clear that this path is shorter, the turning point is closer, and the return to the state of infancy or nothingness is closer.

"Why?" you ask. "Because," answer all the sciences and the wisdom of experience, "everything is based on balance; because calmness of the mind, health of the body, and happiness of the heart live at an equal distance from heaven and earth."

Come close to one extremity, and you will be burned by an excess of life-giving force; come close to the other, and you will be killed by an excess of suffocating force.

196

Confirmed in my propositions by the fire that fell from the sky on twelve heads, I was walking neither slowly nor swiftly on the straight mathematical line that Haller mentally drew from birth to death. I noticed that the line was equidistant from the poles and in general from all extremities . . . The climate was so mild that the words *hot* and *cold* would have passed out of use . . . On the right, in various locations, I saw *goodness, love, south, soul, dream, truth, light, everything, mind, enthusiasm, involvement, attraction, oxygen, sky, fatigue from labor, omniscience*, etc.

On the left were *evil, hatred, north, body, reality, falsehood, gloom, nothing, heart, skill, reflection, nitrogen, hell, fatigue from idleness, ignorance*, etc.

But there were so few people on this path that I should have languished in melancholy solitude if some sense of spiritual and physical health in me had not supplanted all the bright specters that littered that wilderness right and left.

197

Thus, by connecting my life to geometry and boring not only my readers but also myself, I made yet another connection; namely, I laid my hand on my heart and said:

"O heart! Tell me whether I am the cause of your suffering, or you are the cause of mine? . . . Be ever in accordance with me! Agree with me always!"

"Eternally to acquiesce?
Oh no, that's foolish; it won't do.
Believe me, sir, a constant yes
Will in the long run bore you too."

Thus my heart answered me and began to beat more strongly than before.

198

To this I not only said nothing and would not have even thought anything if my enthusiasm had corresponded to my mature age.

That I looked good I could perceive
From every fawning, searching glance.
But all this praise could not entrance
My soul, though trusting and naive.
I've often loved and been loved, yet
I've never had a jealous thought,
And never once have I been fraught
With pangs caused by a coquette.
Who else can claim this? And what's more,
Because of nature's stern decree,
I always was inconstant, therefore
All others constant seemed to me.

Once . . .

But now I set off on my way
After a quick and flighty race,
Each lovely vision I survey;
I marvel at each passing face.
Now for a man in my decade
This is unseemly, or quite odd,
But who among us has not made
An offering, with a cheerful grin,

To that rambunctious, winged god?
Whom has he not led into sin?

199

He who has earned fame by exhausting his strength, through patience and time, is a man of experience; he has amassed a wealth of mind. I respect him and love him . . . though even a rotting piece of wood acquires a certain glow.

But . . . duty calls me to this large tent, where, as Mr. Nakhimov says, mountains of paper rise, rivers of ink flow, and flocks of chirping pens scamper across the table.

200

SENIOR AIDE

Papers from August, but I wonder,
Where's the receipt? Sir, for this blunder
They'll thumb their nose at me, not you!

CIVIL SERVANT

I wrote a draft, though, long ago—it's true!
And sent it to those blasted clerks. Absurd!
(He writes, dictating to himself out loud)
"I have the honor . . . to inform . . . hereby . . .
The *some* of money you transferred
For *itims* 2 and 5 . . . July the *twenty-therd* . . .
Two hundred and six rubles . . . are *recieved*." Now I
Believe that's it, sir!

SENIOR AIDE

Very nice!
You can't be taught the bureaucratic style!
Your writing is so clear and so concise!
But you spelled *sum* as *some*, meanwhile
You wrote down *e* instead of *i*, and *i* for *e*!

My dear philologist, please humor me:
Perhaps you heard that in a formal letter,
The poorer spelling used, the better?

201

But here is Behtirköy!

The signal to march has been given! . . . Look: the camp detail, like a swarm of locusts, has descended on the tents! . . . It seems as if it is devouring them. See how the tent city disappears! . . . It is no more! The entire staff is on horseback. Everything has moved on! Endless baggage trains stretch out along the winding road . . . just as water, held back and then released, slides through the trough of a valley.

Here you can see all the colorful diligences, dormeuses, carriages, calashes, droshkies, brichkas, gigs, wagons, *brașoveance*, carts, kitchens, wains, and boxes . . . They are followed by packs—on horses, donkeys, and shoulders—and finally, two camels, known to the entire campaign staff . . . They are carrying a Kalmyk kibitka. With them are traveling two men from the Orenburg steppe, as well as fat Johann and a former courier of the Constantinople mission.

All this stretches out on the road from Karasu—via Mahmutkuyusu, Musubey, Azaplar, and Çelebiköy—to Pazarcık.

202

Although I am combining several stages of the journey into one, I am sure the reader will not feel at all fatigued, like Suvorov's grenadier, who divided the distance from earth to heaven into only two days' march. I am sure that once he set off on this journey, it only took one day's march.

But speaking of fatigue, being lenient with myself, if not with others, I divide every task into several parts and designate a particular day for each part; therefore, you can imagine that the sun has already passed into the other hemisphere, supplying its deputy, the moon, with a part of its light.

That eccentric Zoroaster considered the sun a god . . .

His prayers flowed to the sun through all his days,
Yet deeper thoughts eluded his intent:
The sun may bless the earth with sacred rays,
But does it bless the endless firmament?

Day 27

203

I was sitting with a book in my hand . . . I do not remember whether I was reading it or thinking about *her* . . . Suddenly a vision appeared before me, as clear as the thought of fulfilling my ardent hopes and desires.

IT

"So do you love to read indeed?"

I

"Do I? . . . ! To heaven's gate I rise,
My friend, when in your sparkling eyes
Your feelings' images I read;
I learn by heart those feelings rare!
Their meaning is so sweet and dear!
Now they're attractive, like despair,
Then suddenly, like chance, unclear!
So tell me please . . . no, do not speak!
But I into your eyes will peek
And read your meaning . . .

Having taken up Champollion's labor, I soon repented . . .

"No," I thought, "deciphering the Egyptian language of friendship and love is Egyptian toil!" . . . and I set off for Bulgaria.

204

Stopping just before Pazarcık, in the Taban Dere Valley, I looked back one more time, then turned my attention to the city.

Hacıoğlu Pazarcık means small bazaar, or marketplace, of the son of the pilgrim . . . So, my dear caravan, have you ever seen an empty city? . . . Here it is . . . Not only the people and animals, but even all the insects seem to have disappeared. What emptiness! What gloom! Just as in a heart abandoned by hope.

205

Go down the street—no one will meet you. Go into a courtyard—no dog will bark. Go into a house—no one will ask you, "Who are you? Why are you here? What do you want?" Go into the harem . . . oh, how unpleasant this emptiness is!

The fountains do not flow; they have dried up. In some of them the water still drips out, but it is as bitter as tears . . . it is poisoned.

Here is the high *cami*, where no more is heard: *"Elin karısını arzulama!"*

The outskirts of the town, to which the Turks, Armenians, and Bulgars migrated for their eternal life, are as large as a mind that shudders at dead bodies and cemeteries could imagine. The edges and environs of the town are covered with granite and marble stones . . . Almost everyone is carved with a turban of some kind, denoting the rank and status of the Muslim who was a guest on the surface of the earth.

206

But I am responsible for your safety, my dear companions, and therefore I advise you not to scamper off or travel far from me! . . . The road to Kozluca runs through a forest . . . Here is the dark Üşenli Valley . . . Throngs of Turks wander through the forest, lying in wait for the unwary . . . Hark, a shot! A whistling bullet! . . . A salvo! . . . Turks! . . . And all this is a dream, imagination! . . . Fear not, my dear female companions! Under my guidance you will get out of danger safe and sound! But . . .

207

My heart is inflamed with a warlike spirit! . . . Give me my armor! My crested helmet! My sword, my sword! It bears this inscription, in golden Arabic letters: "When Chemitszan ceases to favor me, you, my sword, shall protect me!"

My valiant, warlike, male and female readers! A great, immortal feat lies before us! . . . Crowd around me! You young men, prepare your fiery imagination and your lorgnettes! . . . You old men, wise and experienced, put on your spectacles! You lovely archeresses, my Amazons! You girls and women, right and left wings strengthening the center, arm yourselves with fiery gazes!

In charge of such a volunteer corps, I can easily travel the whole world and subjugate the universe . . . to my pen! But this is long and boring . . . By force of arms we will traverse Bulgaria and the Balkans to Constantinople . . . We will fly like a marauding horde . . . no, we will pour, like the Nile, across Mahmud's domains! . . . Does he expect us? Will he have time to publish a *hatt-ı şerîf* calling for an uprising against the unbridled crowd of readers attacking the topographical map of his possessions, storming the maiden town of Şumnu, strolling along the river Tunca, relaxing in the Eski Saray and laurel groves of Edirne, and finally, examining all the curiosities of Istanbul without permission?

208

A detailed map of Turkey lies before us. The field of honor is open. Glory is preparing a wreath for Victory. My friends! "Not numbers, but courage" is the first rule of war. "A herd of donkeys commanded by a lion is more terrible than a herd of lions commanded by a donkey," said the Greek military leader Chabrias. And so . . . but it's already late in the day.

209

Throwing off my armor, helmet, and sword, I hung them on one of the trees belonging to the Commander of the Faithful; I returned to where I had been; I put on . . . not a Roman toga, of course . . . and lost my temper . . .

Next to my room, behind a wooden wall, lived an ardent youth. Often the frenzies of his heart and poetic soul disturbed my sweet sleep. In revenge for the insomnia he gave me, I put my ear to the wall, like the conscience that eavesdrops on human thoughts.

"To love or not to love!" he cried in a voice like Hamlet's.

"Self-love! Prejudice! The law established by Pope Gregory IX! Duties! General opinion . . . oh, so many obstacles!" the young man uttered in despair, like Lear's despair when he says, "Thunder! Lightning! You are not my children!"

"Oh, if only you were free! If my voice did not die on my lips, I would tell you: even before my existence I love you! I love you now! I love you beyond the grave of the universe! . . ."

Yes, I thought, the verb *love* would be a divine verb if it were not conjugated.

"Why should I try to assure you?" continued the young man. "Assurances weaken trust. You are beautiful and virtuous; you are a star shining gently on me from heaven! Two sounds that nature itself has made consonant: *I* and *you*! They were once one being, torn in two by some hostile force so that eventually at our meeting it could revel in our misery!"

This cunning dream retains its hold;
The world of charm now fades away!
You are an idol made of gold,
To which I must forever pray!

210

The shouts subsided . . . Everything grew quiet . . . I began thinking . . . The genius of sleep fanned me with its wings . . .

Sleep well, my little child, and save
Your strength! You've lived ten thousand days,
A toy with which blind passion plays,
Of prejudice the obedient slave!
You're happy in the quiet night,
Indifferent as the restful dead,
You gently slumber in your bed,
Your heart and soul are free from plight!

Day 28

211

I do not intend to devote this day to peaceful wandering around the universe and its events or military campaigns in Bulgaria. This day is as fair as the first of May. But let us suppose it is the first of May, in which case it will not be at all surprising if someone should invite me to ride together out of town, to a garden, to a grove . . .

If the words *come with us!* are uttered by the voice that echoes in my heart . . . if those words are repeated in a glance . . . oh, then I shall certainly go!

212

If my readers' curiosity is following me on this jaunt, then . . . but listen:

"Really?" said one cubic creature.

"Believe me!" replied another creature, whom I know not how to describe.

My God, it is a crying shame
To tyrannize one's wife this way!
Her mischief and naivete
To see as sin, deserving blame!
These values of antiquity!
"Be silent and do not despise
All-seeing husbands' jealousy,
Their selfish love that clings and ties."
It is intolerable! . . .

"Oh, that's true!" said one young maiden, as beautiful as a bride of Oceania. "Men? Flatterers! . . . Husbands? Tyrants!"

> How curious your comments seem!
> I find them puzzling. Surely you,
> At times, if only in a dream,
> Have been in love and married too? . . .

This I said to the ethereal creature who had said those insulting words about the entire race of men.

I do not know whether she liked the ritornello I appended to her song about men, because the moment I said it, I turned onto a different path and stopped beside a grapevine. I plucked a ripe, juicy bunch, covered as if with frost, and . . . I present it to you, my dear, lovely female reader! You angel beside whom even the most sinful creature would be sanctified with new, lofty feelings!

213

> O youth, abandon all your dreams most dear!
> Your treacherous desires and hopes forgo!
> The flowers of your joys are braided here
> Into a stubborn chain of pain and woe!
> Abandon your credulity; gaze on
> The colors that change hue in light's reflection.
> Await the day, O youth; perhaps at dawn
> We shall discern true love, unfeigned affection!

214

Without explaining why this day had wearied me, I invited the sun to slip quickly down to the west and light up all the known and unknown transatlantic countries, where man, according to Cabanis's system, was originally a plant, then a polyp, then an insect, then an orangutan, then a wild man . . .

A herd of wild men grazing peacefully in meadows irrigated by the diamond currents of a river . . .

A herd of wild men living in peace with all animals . . .

A herd of wild men who have no gods on earth, but people in heaven . . .

This herd . . . but what is happiness and peace without that which begets unhappiness and restlessness?

215

"You're blind!"

"That's a lie!"

"Can you see?"

"I see nothing, because nothing is visible!"

> "Go and make sure the sun is not a candle,
> The pallid moon is not a dusky lamp,
> The twinkling stars are not just golden spangles
> Or army medals granted to the sky! . . ."

But blindness is not a sin. But I am retiring from this noise, this frivolity of the heart, this garrulity of the tongue, these prying eyes, this age laden with calamities, and like Jason, with my Argonauts, I board a ship made of mirrors.

From the wharf at Galați, I head down the Danube, through the Beautiful Mouth into the Pontus, then the Propontis, then the Hellespont; then, without touching any island of the Aegean or Mediterranean Seas, I sail straight to the mouth of the Nile and on the Nile to Memphis; from Memphis, I carry the ship on my shoulders, on the same path used by the Argonauts to portage their ships to the sea that divides Egypt from the Promised Land; then I go down that sea to the ocean that waters Arabia, Iran, and India; then I travel on the ocean to the confluence of the Tigris and the Euphrates; and finally, I sail slowly up the latter river to paradise itself . . .

I was in paradise . . .

216

Then it was evening; and now too, it is already evening; and since people in general have come to rely on the morrow as the beginning of good things to come, I appeal to my readers with a question: You're probably tired?

"Oh, not at all!" they reply, panting with exhaustion.

Now thank the gods, if you are free
From riding with your wagon train
Through desert lands of poetry,
Or roads of prose, all wet with rain.

Day 29

217

So, my friends, you heard what the commander Chabrias said. Now give me a telescope, and I will inspect the position of all my readers . . . This telescope is worse than a pair of blind eyes! . . . It disfigures everything, like a biased journalist's criticism! . . . Wipe the lens!

Good! Now listen to the dispositions:

"A detachment of ten thousand of my young warriors is crossing the Danube at Niğbolu. From Niğbolu it will turn to Ziştovi; it shall admire the view, but not wander in the orchards and vineyards, nor tear a single red petal from the rosebushes that adorn the mountains, slopes, and hills—rather, it shall quickly pass Rusçuk. If the enemy makes a sortie, then it shall regard it with contempt and continue on its way via Razgrad to Şumnu.

"Another detachment of ten thousand is going through Silistre. The river crossing will not hinder these brave men. Reminding this fortress about the year 1810, the detachment shall continue via Akkadınlar, Emberler, and Ekizce to the right flank of the fortress of Şumnu.

"I myself, commanding the main forces of my readers, am going through Pazarcık.

"A detachment of five thousand men advanced in years and armed with all types of spectacles is looking at the fortress of Varna from the cliffs near the village of Franka. The chosen commander of this detachment is an old man, decorated by the tsar and by time, who knows by heart all the campaigns of Münnich, Rumyantsev, Suvorov, Potyomkin, Kamensky, Kutuzov . . ."

After reading the disposition, of course, all the groups have returned to their places. A few chosen, talkative female readers beat the tattoo with their lips, and everyone marches on!

218

Fifteen thousand young men and charming, warlike beauties are with me! "Singers, forward march!" I cried. "Ah, gentlemen, my soul fainted with delight when the leading singer, as charming as *she*, poured herself into an aria: 'Di piacer mi balza il cor . . .'"

I quickly move on from Pazarcık to Üşenli through a dense forest and ridge of mountains, hiding the north from Kozluca.

Here, my friends, is where we marched under the command of the tsar in 1828. When we came down from the mountain by Kozluca, the varied ridges of the Balkans opened up to our eyes. Through the lilac distance and the bright future, I already saw the blessed Russian banners waving on the ridge of Haemus and Russian will laying down the law in Mahomet's dominion.

219

While the first two detachments are approaching Şumnu, we shall rest for a day in the gardens of Kozluca.

Here nature makes a wild show!
South to Pravadı we must go . . .
To rest here, friends, would not be wrong;
The road ahead of us is long!
Ahead . . . the world of hieroglyphs!
The sky grows dark on Haemus's cliffs;
Scyths and disputed forebears there
Would graze their flocks without a care!

Day 30

221

The dawn will not break until the next chapter, so before the rising of the sun, I was thinking of the Jingdezhen porcelain factory; of cheerful eyes and a clear face—obvious evidence of wisdom; of lies and stubbornness—vices that should be eradicated already in infancy; of Pliny's phrase "ut externus alieno non sit hominis vice"; of the wisdom and folly of the wise and the folly and wisdom of the foolish . . . etc.

222

The morning was enchanting. Behind a veil of fog stood the Balkans . . . isolated hills, whitening rocks along the Devne Valley . . . the ravines along the right bank of the Pravadı Valley, the sunlit heights above Madara and Şumnu . . . the Kozluca mosque with its gardens . . . the camp of my readers . . . what views!

I came out of my tent and involuntarily glanced at the tent of the maiden tsar with its golden roof . . . My heart fluttered with a desire for battle, and I cried:

O squadron of Life-Amazons,
Beside my tent now form your ranks!

ORDERLY

Impossible, sir, they're unwell.

I

How come?

MEDIC

The moon has cast its spell . . .

I

What timely lunar fits—no thanks!
We must alleviate their plight,
And quickly—we march out tonight!

MEDIC

The ancient treatment's best, I think:
Rosemary water they should drink;
And nature sets the term here . . .

I

Yes!
These Amazons cause such distress!
If only they were like Minerva!
But we'll leave them in the reserve—a
Hospital marching, sick and sad!
But this is really all too bad!
Without them I am bored! . . .

223

Bored, bored! No, not a step forward without them! I am ready to postpone the trip to Şumnu at least till the end of part 3! Oh, to perform great deeds, one needs patience! . . . Angelic patience . . . diabolic patience . . . is that what you think? No, you need mine, i.e., the average of the two.

How patient is he who, having quenched his thirst, hunger, feelings, mind, and heart, lies down in downy waves, and while falling asleep, he feels something crawling on his face, but he is afraid to move, to reach out his hand, lest he scare not only the insect but also the sleep from his eyes . . . How patient he is!

This is still not everything, for everything is bigger than the universe. This is not the end and not the beginning . . . Show me a beginning and an end in something, and I shall say, "No, this is a continuation."

224

Such transitions are familiar from well-known examples . . . or, better yet, from a well-known chord of Mozart's in the overture to *La clemenza di Tito*. Of course, anyone who does not know the thoroughbass of human feelings will not understand the validity of abrupt transitions, only the simple scale is intelligible to him . . . When Haydn portrayed the creation of the world, he began with a depiction of Chaos . . . Everywhere harmony is created from disharmony . . . Thoughts, opinions, speeches, actions, all of life—everything is subject to this law.

225

The rest day felt like an eternity to me . . . I was sad and pensive . . . It is awful to have nothing to do! . . . Picking up Lavater, I began to compare the physiognomy of all great men—but mental greatness depends on the focus of our ideas and our point of view. Here I became pensive again . . . My thoughts, as if chained, did not leave me; I was content. But anything that has wings is not created for permanence. Soon my thoughts rose up and flew away . . . And where did I find them again? On eyes, on lips, on a smile, on a blush, on a bosom, on the reverie of a creature who is as lovely as untasted bliss. They even wanted to penetrate her heart, into every recess of her heart . . . Stop, you daring thoughts! It is night there! . . . The mysteries of the heart are performed in the dark . . . With some difficulty, I brought my thoughts out into the light from the underground dungeon where they had gone astray—and began to write a letter.

I heard about your news today
From one who happened here to stay,
  Who feels for you affinity!
And I rejoiced to hear him tell

That all of you are doing well—
    Give thanks to the Divinity!
Moreover I was quite delighted
That as a family you've united
    In friendly solidarity.
For hours, with pen or book in hand,
You work and answer each demand,
    With loyal regularity.
And every day by nine o'clock
Into the drafting room you walk,
    With great dependability!
There all your duties you observe;
With zeal and carefulness you serve,
    And studious tranquility.

226

I know that you would like to read
How this epistle does proceed,
    O readers most convivial!
But I've no strength for this pursuit,
The ugly verses I recruit—
    Are they not much too trivial?
O you, my being and my life,
My journey with digressions rife,
    My self-encyclopedia!
May all the world read you today,
And from the soul with wisdom say,
    My God, what a *comoedia*!

Part 3

AUTEUR DE st……: Que pensez-vous de mon livre?
UNE DAME: Je fais comme vous, monsieur, je ne pense pas.

—(Lucius Apuleius) Rivarol

Day 31

Οὐ τὸ μέγα εὖ, ἀλλὰ τὸ εὖ μέγα.

227

[*On the shores of Phrygia, Apollo in rags carries stones on a stretcher for the construction of Troy.*]

DAY LABORER

O source of heavenly rays and light!

APOLLO

Say *exile*; that's what I am now![*]

DAY LABORER

A *wanderer* begs you to allow
Him to salute your highness bright . . .

APOLLO

This honor is inopportune!
Where is he?

[*The Wanderer enters, clothed in a motley cover and burdened with typographical errors.*]

[*] Apollo was in exile from Olympus.

WANDERER

O bright sun of noon . . .

APOLLO

No flattery, just speak plain and true! . . .

WANDERER

I—I . . .

APOLLO

You—you? . . . Enough, adieu!

[*The wanderer exits into the world.*]

228

Ah! ah! (il rit.)

Everyone he came across wanted to know his aim and asked him, "Where are you going?" "Behold," he said, "this moth, which is flying along the same road as I."

Of life on earth you are a fleeting guest!
Why do you, too, fly straight into the light?
In darkness can you really find no rest,
Just like the pride of man, so keen and bright?
Look how the distance shines with diamonds white,
But fly not close—your golden wings will burn!
That mystic glow will rob you of your sight,
And all your lofty dreams to dust will turn!
All souls, all things are kept in check by fate,
Step not across the sacred boundary lines!
The *captive spirit* strains to lose its earthly state,
And drag to heaven its prisoner's confines!
Its inner voice keeps rumbling in its mind:
The universe proceeds by law and not by chance!
And men's weak lantern thoughts attempt to find

A way through that mysterious veil to glance.
Ages have passed and more will follow later,
Nations will lie down in a common field,
The mind will never grasp the worlds' Creator,
And nature will forever stay concealed!

229

On the spacious harbor of Troy, having loaded my ship (made of mirrors, as mentioned above) with everything *immaterial*, I involuntarily had to think also about the immaterial *ballast*, so necessary for weight and balance. Everyone will understand that I am talking about *idle talk*, the ballast of the mind, and so, without further explanations, I set forth to the Archipelago.

Just as I am carried by the waves of the Hellespont, which once reflected *Mount Ida* and its foot adorned with the Parian marble and gardens of Troy, my thoughts are carried on the abyss of memory.

It reflects the past: the halls of Priam; high walls and towers; huge temples; the bard who was born in *Smyrna, Rhodes, Colophon, Salamis, Chios*, and *Athens*; his songs on the glory of *Achilles* and *Odysseus*; his *Batrachomyomachia*; and his *Hymn to Ceres*, which languished in obscurity for 2,760 years but was fortunately rediscovered at the end of the last century by *Christian Friedrich Matthaei* in the *Patriarchal Sacristy* in *Moscow*.

230

Continova, *s. f.* continuation
—*Nuovo dizionario portatile*

So that's it! All the past is reflected in my memory!

Here, near the *Sigean* promontory, on the grave of glorious *Troy*, stand the gleaming walls of *Alexandria*. And they have disappeared! Here on the grave of *Alexandria*, irrigated by the Scamander, stand the black huts of *Bunar-Bashi*. And they will disappear! *Inshallah* (God willing)!

As *Süleyman*, son of *Orhan*, before marching to the *Thracian Chersonese*, climbed up a pile of stones, the mortal remains of Troy, gazed upon them with wonder, and went forth to conquer *Gallipoli*, so I, having seen enough of the ruins of true enlightenment, set out with my caravan on my way across the globe.

231

Mare calabalâc!
—A Moldavian

Happy is he whom fate has delivered from storms at sea, in the heart, and in life and from all kinds of storms accompanied by thunder, lightning, whirlwinds, words, threats, and blows!

Forcing my way amid headwinds and tailwinds, with the storm clouds looming on all sides, I moored my ship to the shore and glanced back at the sea. What a picture! Imagine a sea—*blue, white, red, or black*—it matters not. Look: a cloud darkens the horizon and portends an imminent storm. Now you hear thunderclaps, and lightning cuts through the air. In the distance is a ship—a victim of the deep! Winds have ripped off its sails, the rigging has burst, lightning has struck the mast, the mast has shattered, fire has reached the powder in the hold, and the ship has exploded. Look at the fiery cloud! Here is a cornucopia from which men, barrels, stones, timber, gold, cannons, cannonballs, and everything else are pouring into the sea—everything except several tons of that destructive mixture invented by Schwarz. It hangs in the air. Where is its former weight?

It is terrible to explode! I have experienced this myself:

Her coldness when her husband's near—
This I can bear, but day by day,
She's worse with me, and more severe,
How I exploded in dismay!
How I exploded in dismay!

232

Sea, O sea, O vast sea!
Figure of climax, §56, *Short Rhetoric*

When the storm subsided, the clouds rushed away beyond the southern horizon, and the sea swallowed up everything heavier than its waters. I resumed my course. The ship, driven by its willful helmsman, flew like a thought, leaving a fiery wake. The sun had already disappeared, but the surface of the waters sparkled like a vast field of light, and the waves were clothed in brilliant foam. Like *Forster* and many other naturalists, I wished to penetrate the mystery of this light; I thought and thought, and finally decided that it was caused neither by luminous fish, nor worms, nor woodlice, nor polyps, nor roe, but rather by the *friction of the waters*, which gives rise to *foam*, the sparkling and pearl-strewn mother of *Aphrodite*. Q.E.D.

233

Was hat er gesagt?
—Ein Jude

My ship flew quickly, so quickly that *Helen* appeared at the top of the mast. Need I remind the shrewd reader of chapter 151 and the fact that I, a hasty traveler, looked at the islands scattered around the Archipelago with the same attention as the hasty reader looked at the chapters scattered around my *Wanderer*? An abyss of waters separates them from one another; the communication between them is difficult, I agree; but is it my fault that my imagination created a *mental archipelago*? Does it not depend on the understanding of the reader to find gold and diamond mines in *Thasos*; to look at volcanoes in *Lemnos*; to taste luscious fruits and honey in *Euboea*; to remember the naval war fought at *Salamis* in 480 B.C.E.; to learn ant-like labor from the *Myrmidons* in *Aegina*; to learn the naval art in *Hydra*, or in *Nio*; to make a sacrifice to Bacchus in *Andros*; to take a healing bath in *Cythnos*; to climb the ruins of Apollo's temple in *Delos* and regret that he can no longer ask the oracle about his fate; to grow bald in *Myconos*; to pick flowers in the rich meadows of *Stampalia* and weave a wreath for his beloved? This all depends on the reader. In all these islands, especially in *Imbro* and *Milo*, there is plenty of *game* . . . but, gentlemen hunters, get your guns and make ready! I will lead you to places where the snipe have longer noses than any deceiving or deceived *politician*, *slyboots*, or *womanizer*.

234

I have noticed that only *reminiscence* writes well, eloquently, and smoothly. It ought to take up the pen! Yes, let it take up the pen! And this pen will be like *Skanderbeg*'s sword. What *Mahomet* can wield it?

And furthermore:

> He should not deem himself a bard,
> Whose skyward flight is rough and hard,
> Whose pen in drudgery has wrought
> A flow of ink, but not of thought!

235

Hai-hai! Ion zhe ion!
—Little Russian exclamation

While the word *happiness* leads its admirers by the nose, making them want to break off gold and precious stones from the rainbow, I behold the deceptive brilliance of *Isis* with sorrow, for I see how it turns into large drops of rain and drenches the *seekers*—and I continue to write about

> The wicked pastime, ever present,
> Which everyone by heart doth know,
> Which to the poet is so pleasant,
> And which infuses him with woe!

The soul tends to seek nourishment in a variety of objects. Following this attraction, I head to the *source of philosophy* known to some by the name of *good* and to others by the name of *evil*; I sit on a stone next to it and behold the alchemical process that transforms *everything* into gold. Honor, conscience, truth, friendship, love—everything turns into the noble, clinking metal—and the reckoning falls short!

236

$2 \times 2 = 4$
—Multiplication table

"That's old news!" you say. But whoever you are, mortal or deity, as the wandering Telemachus says, give me your hand, be silent for a few moments, bow your eyes to the earth, and turn your ears to me!

I don't believe in honest trade,
That common saying plainly lies:
What fool sells news or merchandise
For "what it's worth"—for what he paid?

237

Tomorrow! Tomorrow!

Day 32

Good dawning!
—*Notes sur le Roi Lear*, 23

238

On the twentieth day of my wanderings, I meditated on the *universe*.

What is the *universe*?

There is nothing more difficult than an intelligent and sensible answer; therefore, the moment a person begins to ask himself questions, his soul grows sad, the sky of his life clouds over, and his mind, like a courtier, must behave cunningly toward the ruling heart, often flattering the tsar's favorites—the passions—to achieve its goal.

If I took it into my head to ask any being endowed with the light of reason what the universe was, he would look upon me with surprise as an *ignoramus*, and without answering, would turn away from me, like an advanced student whose pride is wounded by the offensive question "What is grammar?" To whom then, after such an event in the universe, should I pose the question, if not to myself?

Imagine now, dear nations, that the *universe* is nothing other than that lovely, perfect thing, the daughter of eternity from whom imagination has copied all its dream forms and images, and who floats alone in space, now sad, now joyful, now terrible, now majestic, depending on the mood of the person thinking about her.

Will this beautiful woman ever cast off her ornaments of brilliant, many-colored suns and her ever-blue, transparent clothes?

Will it be only when the foretold *dragon* flies into space, flicks the moon and stars out of the sky with the whirlwind of its wings, overturns the vessel of light, squeezes the earth in its claws, soars up like an eagle—and drops it from a great height? . . . But whither will it fly?

239

During the abovementioned flight of the earth in an indeterminate direction, would it retain its centripetal force? If not—then, dear friends, I lack the force to continue this chapter.

240

Le génie (*seul*)
(*on entend une douce symphonie.*)
Mais quels doux accents succèdent aux cris de la douleur?
—*Divertissement* de Saint-Foix

Having deflected my attention from my frightened imagination, I take my staff, *walk out of the room, step off the porch, go through the gate*—and walk down a secluded alley. Everything is dark, quiet, and asleep; seldom does a ray of light shine through the shutters or a watchdog bark behind the gates. Thoughts crowd in my head. I ask myself questions and answer them myself. "Yes!" I say mentally,

"It's hard to live on earth, no doubt!
But what is life's true meaning now?
To love with wisdom and without,
Both knowing and not knowing how."

"But who doesn't know how to love? Is love such hard work?" I cried and stopped, so I could think more comfortably about whether I had told the truth.

"Lie!" replied with one voice all the wise and great men described by Plutarch. I blushed and ran away from myself in fear.

Haste always throws an obstacle in the way; nonetheless, I arrived safe and sound at the gate of the house where the heart wonders about its own fate. Neither a sphinx, nor a lion, nor a dragon guarded the gate, so I made several steps in the yard without hindrance, when suddenly my heart began to beat. And how could it not beat when I was already close to the steps that are easier to ascend than to descend; so close to the walls into which I wished to transform my embracing arms!

Placing my right foot on the first step of the porch, I stopped and looked around: had anyone noticed me? No . . . thank God! Then . . . I stole away and headed home with rapid strides.

Such indecisiveness is a phobia based on presentiment; it is a tardy deliberation of the heart, the out-of-place question "To be or not to be?," a characteristic trait of love, a whim of reason, nervous debililty, numbness of feeling, discord between the soul and the body, animal laziness, etc., etc., etc.

241

Returning home, I asked myself: Why have I come back? Since people usually answer themselves rather slowly and hesitantly, I followed this habit and kept silent for a long time, as if waiting for someone to answer for me. This did not happen, and therefore the question remained unaddressed. Being bored of sitting at home, I left town to breathe the pure, fresh air.

242

Mais il est vrai que l'air pur n'est pas fait pour l'homme,
comme on le démontre en chimie.
—Rivarol

"Patience! And what is patience?" said 5,171,003,405 people entering my room.

"Oh, if it is my turn to answer this question," I said, raising my head and voice, "then I am ready to assure you, at every step and every minute of my life, that patience is the true talent of a genius, a true shield against real and imagined misfortunes, a cure for all diseases, a constant occupation of the soul, true labor, the philosopher's stone, the squaring of the circle, Greek fire, the best token of existence . . . . . ."

In meek docility I'll bear
The scorns of men and destiny,

Patience for this I have to spare,
But there is honor too in me!

This means that for human patience one needs a great soul and not long ears, a strong spine, and a tough hide.

243

Il n'y avait rien de si facile que de découvrir l'Amérique,
puisqu'il ne s'agissait que d'aller pour la rencontrer.
—*Les envieux*

Not knowing how to return to the place where my main thoughts and military actions had stalled, I thought, like Aristotle, about the dignity of writing and books.

"A good book is one," he says, "in which the writer says *what he should*, does not say *what he should not*, and speaks *as he should*."

"*Virtue in everything holds to the mean*," says Aristotle as well.

And therefore, I am perfectly right if I write *not exactly what I should, not exactly what I should not, and not exactly as I should*."

For example, how could I possibly skip the next chapter and not clean the air of the rumors spread by a wicked tongue?

244

(Pudet dicere.)
—Florus

She'd been a widow for a year
And meekly lived with mommy dear . . .
Though winter's always long and slow,
Among her friendly family
My idle hours did quickly flow,
In innocent activity.
But wicked tongues said with delight:
"He spent the day there and the night!"
Spent I the day? . . . Spent I the night? . . .

Day 33

Ein armer Teufel sang und trallerte vom Morgen
Bis in die Nacht, entfernt von Gram und Sorgen.
—*Deutsche Geschichte*

245

Many times have I heard, and long have I thought myself, that poets were created to add variety to the world, that they, like all artists and artisans, exist to practice their trade, but . . . what could I say to refute the opinion of this cold age? Let us consult the oracle . . .

The oracle is far away,
Too far away, my friends so dear!
I lack sufficient strength, I fear,
To travel to the east today.
But no! For you, fair deities,
I'll soar up like a wingèd thought,
Across the Arab deserts hot,
Across the mountains, steppes, and seas,
To lands where glows the rosy dawn,
I'll fly! I'll fly, my little dears,
You playful girls! . . . Now I have gone
Ten thousand versts, ten thousand years;
Thank goodness, I'm alive and well.
And are you tired, tots? You've slowed! . . .
A pity! . . . Was it my mistake?
But tell me, please, why did you take
Your prejudices on the road? . . .

"A heavy burden, God save us, what a heavy burden!" Aleksandr Vasilyevich would also say—that Russian soul, that great soul, that pure, fiery soul!

But here is the temple of Ammon; here is the oracle. Listen to its answer:

May he lose feeling from his heart
And be by everything betrayed,
Who deems a gift to be an art,
And soulful work to be a trade!
I am no wretched slave, but free,
The pure conductor of the fire
That drives the universe entire,
And pours from heaven into me!

246

That sky is no longer above me, which, like a blue canopy, sheltered the high mountains, the deep sea, the green steppes, and the magnificent gardens. That time is past, in the whole universe, in which my and my whole generation's blooming youth flowed by. More layers of air weigh down on me; my feelings have become more attentive to life; but the fire in them is the same: the soul, the invisible vestal virgin, has preserved it! Blessed is he who has not used up all his joy!

For he who knows his own true worth,
Whom others also highly rate,
Need seek no other joy on earth
Or try to change his happy state!

247

I will fly like a cuckoo down the Danube!
—*The Tale of Igor's Campaign*

My dear readers, with a happy heart, a clear soul, and a clean conscience, step aboard this barge!

If I had a brush in my hand instead of a pen, a palette before me instead of ink, and a canvas instead of paper; and if my poetry—*mental painting*—were to transform into ordinary painting, you would certainly be more pleased with me. Pointing a finger at the picture, you would say, "Here is the Danube! Here is an island in the Danube; here is the barge on which we are floating; here is the Turkish fortress of Hırsova! See how the stone walls are joined to the rock! Here is a ship sailing on the Danube! And there, there, what a flowery prospect! See how the river gradually hides itself in the greenery and disappears in the shade of the high cliffs of the right bank!"

That is what you would say. I would also paint a self-portrait for you. "Here he is!" someone would say. What more could be said?

248

The readers who ran their eyes over chapter 201 might have thought it complete because there was no note saying *continued in chapter 248*. This is excusable: on account of the long distance between these chapters, I myself could not see from 201 what would be in 248.

> The word of the Old Testament,
> Who spoke it o'er the deep at night?
> Whose self-begotten spark was sent
> To make unbounded Chaos bright?
> Sun, was it you? Did you decline?
> Did your bright gaze go west to sleep?
> And where is Bel's majestic shrine?
> Where is your face that Vestals keep?
> Of all your power be not too proud!
> All things extol your rising flight,
> Until you die, and from your shroud
> Another Sun brings forth its light!

249

It is strange! Choose any point in this wonderful universe, look from it with your two human eyes, and everywhere you see the same thing! Everywhere there is a sky dotted with ever-burning sparks; everywhere there are certainties and laws; in everything there is life and balance; everywhere there is God!—ocean of existence, of light, of wisdom, of bliss!

Oh, if only my arm were as long as my line of sight, then . . . then I should not know what to do with it! . . . And especially at this moment, when my heart is offering my arm a new Armida, to help her climb a narrow path that winds among thick vines to a high hill in the *Carpathian Mountains*, from which is seen in the distance a desert plain and the rocks of Maçin, and nearby the trickle of the glorious Râmnic.

"Is this really the same Râmnic in which the whole Turkish army perished and in which Suvorov's son drowned?—This is a stream!"

"Yes, and no larger."

The streams that in high mountains rise
Can drown a man as oceans do.
In this case, readers, it is true;
The story does not Aesopize.
Though Râmnic is no mighty flow,
For swimming it is quite unfit;
In spring it's fast, and wide, and deep;
A devil too could drown in it!

"That's astonishing! But we've fallen behind the rest; where are they?"

"To the right, I think."

"To the left, I think."

"I didn't notice."

"Let's go look for them! Catch me!" *She* started down the mountain like a chamois; I ran after *her*. Meadows, gardens, vineyards flashed by us. She flew fast, and I followed her. We were not far from the goal, and I despaired of capturing her . . .

But thanks to skillful nets I planted,
She fell into my grasp with ease.
I was a new Hippomenes,
And she a second Atalanta.

250

How annoying, how very annoying, is this rule that a person, willingly or not, must leave places, people, habits, desires, etc., etc., for new places, people, habits, desires, and so on! Whether I tell myself or others tell me, "You are not in your place," I must walk on. Whether I remark to myself or others remark to me, "You are not loved here," I must walk on. Whether I become accustomed to someone or someone becomes accustomed to me, I must walk on, so that the habit does not turn into a fatal passion. Whether I desire happiness for myself or others desire happiness for me, I must not walk, but run on, because happiness is like swift Atalanta. Thus time goes by and we go on. But I am tired of walking; I shall sit down in the wagon and ride. Berka, a Jew, urges on the nags; they slowly drag their eight legs; boredom overwhelms me; and I fall asleep.

Day 34

251

My sleep was sweet, and sweet was my awakening. Silence surrounded me. Like one who has lost his memory, I knew not where I was. I wanted to look around and I tried to raise my eyelids, but they fluttered shut, and all objects were hidden from my view. Sleep overcame all my efforts. Again I plunged into waves of oblivion. I dreamed I was on top of Olympus, at Jupiter's feast. Thirst tormented me, and I besought Hebe:

Juventas-Hebe, pour me nectar bright!
My lips do burn for that refreshing cheer!
Like thoughts of bliss and heavenly light,
That stream is wondrous clean and clear! . . .
How languid is your gaze, though sweet!
Your breast disturbed by storms, but why? . . .
Wait, wait, don't go! . . . I'll be discreet . . .
And I will drink! . . . But let me sigh!

252

I sighed deeply and awoke. I look around. Where am I? I am lying in the wagon; the unharnessed horses are calmly eating hay. To the right is a forest; to the left is . . . noise . . . a secluded inn . . . Where is my Berka? Swindler!

I enter—all are drunk inside!
And Berka too! But why, oh why?!
This idler could not, if he tried,
Tell Haman now from Mordecai!

I did not have a stop in view!
"Now will you get the horses ready?"
"*Ni, shabas, pane!*" says the Jew.
Happy is he who's calm and steady!
But if this man were forced to stay
With these Jews on the Sabbath day,
I'd like to watch!!!

Day 35

Most honorable sir, at the post entrusted to me everything is satisfactory; there is nothing new.
—*Garrison Service Rules*

253

I believe everyone remembers where my expedition stopped in part 2; everyone knows the reason for the stop; and therefore, after a short or long time, I return to my camp at *Kozluca*.

Quietly, without cleaving the air, I approached my tent. What a mess in the whole camp! My bodyguards, my *Amazons*, in their morning half-dress *à la fille d'Yémen*, wandered around the gardens, forgot their duties and zeal for service!

What if, during my absence, a crowd of Turks had come to the camp? Would I have enough body and soul to answer for the fear, tears, despair, fainting, and all kinds of female fits that my *long-skirted knights* might undergo? "Oh!!!" I roared like a Numidian lion, and breaking a horn from the head of a giant ox that stood by me, I blew into it, sounding the alarm and muster.

"Women!" I cried to my assembled army, and after a long silence I continued, "Go! There is no other word in any language that could better express my reproof."

"It's strange!" said several girls, withdrawing from the muster point. "Why didn't he say anything to us?"

254

After putting the camp in proper order and sending out the next day's dispositions to all parts of the army, I walked to the tsar-maiden's tent. Near the entrance . . .

I cleared my throat before I went,
And dabbed my face and fingers dry.
I mused: should I from clouded sky
Fall down as rain into this tent,
Like Jupiter, then . . .

Here I stopped, took out a pocket mirror, and could not help laughing.

For I looked so much like the *Face*,
With grape-red spots all speckled o'er,
Of one who steps up to the door,
Gives his *report*, and waits in place.
You see his blackheads, perspiration,
Tobacco marks, preoccupation . . .

I resembled him so much that I was afraid of myself, but nevertheless I moved my body forward—and soon forgot all that!

255

I did not notice what happened to the sun; either it *set* as usual or disappeared from the sky without *setting*. A dull moon dived into the clouds like a *flounder* and like a *cold creature* looked indifferently on everything and everyone. No wonder: for a long time it had gazed down at trickery and listened to sighs . . . ; and it had grown tired of all that!

Meanwhile, as the moon floated on and the stars arranged themselves according to the disposition given to them on the day of creation, nothing violated the heavenly order, but as for the earthly order . . . On earth it is different: today is not the same as yesterday, yesterday is not the same as the day before, etc., according to the infinity of *Newton's binomial.*

Day 36

256

Here is Şumnu. My dear female companions, who are accustomed to victories, make ready!

> You'll win not just the Turkish realm
> But Eden too—you have the skill.
> For you have learned to overwhelm
> In the mazurka and quadrille.
> Your gentle look, your heartfelt sigh
> Is awful, threatening, and fraught!
> Hurrah! . . . We've won! . . . Thank God on high! . . .
> But any traitors will be shot!
> "What, we'd be shot? Just out of hand?"
> The murmur spread across the field;
> "Our freedom we will never yield!"
> And now I've lost my martial band!
> How hard, an army to command!

257

Like *Sulla* at *Orchomenus*, I grabbed the *Ternaux shawl* from the hands of the standard-bearing maiden and exclaimed, "Leave me, leave me! I alone will penetrate the walls of Şumnu and climb the tall *Yeni Cami minaret* to break off its crescent moon! If I fall from the height of the minaret, tell everyone—everyone who can read Russian books or even just spell out the letters—that I fell, without help . . .

N.B.: Happy is the man who has no friends to help him fall!

My words worked. My heroines, like flowers endowed with life, gathered themselves again into a magnificent bouquet, and I set out to perform a great feat!

258

Aidez-moi Johannot!

Scarcely had the sun . . . or rather, scarcely had the earth come to the position in which the Eastern sun, as seen from the Bulanık heights, sends its rays from Ararat, over the Black Sea, through Varna, and along the Pravadı Valley—and the hill of Şumnu looked like an old Turkish woman, sitting cross-legged on the luxurious carpet formed by the Bulgarian landscape. Imagine now the crossed legs as the fortress walls; behind these walls, in a huge ravine, lies the town of Şumnu. This picture would well deserve the quaint brush of Johannot.

259

So, the eighth of July was fixed for the attack on Şumnu. I awoke under the light blue sky of Bulgaria with my whole Russian army and with Aurora, who parted the thin cloudlets veiling her bed and cast a curious glance at the magnificent Russian camp. I recollected that the eighth of July was the first day of my life and thought it might also be the last. I sighed, and then having forgotten what I was recollecting and thinking, I mounted my bay horse, Turchonok, made him dance, bend in a ring, stand on his hind legs, twist a dozen times on one spot to the right and left—and then I set off for the rallying point, the imperial tent.

Meanwhile, the advance guard . . .

But in order that everyone knows what happened on the day of my birth, I shall pull a report I compiled out of my traveling chest and present it to everyone who loves Russia, its tsar, and Russian glory.

260

Two poets great in days of yore—
Immortal Virgil, Homer blind—
Left us examples quite refined
Of versified reports of war.
But what use is the muses' strain
When thoughts are grand, but words are plain?
—*The Wanderer*, part 3, chapter 260

Occupation of the Position at Şumnu

The decisive and glorious crossing of the Russian troops across the river Danube on the twenty-seventh of May, ordered by the tsar himself, gave them free access to the fortresses of Varna and Şumnu. The retreating enemy dared not block either the forest defiles between İshakçı and Babadağ or the mountain ones between Pazarcık and Kozluca. An advance guard action near the latter cities was its one futile attempt at resistance.

From the day of the Danube crossing to the middle of June, victorious Russian banners were already waving on the walls of İshakçı, İbrail, Maçin, Köstence, Hırsova, and Tulça.

On the seventh of July all the forces concentrated in front of Yenipazar. The enemy was in sight of our advance guard and seemed to have halted with a determination to fight; but on the eighth they were forced to yield the final stretch of the approach to Şumnu.

According to the plan of action approved by the emperor, the troops moved toward their goal in two columns. The left column consisted of the Seventh Corps reinforced by the hussar regiment of the Prince of Orange and commanded by Count Diebitsch; this column set out an hour earlier. It moved through the *Pravadı Dere* Valley, keeping close to the mountains. The purpose of this detour was to flank the enemy and cut them off if they should decide to engage with our main forces.

His Majesty the Emperor was present with the Third Corps. *In column formation*, this corps marched straight to the fortress, leaving *Yenipazar* on their right. The first line consisted of the brigades of the Ninth Division with their artillery, under the command of

General Rudzevich. Their left flank projected forward to join the Seventh Corps. The Second Brigade was followed by the Fifteenth and Sixteenth Jäger Regiments along with twelve guns. These regiments were intended, in case of a raid by enemy cavalry, to form a stronghold around the Russian tsar.

To the right of the jäger brigade were three hussar regiments; behind them, in two rows, were 108 pieces of reserve artillery, under the cover of a brigade of the Eighth Division. The right wing consisted of the First Cavalry Division, under the command of General-Adjutant Count Orlov. In the rear guard was a light *Wagenburg*, under the cover of the First Brigade with its artillery.

The field ataman, Major-General Sysoev, with his Cossack regiments, guarded the right flank of the army.

During the march up to the ridge near the village of Bulanık, only the retreating Turkish vedettes could be seen, but after the ascent of this ridge, which had hidden the enemy's position, their forces appeared in several columns of infantry and cavalry, placed on the right bank of the river Bulanık parallel to its current, with as many as ten thousand men, excluding the auxiliary troops hidden behind the ridge, several cavalry units near the village of Bulanık, detachments protruding separately from the enemy's right flank, and detachments hidden on their left flank, behind the forest, near the road to Silistre . . .

261

At the beginning of the previous chapter, most of my female readers—already foreseeing the fierce battle and gushing blood and anticipating the fear that this terrible picture and the thunder of several hundred guns would instill in them—quietly disappeared . . . Instead of undeceiving them with assurances that the danger is not as great as they imagine and that the Turks are cowards, I shall, like Night, throw a veil over this military report.

Here I must notify my readers that, contrary to the premonition I expressed in chapter 259, Providence did not deprive me of any signs of life on this day.

Around midnight I could not have been more alive and was riding all alone, as my Cossack orderly—shame on him!—had fallen behind. I was riding across the battlefield on the right flank. The horse often snorted, stopped, shied, and jumped; perhaps he was frightened by those who had lain down to rest in the damp earth, on the field of honor. Having found the village of Mayna, Mayka, or Makak on the map, on the right flank of our new position, and having taken the battalion of the Eighth Division there, I returned calmly and thought about how to find the *headquarters*, my orderly, my pack, my tea kettle, and all the accessories of a military camp.

All this I found. Fatigue lulled me, and I was soon carried . . . into the next chapter . . .

262

I was flying along with post-horses. The bell could not manage to make a sound; a cloud of dust spun around me and concealed from my view *all objects* except the sun, which, as if eclipsed, seemed rayless but still burned with an ungodly light.

I was in a hurry; an incomprehensible feeling drew me on; my thoughts and eyes were fixed on the distance that lay before me. I felt that my spiritual self was already *there*, eagerly awaiting the approach of my material self.

Some buildings appeared on the left. "What village is this?" I asked the driver.

"*Alef!*" he replied.

There must be a station here, I thought, for we had already galloped about thirty versts; and indeed there was. Coming up to a small house, the horses stopped dead, the bell tinkled, and I jumped out of the carriage, ran onto the porch and into the hall, opened a door to the right, and entered a small room.

A thin pale man in his morning dress and cap sat by a table covered with books and papers. Beside him, on shelves, chairs, windows, and the floor were scattered books of various sizes in wooden, leather, and parchment bindings.

"Stationmaster, horses, quickly! . . . What is this station called?"

"*Alef!*" said the stationmaster, ignoring me.

"Listen, pal! When you see a uniform and epaulets on somebody's shoulders, you ought to take off your cap and set to work!"

"*Bet!*"

"*Bête*? Why, you old stick!"

I grabbed the stationmaster by the chest, and his cap fell off his head. "*Gimmel!*" he cried.

"Ah, so it's German now! Go on, take the post-horse order, write it down! . . . And the horses! Quickly!" He took the order and silently turned it all around.

"What are you thinking?"

The stationmaster looked at me and began to whisper, "*Alef, bet, gimmel, dalet, khe, vuv!*"

"Listen, friend! I've had enough of your stupidity or pranks, so here's some money for tea, vodka, bread, whatever you want, just give me some horses!"

Glancing at me, then at the few small silver coins that I had laid before him on the table, the stationmaster left the post-horse order and began to examine the coins one by one, saying, "*Alef . . . gimmel . . . vuv . . . khes . . . kuf . . .*"

Someone endowed by nature with the wonderful virtue called *patience* might enjoy this scene, but I could not stand it. I threw all the money onto the floor, grabbed the order, and stuck it into the stationmaster's hands. "Read! Write! And have the horses harnessed! . . . Or else I . . ."

Taking the order again, he looked at it, thought for a moment, stood up, went to the shelf, and took down a huge folio volume. Returning to his place, he opened the book, laid the order in front of him as well, glanced at it, and began to flip through the pages.

The huge book was some kind of dictionary!

"Have you lost your mind? What language are you translating my order into?"

"*Lammed, mem, ayn, zammekh, all, pay, fay,*" said the stationmaster instead of replying, raising his voice, but I did not let him finish his incomprehensible speech.

"Demon! Sanskrit!" I cried, tearing the book from his hands and throwing it aside. It hit the shelf, knocking a pile of other books directly onto the strange man. The same movement made the table collapse. And with the table the stationmaster too fell to the ground, repeating, "*Alef, bet, gimmel . . .*"

Horrified, I ran out of the room into the passage, into the yard, into the street. Not a soul was there.

On the road I heard the intermittent tinkle of a bell.

An empty post troika was passing by at a walking pace. The coachman was sleeping in the wagon. I jumped into it; he gave a start and woke up.

"Listen," I cried, "here's a purse with some money! . . . Take me quickly to the next station! . . . Not a word! No time to talk! . . ."

Grabbing the reins, the coachman lashed the horses with his knout, and they galloped faster than an arrow.

"Thank God!" I thought, "at least I've escaped that cursed *Alef*!" and I lay down in the hay that was stacked in the wagon. I was already falling asleep, when suddenly I felt a terrible shaking.

"You've gone off the road!" I cried and looked out of the wagon. We were riding across a plowed field.

"Hey, beardy! Where are you heading? Where's the road?"

"*Alef!*" sounded in my ears.

"Not *Alef* again! Get back on the road!"

"*Bet!*" continued the coachman.

"On the road, you rogue!"

"*Gimmel, dalet, he, vuf, zayn, khev, tet!*"

"What's happening to me! . . . Where am I? . . . In what country? . . . Where have all these damned *Alefs* come from?" I cried furiously. I grabbed the coachman by the collar with my left hand, and wanted to hit him . . . but I had no right hand . . .

"Oof!" I yelled.

"*Tuf?*" said the coachman in a questioning tone, and he suddenly stopped the horses.

"Evil spirit! Devil! Alef! Get back on the road!"

"*Alef?*" the coachman said, glancing at me, and suddenly he whipped the horses and started off across the field at full speed.

I lost both strength and voice.

We rushed downhill and uphill, over rocks and mud; here a pillar of dust rose around us, and here we were splashed with mud and water. The bell stopped; the only sounds in my ears were the broken exclamations of the coachman: "*Pay, fay, ayn, all, kif, resh, shin!...*" Once we reached the top of a terrible mountain, I glanced fearfully at the steep slope we were about to descend.

In the valley gleamed a broad river, across which stood a huge building surrounded by bright gardens and heavenly meadows.

"What is this building?" I asked.

"*Zammekh!*"

"*Zamok?* What castle?"

"*Ayn, pay, fay, tsadyk...*"

Before I could finish a few angry words, the horses rushed down the mountain...

Like a rock torn from the mountains, we collapsed into the river.

It is impossible to define the feeling that fills the soul during an unexpected fall. This feeling is not fear, for fear is unpleasant; it is more like the sinking of the heart and the senses when a *leshy* tickles us; it is closer to enjoyment, and one could love it if death or the loss of precious limbs were not the result of the fall. This feeling is the momentary absence of thought, and therefore I do not remember plunging into the water; I do not remember how the horses carried me to the other shore, and how the coachman fell off the wagon and disappeared under the waves, and how I drove the horses while standing.

As Asphalius, Dagon, or Neptune emerges from the sea in a shell drawn by dolphins, so it seems that I too appeared on the opposite side of the river.

Jumping to the shore, the horses shook themselves and started uphill, as if pierced by the trident of Neptune, and their dashing driver shouted, dropped the reins, and gave full freedom to their impulse. Before I could pick up the reins again, they had brought me up the mountain and stopped dead near a huge palace, where a large assembly of people stood on the terrace. Everyone's attention was directed at me.

If someone should ask me what I looked like in this strange and wonderful moment, I should laugh involuntarily in his face and ask him, "What does an impossible dream look like?"

My appearance produced unusual excitement in everyone. Petrified, I stood in the wagon and kept hold of the reins. Suddenly a general cry of joy, fear, regret, and surprise was heard on the terrace. All the men and women, young and old, rushed to me. It seemed as if crowds of people had poured out of a masquerade ball and surrounded me with the cry *Alef!*

My hair stood on end, and cold sweat rolled down my face. With a frenzied joy, several men dressed in various sumptuous garments of all ages and parts of the world grabbed me by the arms and led me to the house. All the other men and women crowded behind me as if I were a miracle on which their life and happiness depended. I lost the rest of my memory and was not aware how my wet clothes and tight-waisted military coat disappeared, or when they managed to clothe me in luxurious, comfortable, soft, and seemingly Oriental garments, because I had no time to pay attention to myself.

I regained consciousness somewhat when I was led into a magnificent, festive hall, where all present, of both sexes, seemingly representatives of all nations of the earth, stood in some kind of expectation.

At the end of the hall, on a dais, sat a maiden; in front of her was an altar with a burning flame. I glanced at her and lowered my eyes involuntarily; she seemed a deity before whom I was brought to justice. I remember that her eyes were fixed on the ground.

When I approached her, she seemed to come to her senses, cried out, and stood up.

The charming sound she made was not like the rapturous French *ah!*, the dry Greek *ἆ!*, *ἰού!*, or *ὦ!*, the proud Latin *iah!*, the sentimental German *ach!*, the sharp Italian *ah!*, or the silly Hebrew *okh!* No, it was a tender Russian *akh!* amid the profoundest silence. It penetrated deep into my heart.

Not daring to raise my eyes, still I noticed that the beautiful, majestic, young creature gestured to me with her hand to sit next to her. I dared not resist.

All present also sat down.

I waited for what would come next.

All were silent, and all eyes were fixed on me.

In some kind of expectation the girl was sitting silently with downcast eyes.

What was I supposed to do in this situation? . . . Stay silent? . . . I was silent, and all were silent.

Impatience began to affect me. "Well," I said to myself, "if it's up to me to get us all out of this silly situation, then I'll break the silence first!"

"I don't know what deity has turned her benevolent gaze upon me and granted me the happiness to be here?" I said quietly, turning to the charming, silent maiden.

She looked at me tenderly, and the word "*Alef!*" burst with a sigh from her lips.

"*Alef! Alef! . . .* " sounded throughout the hall, in a whisper. A chill of horror ran through me.

"I don't understand these mysterious words," I continued; "everything here is mysterious to me; explain it to me or let me escape these enchantments!

"*Bet!*" said the girl softly.

"*Bet! Bet! Bet!*" repeated thousands of voices quietly.

I jumped up.

"I cannot bear this!" I cried.

"*Gimmel!*" cried the girl and rushed into my arms.

I grew numb.

"*Gimmel! Gimmel! Gimmel!*" sounded loudly throughout the hall.

Suddenly an old man in white clothes appeared; from under his two-horned hat, like those worn by ancient priests, snowy locks fell to his shoulders. He approached me, took my hand, placed the maiden's hand in it, and began to say slowly, "*alef bet gimmel, dalet ge vuv, zayn khet tet, iot kaf lamed, mem nun zamekh, ayn pe tsade, kuf resh shin, taf!*"

All present repeated these words.

Horror engulfed me, my eyes darkened, the day disappeared, and darkness covered everything. The maiden's hand was cold in mine.

"Your honor! . . . Your honor! . . ." sounded in the distance.

"Oof," I cried, and woke up.

Before me stood the courier and the orderly; the evening sun shone through the tent; my left hand convulsively grasped my saber, which was lying next to me.

"Oh my God! It was all a dream!" I said and jumped for joy, for I had rid myself of *alef, bet, gimmel,* and all the other letters of the Hebrew alphabet.

Day 37

Jetzo gehen wir weiters.
(*Überzeugender Beweiß der Unsterblichkeit.*)
—1s Haup. II. Abs.
Israel Gottlieb Canzen.

263

Everyone in general and everyone individually who has not seen the fortress of Şumnu with his own eyes and knows it only from the above description ought to know that Şumnu is not a simple, ordinary Turkish fortress, but a fortified position more than forty versts in circumference, and therefore neither Coehoorn, nor Vauban, nor Cormontaigne, nor Bousmard, etc., etc., nor tricks, nor underground warfare will avail to take it, but only the words, "Well, boys, God is with us! Hurrah!"

But it is hard to resolve to attack this *old woman* if one is not ready to sacrifice at least ten thousand souls tempered in the fire of war. This calculation confirmed the need to conquer first Varna, which would reliably support the left flank of the active forces and defend the supply of provisions by sea.

Thus, a significant part of the army, reinforced by the Guard Corps, turned with its thunder to ancient *Odessus*.

264

Varna, like sad Hero, sits in her garden, under the cliff, on the seashore, and looks at the waves, waiting for Leander.

The ill-fated Polish king Ladislaus III, wishing to save this beauty from the Muslim yoke, broke the solemn treaty that had just been sworn with Murad on the Koran and the Gospel, and stretched out his arms to embrace her. But the brutal janissary flew at him, cut off his head, which had born the crowns of the kingdoms of Poland, Hungary, and Lithuania, stuck it on his *jerid*, and carried it through the crowd of Murad's army. The lips that had just kissed the Gospel as a sign of eternal peace with the Turks continued to babble something, but the Turks could not understand the last words of Ladislaus.

265

In 1828 the fighting at Varna began and continued otherwise than in past centuries.

By the middle of July, Şumnu was already under siege. On the sixteenth and seventeenth the heights near the village of *Straja* were occupied by the right hand of the besieging army. It was necessary to keep Hüseyin Paşa and his thirty thousand Şumnu troops occupied with something to divert attention from Varna, and therefore the construction of redoubts began along the whole front. Their main purpose was to allow the front to be held with a small number of troops, so that the rest could assault the flanks and rear of the fortress and scout out Eski Cuma, Eski İstanbul, Hezargrad, and so on.

On the twenty-first of July, His Majesty the Emperor, having given the necessary orders to support the capture of Varna, left us on the heights near Şumnu and, bidding us be clever, brave, and cautious, as a soldier on watch ought to be, he left for Varna, where glory was already preparing new laurels for the tsar of Russia.

266

Imagine, my dear companions, the fortress of Varna as the faithful brush of a painter or the pen and compasses of a *military topographer* might represent it to you on paper. Then imagine that the walls of the fortress are lined with 250 guns and fifteen thousand Turks armed from head to foot; that each of them, trusting in *Allah* and his Prophet, drinks his coffee, smokes his tobacco, and fires several stout rounds every day over the fortress wall.

At the same time, my good readers, imagine how the Russian field regiments have pressed in upon the fortress with everything they have; how the Russian guard, the flower of the Russian people's courage, strength, health, and beauty, is stationed on the heights in golden-topped tents; how a squadron of the Black Sea fleet, like a huge flock of proud pelicans, surrounds and constrains the Turkish Varna flotilla, like frightened fish, by the shore. But to crown a great event in the annals of Russian glory, O Russians, recognize your tsar! Imagine him pronouncing his will from the flagship *Paris* and ordering his men to vanquish the intractable enemy.

The siege artillery, from the newly built fortifications under the walls of Varna and from all the ships of the fleet, casts seventy thousand cannonballs, bombs, grenades, and rockets into the besieged fortress, smashing walls and houses and forcing the captain-pasha to beg for mercy. Mercy is granted. Varna is captured, and victory has inscribed in the annals of the world: "The Russian tsar Nicholas conquered Varna."

267

If my imagination could remain in one place for long, I would fill hundreds of volumes with detailed descriptions, and my book *The Wanderer* would be the size of the Mongol book *Ganjuur.* But this is incompatible with the goal of someone who stops only when he is stopped by a great event, by curiosity, by a fork in the road, by Janus's two- or four-faced head, or by an unresolved question, for example: Why was Janus's temple opened only during wartime? Because, he answers, during peacetime there is nothing to ask a god of war about.

But this answer will seem unsatisfactory, for it is a rare scholar who is satisfied with pure reason, without commentaries, citations, and facts.

Day 38

Le métier qu'on croit particulier aux comédiens et aux bateleurs,
c'est le métier de tous les hommes.
—Hippocrate

268

Gli uomini si rendono miseri col desirare il superfluo.
—Minerva sotto la figura di Mentore

. . . . and so on.

269

*

. . . . ?

Oh yes, it's clear, and understood
By minds in women's schooling made;
Such cryptic questions never could
Be in another form conveyed.

270

Having thus explained why I retired for a time from the sphere of military operations, I was, as usual, riding post. My surugiu, cracking his long whip, beat the rump and head of the horse he was riding with the stick he held in his hand. I should have been at the station at least an hour earlier if the wheel on my brichka had not shattered and if the following conversation had been less entertaining.

---

* Ces exagérations sont permises à la poésie, surtout dans la manière d'écrire dont je me sers. *Fables de La Fontaine*, liv. 11, fab. 9.

While the wheel was being mended, I strolled about the place. My curiosity led me to the gate of a hospital. I looked inside. Two soldiers were carrying a basket full of medicine bottles. They stopped by the hospital porch and entered into conversation:

"Wait, brother! How my stomach aches! It's quite a shock!
But I won't ask the doctor for a cure!
No sir! Whoever gets *perscriptions* from that doc
Will soon end up in heaven, that's for sure!
He's good at doing people in! You know
That uhlan soldier? Well, he got a simple rash,
And then . . . he bit the dust! Hey brother, take it slow!
I need to rest. I'll drink this *mixter*—just a dash."

[*He looks at the bottle in the light, then drinks.*]

"Like beer! . . . But trash! Can hardly down the cup!
What a *decaution*! Guess the devil taught him how.
This hospital perportion—once you drink it up,
You'll swell up like a dead and rotting cow!"

[*A sick soldier comes up.*]

"What's wrong, Khadei? Say, why the frown?"
"I've got a fever, mate! Since break of day
I've just been burning up! It's really knocked me down!
Some medicine, brother! Make it sour; pour away!"
"Well, you may ask for sour or salty, bitter, sweet,
But druggists don't prepare things to your taste."
"And you? You had a side ache, as I understand?"
"Oh yes! It must have been for some great sin!
I couldn't drink or eat or sleep! I thought I'd die!
But then the doc gave me a plasser, just to try,
And so I ate it with a bit of bread, and within
A day I'm better!"
"Really?"
"Swear to God, I'm fixed!"
"All right, let's go . . ."

[*They pick up the basket.*]

"What's this?"

"*Decautions* and some *mixt'*!"

[*They exit.*]

271

I wanted to lend credence to the above story by taking all manner of oaths that only a reader could have devised on this occasion, but my horses are already running faster than a whirlwind, and objects to the right and left are also rushing somewhere. Beyond the vast plain only the morning sky is visible. It seems that in two or three versts, plop!—we'll fall off the globe! What a prodigious leap!

272

But . . .

A man of reason will be glad
With this assertion to agree:
A thing is good if it *may be*;
If it *may not*, then it is bad!

273

Here I must confess to posterity that there is nothing sadder than a camp outside a fortress—especially, my friends, in desolate Bulgaria. "Why," the medical faculty will ask, "why was the trans-Danubian air so poisonous for us? What vital element did it lack?" None of them will find an answer.

What it lacked was a woman's breath.

In vain did the military music try to cheer up my soul, by playing first a Russian song, then an aria from *La Dame blanche*, then one from *Der Freischütz*, then a mazurka, then a *quadrille française*. All this only increased my melancholy, for it reminded me of *many things*.

This same melancholy settled upon the headquarters and the twenty-seven sentry redoubts.

274

All these operations were directed at Varna and at Milyon Paşa, who had been sent to defend it. The greater part of the troops who surrounded Şumnu secretly moved to the left flank of the front line, to the river Kamçiya, to block the thirty thousand auxiliary troops approaching Varna.

In addition, diseases filled the hospitals so much that neither wise management nor all possible measures to protect the troops could stop the flow of ambulance wagons, biers, and vans coming from the Şumnu camp. The tents were emptied. Hüseyin Paşa hoped to trounce us with two decisive nocturnal sorties, but both times he met a Russian *unit* in an open field that, like a bogatyr's club, laid the Turkish hordes to their final rest in the open field.

In vain did Hüseyin, on the fortress walls, lash his *Nizam-ı Cedid* with grapeshot, in vain did he curse them and threaten them with death—they fled back to seek salvation from the Russian club in the embrace of the walls of Şumnu.

275

Now inexplicably annoyed,
Within my tent I took my station.
The siege was then in preparation;
And I in countless tasks employed.
By me, like rows of tumuli,
Stood stacks of papers, near collapse.
Behold our age! One can't get by
Without these letters and these maps!
Our age! A miserly old man,
Encumbered by some weighty plan!
Recall the days, when on campaign
Darius could with perfect ease
Take beds instead of chancelleries;
Not scribes, but women, formed his train.
Those were the days! Without regard
For plans, they simply aimed at glory.
They had a poet tell their story,

Like Ossian, that immortal bard;
Upon the field there burned an oak,
As he their heroes would invoke!

276

But now they have brought in a prisoner for interrogation.

He was with youth and beauty blessed
And like a girl, with passions new;
He was in Turkish style dressed
A pike had pierced his shoulder through.
Russian knew he not too well,
But still he lucidly could tell
In Şumnu how he'd lived carefree,
In the Çifte Hamam he'd sing;
In Russia, with the embassy,
He met a girl, a "preety ting,"
And "'coz of her" he wept and wailed.
He then returned to Istanbul,
Where the *emir oğlu*, most cruel,
Once almost ordered him impaled.

277

Alme was the cause of this misfortune, and here is what Emin recounted:

Oh, she was young, and she so good,
The sweetest gurl I ever saw!
The best gurl in the neighborhood!
Ah! *La 'ilaha 'illa llah!*
The pasha fell in love with she,
But what is it? And why I care?
Pasha have many wife, you see,
In harem, pretty gurls and fair,
But Alme's not for him, I said,
Like my *pistoli* and your gun;
Trying kissing my *hançer* instead,

We see then who's the stronger one!

. . . .

Here the young Turk began to curse the pasha in his own language—I did not understand; and meanwhile the day ended.

278

And every year doth dissipate
Life's finite riches, crumb by crumb,
We squander at a growing rate,
And we approach the *total sum*!

Day 39

Celui qui n'a pas un grain de chimère dans la tête,
pour se consoler de la réalité, je le plains.
—Dolomieu

279

A new day began, but I, still as sad as the future of a hopeless person, knew not where in the world to escape my melancholy—so I rushed away to the desert that lies between Senegambia, Nigritia, and North Africa.

Fearing neither predatory Arabs, nor predatory beasts, nor predatory birds, nor tempestuous whirlwinds stirring up the billows of the sandy sea, I sat on a high embankment in the very center of the Zaara and looked at the brazen sky.

Then I saw all the riches of the sun and its misplaced generosity.

It scatters its rays excessively and does not allow a single cloud to fly over the desert to quench the earth's thirst or a wind to bring coolness. It just wants to be kind and generous.

Who can say whether an excess of good deeds is not really an evil?

Look, can this desert be grateful to the sun for turning it into a hell by its generosity?

Farewell, poor Zaara, barren and desolate land! Are you guilty of your excesses and defects, which, over an area of 5,895,760 square versts, give no shelter to poor humanity, which is so cramped on this earth!

280

When I was still a child and refused food out of anger and frustration, my nanny would try in vain to persuade me to eat. What would

I do now, when I am angry at the brazen sky of the Zaara, and in the same mood as Xerxes when he punished the Hellespont and called Mount Athos to battle?

To the words:

> Dear friend, I repeat,
> Really, you must eat!

I would reply:

> No, I don't want bread!
> Just a southern sky above my head!

281

That is how I would answer my nanny and anyone who would think of giving me empty land, for example in the middle of the Gobi Desert.

As an inhabitant of the Gobi, a person may not know the pleasures of life or even understand that there is prosperity on earth. Is it his fault that he was born in the middle of a desert steppe? There are no forests, no water to quench his thirst. In summer, prayers for rain are offered in vain; winter threatens to exterminate the herds. Water as salty as the sea, poisonous *suli* grass—these are the ornaments of an environment in which a being endowed with reason is sometimes destined to live.

But this matters not. A person who resembles a Gobi dweller ought to think and feel like a Gobi dweller: "Someday I shall quench my thirst in the miraculous, sacred spring of *Arashan*, sweetly bubbling amid the paradise intended for righteous Mongols; someday I shall be as imperishable as gold and shall shine like a precious stone; someday I shall mount my *tarpan*,* drive three thousand horses, and receive rewards from the *Khutagt:* a gun, a coat of mail, fifteen bulls and cows, fifteen horses, a hundred sheep, one camel, a thousand bricks of tea, twenty pieces of satin, and several fox and otter skins!"

---

* Wild horse.

Imagining such incalculable wealth, the inhabitant of the Gobi decorates his entire future with it, builds *Rehe*[*] in his mind—and is happy.

[*] Palace of the Bogda.

Day 40

Celui qui est assis, travaille pour se lever; celui qui est dans le mouvement, travaille pour être en repos.
—Hippocrate

282

Du, lieber Berg!
—*Gesangbuch für Kinder*, von Stoy

Returning from the steppes of Africa via the Gobi Desert to my camp, I was greeted by the embrace of my good comrade.

"Why are you so gloomy?" I asked him.

"That cursed Jew has annoyed me again!"

I understand!

> Alas for you: *birds of a feather*—
> The saying's true—they *flock together*:
> For you are everywhere pursued by sober fate,
> But Berka's followed by a stupid, happy state!

283

We entered the tent.

284

[*In the tent.*]

And this poor heart . . .

SBITEN SELLER

[*behind the tent*]

It's boiling!

ORDERLY

Even in trusty hands, coins don't last long,
Like wicked women who have no remorse;
So, kopeck, stand up on your edge, stand strong!
I've saved you for a capital divorce!
Hey, drink man, over here!

SBITEN SELLER

It's hot!

ORDERLY

Well, pour me some!
How much?

SBITEN SELLER

The prices vary.
This sbiten, like your tea, is quite extraordinary!

ORDERLY

Well, brother, did some devil bring you to the war?

SBITEN SELLER

Devil? No, Savelyich—he's my master, nothing more.

ORDERLY

And beardy, say, you've seen some scraps, no doubt?

SBITEN SELLER

Oh, have I ever! Kamensky had us go
Down to Silistre, Rusçuk, and then all about
Pazarcık, and then Batın, where we fought the foe.

ORDERLY

Aha! So, brother, you have really served, no lie!

SBITEN SELLER

Yes, five years as a sutler in a regiment,
And then a year with a division, then I went
To Şumnu, by the Balkants, with their peaks so high!

285

It was already about midnight. I had to go to the left flank. A Cossack, some nameless Yermak, brought me a horse and a whip, and I jumped into the saddle and rushed down a wide path near the camp. Someone was trotting in front of me and muttering something to himself. I followed him quietly. My curiosity induced me to listen to his words. They were complaints to himself, *military envy*:

We have the constant din of arms,
Crackling grenades and whistling shot,
Our heads ache under these alarms;
But here the calm cook stirs a pot
And for his master fries a steak! . . .
The soup gives off a smell sublime! . . .
My stomach grumbles right in time! . . .
The soldiers here have caught a break! . . .
Under their tents of canvas made,
Their dreams are flying, soft and light! . . .
And everywhere you see displayed
The signs of quiet and delight! . . .

The Petersburgers drown in beauty! . . .
But in the meantime, I must go
To where two lanterns brightly glow,
Where I will find the men on duty!

The detachment officer turned to the left, and I to the right; thus we parted without ever meeting. Could he have guessed that I had overheard, with a criminal ear, the words he had spoken to himself, and which I then brought to light, tacking on a fringe of rhymes?

286

The darkness of the night obscured the road. Lost in thought, I rode across the fields instead. Suddenly a question sounded in my ears which everyone (even a hungry dog) is obliged to answer: "Soldier!"

I consider this question, posed to me at night by a sentry on the front line, the happiest and cleverest of all those I have had to answer. Without it, under the cover of night—on the assumption that even a stocky Nekrasovite with a thick beard, wearing a belted Russian caftan and a high, fur-lined, cylindrical cap bent to one side, standing on the Turkish front line, would not have noticed me—I would have wandered into the enemy's advance fortifications and surely would have hit my head on something belonging to Sultan Mahmud.

What an unpleasant feeling would have filled my soul if the natives of Bulgaria, Rumelia, Albania, Bosnia, Macedonia, Anatolia, Armenia, Kurdistan, Irak Arabi, Diyarbekir, and all lands and islands belonging to the Sublime Porte had surrounded me, exclaimed "*La 'ilaha 'illa-llah! Gâvur!*" and taken me to Hüseyin's headquarters.

Sitting on a long velvet cushion, the seraskier would have asked me how I had ended up in the Turkish camp.

"I lost my way," I would have replied.

"It is not a lost way, but the right way, which leads to the shelter of Allah and his Prophet," Hüseyin would have said, ordering me to be sent to Constantinople.

287

He would have kindly given me
A stubborn mule, unfit and scarred;
Thereafter some Ahmet-Bashi
Would have conveyed me under guard;
And long would he have led me, 'cross
To Karnobat, or to Aydos,
To Kırkkilise, Istanbul.
I should have bid my youth goodbye!
How many times I'd give a sigh,
And you'd have sighed within your soul!
You would have shed tear after tear,
And I'd have had no comfort near! . . .

288

Fortunately, this did not happen; my sighs and tears remained intact. Meanwhile, it was time to head to winter quarters. Following the historical personages of 1828, I rode post from Varna via Mankalya . . . Psst! Beyond a strip of land separating a small lake from the sea, on a gentle slope to the sea, a small, deserted Asiatic village came into sight; apart from one or two mosques, a steeple with a cross gleamed white—this was a church.

So this is the place where Ovid lived, exiled from Rome for a reason unknown to posterity! Here is the same city of *Tomi*, where his tombstone lay with this epitaph:

Hic ego qui iaceo, tenerorum lusor amorum,
Ingenio perii Naso poeta meo.
At tibi qui transis, ne sit grave, quisquis amasti,
Dicere Nasonis molliter ossa cubent.

289

For the most part, people solve tangled knots with no more subtlety than Alexander the Great. So who will reproach me for translating an ancient Latin manuscript explaining a mystery that is important to the learned world?

290

[*Octavius Augustus and Ovidius Naso in the hothouse of the Pantheon.*]

AUGUSTUS

Lie down, dear Naso! . . . Once you've steamed your bones, it's pleasant to lie down and take a rest!

I feel as if . . . together with my sinful body, my mind and feelings have been washed, and all my cares have been wiped clean.

Read me your recent work; I'm ready now to listen.

When I am in my baths . . . I am entirely free . . . just like a singer's wingèd thoughts!

Here, having rested from the weight of power, I feel . . .

And everything within me says, "You are a poet in your soul!"

Oh, had it not been my true fate to govern Rome and glorify my country, I'd have devoted all my life to pure delights, just like the holy fire preserved by Vesta!

To love and to sing of love . . . these are two purposes: the sacred destiny of people and the goal of life! . . .

Oh, I'd have been a splendid poet! . . . My age would know Octavius!

Between the author of the Iliad and the god of song there's ample room!

Our age is lacking in those worthy of the noble name of poet! . . . [*Sighs.*]

Horace? . . . They're unimportant singers, glory's hangers-on.

Judge them yourself, dear Naso!

OVID

Their judges are posterity and time.

AUGUSTUS

No, no, speak freely! . . . You have the right to state their worth . . . For Naso glorifies the Roman Muses.

OVID

Such spongers in pursuit of glory are in plenty!

AUGUSTUS

Take Virgil's tales of Aeneas—I listened, listened, and then fell asleep.

The language is polluted, dense, and swampy, like the foul air of the Pomptine Marshes . . .

Only the eclogues and the ending of book 6 are . . . adequate and tolerable . . .*

But I could not forgive his folksy foolishness and raptures when he read a passage on the stage; for, Caesar's honor . . . it suited Virgil as a toga suits a monkey.

I sat him down with Horace at my table . . .

Like living statues! . . . Nothing could move them from their places; but they're endowed with stomachs that I envy! . . .

[*Laughs.*]

One sighed, the other shed some tears . . .†

I laughed . . . Well, laughter's good for my digestion . . .

So, Naso, you're acquainted with the tribune Horace? . . . And do you know he ran from battle? . . . A poet cannot be a coward.

And all his odes are so intolerable! . . . More puffed up than old Aesop's frog—it seems their fame's about to burst! . . .

OVID

Yes, it is so . . . But envy of the bard, it seems, will burst before his fame! . . .

AUGUSTUS

Toward Horace you are biased, out of friendship.

But listen now to how Octavius taught him once a lesson:

He never had the least idea that Caesar could become a poet.

Once I was joking with him and suggested that he school me in the art of poetry.

And so? All of a sudden Horace comes to me with an enormous scroll.

* The eclogues in honor of Augustus. At the end of the sixth canto Virgil sings of Claudius Marcellus, son of Octavia, sister of Augustus.

† Virgil was often short of breath. Horace had fistulas in his eyes.

Here is, he says, the *Art of Poetry*; shall we begin the lesson?

The lesson? . . . Have a seat! . . . and then I listened both with patience and with laughter.

Then with a look of deep importance, he expounded on *caesuras* and *hexameters* and the *Alcaic* meter, which must be his silliest.

I promised him to learn it all by heart, but then I asked him for a subject to describe in iambs for the following day; and then I slyly turned the conversation to splendid Sicily.

He did not see my trap, and he himself proposed I sing of Sicily.

So on the next day I appear triumphantly, a great success, before my tutor.

I read the third song of my own *Siciliad* . . . * You know yourself, dear Naso, how superb it is!

What do you think that whining Horace did? He did not understand its beauty! And he tried to count out my mistakes.

My friend, you're looking rather dumb!

Go take your art into the countryside! Learn first before you try to tutor others!

OVID

He's not the only one you taught a lesson!

AUGUSTUS

Well, how about Tibullus? The bard who sang the love of fair Sulpicia and Cerinthus, do you like him? . . . Well, I feel sorry for him! . . .

And not for nothing did he slobber over all those elegies: I think Cerinthus, out of friendship, gave him leave to sit down by the bed and copy all those passionate delights from nature!

[*Laughs.*]

Wait . . . excellent! . . . An epigram! . . .

> Alas, to this hard life he has been fated:
> When others drink, he gets intoxicated!

---

* Suetonius.

Like Metis, I have given birth, straight from my head, to armed Minerva—to this epigram!

Well, Naso, now begin!

OVID

[*Unrolls the scroll.*]

AUGUSTUS

What, isn't this the *Art of Love*?

OVID

Oh no, it is the *Art of Hate*, a tragedy.

AUGUSTUS

A tragedy? . . . How excellent! I seem to have conspired with you! . . . I've recently refined a tragedy all of my own, and once I've rested I shall read it to you.

What's your title?

OVID

Medea.

AUGUSTUS

What, *Medea*? . . . Naso, surely you must know that *I* am writing a *Medea* . . . and you're making fun of me!

OVID

I have no reason to make fun of you! Whose fault is it, great Caesar, if Melpomene inspired both you and me with an identical idea?

AUGUSTUS

You didn't know that I was writing a *Medea*?

OVID

I only knew one thing: Augustus is the emperor; his duty is to write the laws for Rome!

AUGUSTUS

Are you not trying to impose your laws on me as well? . . . But that's enough, let's put our hearts aside, for reason now will reconcile us . . .

But if you wrote your own *Medea* and you have no hidden purpose, simply prove it!

[*Claps his hands; servants appear.*]

A censer with the sacrificial fire!

Give me your scroll!

OVID

What for?

[*They bring the censer.*]

AUGUSTUS

To make a sacrifice to friendship. For I desire to try my hand alone in competition with Euripides!

OVID

So, when your son was born . . . did you command all other infants to be put to death . . . so there could be no other like your son? . . .

AUGUSTUS

Your sarcasm is unkind! But I'll forgive you once you have complied with my request.

OVID

I love these works as my own children! . . . I will not sacrifice them even to the gods!

AUGUSTUS

[*Snatches Ovid's scroll and throws it on the fire.*]

Behold now all your blazing glory!

OVID

[*Grabs Augustus's scroll and throws it on the fire.*]

Behold the execution of your own *Medea* and the smoke that's left from Caesar's toils!

AUGUSTUS

Guards, guards!

[*The guards enter.*]

[*Pointing to Naso*]

He's banished to the Scythian border, in captivity!

OVID

[*Carried away by the guard.*]

Medea! . . . You are guilty! . . . And I receive the punishment of heaven because I wished to sanctify your memory and justify you to posterity!

Day 41

291

[*Evening.*]

[*A company is seated around a table reading a poet's new work.*]

UNE DEMOISELLE

[*Enraptured and brought to the seventh heaven by the poems.*]

"How good he is, how very dear!
How wise! . . . I didn't know all this! . . .
Ah, if right now he should appear,
I'd surely offer him a kiss!"
And now, the poet's on the spot,
Quite shyly, unexpectedly.
"He's here!" they whisper.
"Surely not!"
"Upon my honor!"
"It can't be! . . ."
I don't believe it, it's not he!"
Indeed, who will believe this claim:
That fate treats talent shabbily
And keeps it in a *swarthy frame*!

I

[*To myself*]

O memory, make me not grieve!
Can all in life be so amiss?

Alas, I shall not now receive
That previously promised kiss!

292

The poet was invited into the circle. He was quite timid.

I looked with regret at his painful position between two ladies, who *in their own way* were examining his mind and feelings and were visibly surprised at the simplicity of his answers. And he—so courteous!—pulled himself into a mathematical line, so as not to brush shoulders, elbows, or hands with either of his neighbors; but—alas!—they began to consider the *portrait of the eye* of one of the ladies; they suggested that he look as well; he reached out his hand and—bumped his elbow on the face of the pretty neighbor on his right.

"Compose an impromptu poem on this portrait of the eye," said his neighbor on the left.

The poor poet did not know what to do first: answer the proposal or apologize for his carelessness.

On both sides he was at fault, and all sides noticed his awkwardness.

He blushed; a poetic frenzy seemed to come over his face.

"Write the poem!" repeated the neighbor on the left, pushing some paper and ink toward him.

"What do you want me to write? I don't know . . ."

"For example, find a mistake in this image of an eye."

"But if this is your eye, then . . ."

"Then write!"

The poet took a pen and wrote:

I'm glad to locate the mistake—
Though feelings strong my words entangle—
I think the form your eye should take
Is not a square, but a . . .

The poet paused, thinking about the rhyme.

"Fine, fine, I'll choose the rhyme myself," cried the capricious neighbor. "Now write something else: the dedication of this eye to my friend, only in French."

"I don't know how, madam."

"Write, write, I tell you!"

The poet did not know how and dared not excuse himself. Poets, not women, are the weaker beings, I thought.

He wrote:

> Mon amie! que cet œil vous rappelle les yeux,
> Qui aimaient vous chercher, contempler et comprendre;
> Qu'il vous souvient toujours les regards tendres,
> Et les larmes qu'ils versaient au moment des adieux.

"Good! . . . Now a poem for an album, and no excuses! This is easy for you."

"No, it's difficult," replied the poet, stammering.

"No more difficult than for us to tie together a pattern from a handful of beads. Here's a handful of words for you: *cœur, souffrir, souvenir, oubli*; make some sense out of them."

"They want to turn poetry into mosaic work!" whispered the poet, and he began to write:

> Deux choses qui font le cœur souffrir,
> Qui le tourmentent pendant la vie:
> C'est d'un côté le souvenir,
> De l'autre côté l'oubli.

"Bravo, bravo, and again bravo! This is fit not only for the album but also for a new edition of bonbon mottoes!"

The poet did not take offense at the suggestion, for he knew that poetry is a *sweetness* that aids the digestion of truth, especially for those who find philosophical food heavy and indigestible.

293

"Please tell me," I thought to myself, "is poetry nothing more than mosaic or beadwork?" "It's not hard!" "Then I will write poetry too! I'll write—and that's it!" *A handful of words, a little sense, a musical ear, a bit of skill*—those are all the materials needed to produce poetry.

Reader, let us write poetry! Believe me, in a day or two we'll beat down the price of all poems, operas, vaudevilles, etc., not to mention the petty rhymes that are written in one sitting and even *impromptu*, as you saw in the previous chapter. We'll humble all those pampered minors who style themselves poets.

Good heavens! As if beets couldn't replace sugarcane!

294

A ring with jewels finely hewn . . ."
. . . .
—*The Wanderer*, part 1, chapter 107

. . . . since that day
He's driven all my sleep away
And filled my soul with sad unrest.
How often have I cursed and blessed
The care she gives me every day,
And later lain awake and raved!
On one occasion, weary, frail,
I looked at her and craved
To be resilient, strong, and hale.
I see the army junker now;
He steps into this humble hut;
I would not normally allow
A brother in this room, with but
A simple table, walls, a floor,
The gentle sex, and nothing more.
My host must know, without a doubt,
That though I love my neighbor dearly,
I lose my temper quite severely;
But like a hermit, all worn out,
I suffered all and even did not
Chastise my batman as I ought.
Then like a chamois, having spied
Her junker, up my hostess ran.
And he, as timid as a bride,
Came in, bowed, and soon began
To doff his pack from shoulders weak;
And on his sword belt was a streak,

Which he then rubbed at with his cuff;
He hung his shako; sore enough
And wearied by the heavy heat,
He'd long have struggled with his clasp
Had not the hostess, kind and sweet,
Jumped in with help, and eased his grasp.
"*Muscal săracu*,[*] young and bold!
How can your young and weary back
Endure the heat and bitter cold,
The rifle and the soldier's pack?
Aşteaptă![†] I will now undo
This buckle!" Shortly after that,
She took his jacket and cravat,
Gave him a kiss, then gave him two,
Then asked him please to take a seat.
This honor and reception sweet
He answered with ingratitude.
"Mistress, I'll have a bite to eat!"
Replied the junker, strangely rude.
And I, though indisposed and thin,
Forgot that I was tired and grim,
As if the junker, coming in,
Had brought my health back in with him!
. . . .

295

Oh, shame on you! There was no need
To take my notebook without leave!
And from this act, I do perceive
That you, it seems . . . know how to read!
[*Aside*:]
Not what I meant to say, indeed!

---

[*] Poor Muscovite!

[†] Wait!

296

Angered by the indiscretion of a neighbor who read, without my permission, the continuation of the poem I found in Lozova about *mititică Mărioliţa*, I sat down at the writing desk and cast my gaze at the map, but my eyes could not concentrate. What could I do without eyes? Like a disciple of the abbé l'Épée, I ran my finger along the map and felt the Caucasus Mountains. In my imagination I created a complete logical idea about them.

Look at the wilderness enriched by the sky, the cluster of mountains, the bright streams of living water, this lavish, virgin land untouched by the plowshare, these fertile forests, these slopes dotted with flowers and valleys covered with dense greenery, these layers of snow, by which one could determine the age of the universe, this air as fragrant as the rose that blossomed during the creation of Eve! Look, look, gentlemen readers and dear lady readers!

The envious sun with its brilliant light hides from view the countless luminaries floating in the sky; in the distance, the eternal snows resemble a canvas spread across the peaks of the blooming Caucasus; neither wave nor leaf murmurs at the restless wind. Surrounded by a stillness as I have never known before, I hear only the beating of my heart; but suddenly a voice rings out . . . and what a voice! Listen, listen, gentlemen readers and dear lady readers! . . .

297

Having thus engaged the eyes and ears of my companions and fair companionesses, I steal away from that crowd again and ride up the seashore from Mankalya. Counting out three hundred stadia, according to the calculation of an *unknown seafarer on the Pontus Euxinus*, I approach ancient Istros, transformed by time and the descendants of the Torks into Köstence.

My good friend P. P. L., a man with a fine soul and friendly heart, was there. Having paid his debt to the climate and hardships of the campaign, he had just shaken off the fetters of disease.

I was unaccustomed to a warm welcome, a soft bed, and delicious food, and it was strange to me to find all this luxury combined in the former house of the pasha of Köstence, where L. lived.

This calm was quite peculiar to regard,
But here I must declare: it is not true
That losing habits is in fact that hard
Or that they're difficult to gain anew.

298

After enduring the fickle roof of heaven for six months, it felt so good to see above me the carved ceiling of the former harem, so good to be confined in walls again! . . . Sleep would have been the death of me, if the need to arise had not broken the soporific chains in which I was entangled. My heart and imagination were resting serenely; my pulse had subsided; my blood was humbly circulating. How hard it is to part with such sleep!

Since during the war every fortress was converted into a hospital, all the curious eye could find, even in Köstence, were a few *băcălii* with Jewish, Greek, and Armenian hucksters and Russian sutlers.

Whoever had need of lard, *balyk,* black bread, and sour wine could buy all these vital supplies at a reasonable price.

On the fortification walls there were still huge fortress guns, ancient trophies of Turkish victories in Germany and Poland. They gazed silently out of their embrasures like the heads of tortoises from their . . . what are those called? . . . like the two shields in which the body of Alaric, the brave king of the Goths, was buried.

Seeing no need to describe how the *Black Sea* splashes about the granite foot of the ancient, glorious city of *Istros,* I am even less inclined to persuade my readers that the Danube once flowed into the sea near this city and that the Karasu Valley was its ancient bed.

Though you, my Danube, swiftly flow,
Without a miracle you could not force
Your water o'er the mountainous plateau
Near Istros, once it chose to block your course.

Day 42

299

Pour ne rien laisser en arrière je vous dirai, monsieur, que . . .
—*Lettre sur les têtes parlantes*, Rivarol

I travel on, through the barren *sancak* of Silistre toward Hırsova. After six hours of riding, the horses were tired, my stomach was empty, and I was obliged to seek shelter from the rain. Here, on the side of the road, one can see a *köy*. Let's look at the map. *Karamuratköy*, *Danaköy* . . . God knows! *Danaköy* or *Karamuratköy*? . . . Judging by the distance from Hırsova, it must be *Dana-Köy* . . . but *Danaköy* is on the left of the road from Köstence! . . . But then *Karamuratköy* is also . . . yes . . . not more than three versts on the map . . . but how many in reality? . . . "Maps help those who help themselves," says a military proverb.

While I was reasoning thus, the brichka moved forward, leaving the *köy* about two versts behind. "Wait!" I cried, "Go back!" Does it really matter if it was *Karamuratköy* or *Danaköy* But there's smoke in one chimney! . . . Turks, perhaps? . . . No! . . . I see a brichka . . . I drive up.

"Well, well! V—!"

"Ah, N—!"

"What are you doing here?"

"Come in and see."

One Bulgarian mud hut survived the complete destruction; it still had a roof on top and a hearth inside. In front of the fireplace, in which the reeds were already crackling, lay a huge trunk; on the trunk was a tin bowl; out of the bowl rose a cloud of steam, as from Vesuvius.

I will neither confirm nor deny the reader's guess that the bowl contained a soup made like French soups with water, like German ones with chocolate or beer, like English ones with wine, like Chinese ones with brick tea, like Oriental ones with all sorts of things, etc.; I will not argue the probability of the supposition that it was Russian cabbage soup, Polish borscht with beets, Little Russian borscht with cabbage or cucumber juice, or Moldavian borscht with grape leaves; I will not say whether the conclusion is true that the bowl contained fish soup as fat and tasty as Demyan's fish soup.

And it would be strange to argue what I had no time to investigate myself, since what I rashly gulped down was uncommonly hot. My tongue burned, my eyes shed tears, and my appetite disappeared.

300

The burn deprived me of my memory and attention for about three hours; so in but a few words I transport myself and N— along the muddy road from *Danaköy* or *Karamuratköy* to Hırsova.

The reader can imagine the blue ribbon of the Danube flowing through the wilderness on the left side of the road and the mountain slopes on the right. Behind us is the road we have already taken; before us is the glacis of the fortress of Hırsova, a bridge across the moat, and a stone gate in the middle of the curtain; above us is the evening sky, with all the signs of bad autumn weather.

Thus, marching ceremonially along with the whole universe in the face of *Time*, we rushed across the bridge, through the gate, and rolled down the street in Hırsova to the commandant's house. The commandant was not at home, nor was his adjutant.

The evening was already hanging by a thread.

A soldier undertook to find us *proper quarters*.

For a long time he led us among dilapidated wooden houses scattered throughout the fortress and serving as hospitals and magazines. Finally, as if by accident, he found an empty house.

We entered.

"Soldier, there are no windows or doors here! The fireplace and chimney are broken!"

We walked on.

"Here is another house, suitable for an apartment, your honor!"

I open the door and enter . . . it's dark . . . Stepping on something soft, I stop involuntarily . . . I look under my feet . . . "My dear friend, there are already lodgers here! . . . If not alive, then dead! . . . Look how many of them are strewn all over the floor!"

"My fault, your honor!" replied the simplehearted soldier, "This is actually the *hospital store* where the dead are kept."

We resumed walking and riding around.

Another apartment was shown to us by our guide. It was warm and attractive; but an officer who had a *fever* had just passed away in it.

"This apartment is no good! Show me another!"

"There are no more, your honor!" replied our billeting officer.

Our situation was not very pleasant: nighttime, in the rain, on a muddy street in Hırsova. It soon improved, however. Learning that the commandant's adjutant had left the fortress for some time, we settled in his apartment, which was warm and equipped with all the necessities for military tranquility.

Day 43

This day was to begin with chapters 307 and 308, but since they did not appear in their proper places at the appointed time, I detained them for twenty-four hours.
—(Note)

301

Even if the thread of your memory were shorter than the distance between the head and tail of the *Great Bear*, surely you would not refuse to string onto it this beautiful rule of life:

Be what you are;
Don't wear a mask;
All flattery bar,
For kindness ask.
Love wide and deep;
False shows abhor,
Don't oversleep,
Drink water more.
Oaths never trust;
Be shrewd and just;
Give flesh no heed
And do the deed.

302

Thus, if in your youth you string onto your memory all that is beautiful, useful, and lofty, then in your old age, with nothing else to do, you will be able to turn over these beads in your mind.

How sweet is memory, and how fine is old age when it is a quiet reverie of the past!

Our life demands that every deed be preceded by a thought and followed by a new thought.

Do *you* remember . . . *you,* whom I know not what to call . . . *you,* who are so like everything with which poets have compared beauty and virtue—do you remember your feelings at the moment when your heart told you, "You did a good deed!" and everything around you thought, "How perfect she is!"

303

If my thought were as deep as the ocean where Forster measured it and as high as the layer of air to which Gay-Lussac flew, then such an eloquent thought would not find a tongue to suit it and would have to be expressed in eloquent silence, because, as everyone knows, eloquent silence is more powerful and expressive than verbal eloquence. This will be confirmed by all my female readers. Their delicate, sensitive hearing can better understand a *rest* between two charming *chords,* that secret sound heard only by a pure, innocent soul.

304

Do not be angry that in this chapter you cannot hear the scratch of my pen. This is a *rest.* Here my thought is expressed by silence.

305

After a three-day stay in the Hırsova fortress, owing to the impossibility of crossing the Danube, finally on the morning of the fourth day the sun began to peer through the remaining clouds, and I moved on.

I will not describe how I arrived in the city of Galați, where the headquarters of the acting army originally intended to winter.

> Galați may be already known
> To you from a poetic tale;

Recall: the hero, barely grown,
Though kind and honest, strong and hale,
Did fear a prison full of mold,
And cold Siberia far away,
And so he fled. He was a slave;
A fair Greek maiden did he save;
And from the plague he passed away.

And therefore I will not depict Galați either. It is a small town on the bank of the Danube, compressed by the rivers Siret and Prut. At a certain time, a few dozen merchant ships flock to a small pier and trade Archipelagic wine, Turkish tobacco, olives, oranges, lemons, and oil for rich Moldavian wheat, and then—they go where they ought to go.

306

My hope of remaining in Galați and settling down in a quiet apartment was disappointed, but in a pleasant way.

As soon as I entered the courtyard of a certain resident of the city, a messenger from the commandant brought me an order from headquarters that I was to spend the winter in Iași.

To Iași! . . .

Day 44

Vulcain (à part).
Ah, nature, nature! va, je t'abandonne à qui voudra te prendre!
—*Pandore,* Saint-Foix

307

A person is happier, calmer, and more satisfied with life when he has to deal with nature itself and not with people.

With what gratitude and generosity can nature's gratitude and generosity be compared? Who better rewards labor?

Reliable creditor! Faithful debtor!

Free and healthy in body and soul is he who is betrothed to you in body and soul!

308

My friends, have you ever experienced moments in which an earthly calamity surrounded you with all its visible and invisible properties and attributes, but your heart was unassailable, like heaven, and you smiled, like angels, at the presence of patience and hope?

These are the best moments of life, in which

I've left the earth; I'm full of something;
There is no place for thought in me!
And I am peaceful, glad! For thought
Is nothing but the germ of grief.
A sigh for my departed bliss
Lies dormant in my carefree soul,
And still the future lies ahead . . .
But what is happiness to me? . . .

I'll build a world from my desires,
A world that I will then despise.

309

Mes regards veulent pénétrer dans la profondeur du passé; mais je n'y vois qu'une lueur incertaine semblable à celle des rayons de la lune réfléchis par la surface d'un lac éloigné. Là brillent les flambeaux de la guerre; ici je vois une génération faible et vile, passer dans le silence, sans marquer les années d'aucune action éclatante.
—*Cathloda*, chant 3

Now, my dears, I am waiting at the Bordea post office until my four skinny *cai* are harnessed. But I already see the river Bahlui and the city of Iași with its long *Ulița Mare*, its burned princely palace, and its churches and monasteries, which stand like individual ancient castles on vine-clad hills; beyond the city, I see an extensive carpet of green . . .

Copou, *Copou*, O lovely, green *Copou*!
Where Cupid joins the *mititică* dance!
The *cobză* and wild melodies entrance,
And *po-o po-o pomerani-po*!

O power of imagination! Imagine, I feel as if I am already in a crowd of Moldavian beauties; I'm walking through a field that is enchanted by their charm! Now one who is prettier than all the rest has moved away from the assembly; I pursue her; she stops, and I do too; she looks at the surrounding greenery of Iași, and I do too . . .

I

The world is wondrous beyond words,
In beauty clad!
The grove resounds with songs of birds,
[*Pointing to his heart*]
But this . . . is sad!
My vision of a happy fate
I cast away!

[*After a pause*]

You sit in such a silent state!

SHE

What can I say?

I

What can you say? Well, that is new!
I comprehend
What's spoken wordlessly by you:
A total end!

SHE

But what's the cause of your distress?

I

Nothing and all!
For you . . . my words cannot express . . .
My tongue doth stall!
Because . . . your fondness made me weak,
I lost my mind!
And what in me did you so seek,
And never find?
Perhaps from some external view
Did I not please? . . .
Or is my love not suited to
Southern degrees?
Or . . . being early sated you . . .
I feel your plight!
But you're Moldavian, that is true,
And I'm a Muscovite!

Farewell!

310

All this was but a dream I had on the way to Iași, but the indifference of the beautiful woman in my mind affected me so much that I ordered the driver to stop the horses, and I jumped out of the *căruță* and walked off into the forest—imagining that I was moving far away from the cruel Moldavian woman.

"What!" I cried, stopping before a deep ravine. "What!" echoed in the forest.

I looked all around me.

"Where is she?" "She is not there and never was," said my heart, coming to its senses.

"What!" I repeated, "Can grief, melancholy, sorrow, and ecstasy really arise equally from true causes and imaginary causes?"

"Yes," replied a Mathematician, "because $+a^2$ results equally from $(+a) \times (+a)$ and from $(-a) \times (-a)$."

"I see."

Convinced by such a clear argument, I returned to my postal *căruță*, sat in it, the *surugiu* slapped the horses with his whip; they faltered and pulled apart; the second blow convinced them—and off I went.

311

In the hope that drops of *wisdom* falling from the sky will someday gnaw through the stumbling block of ignorance, which is as large as the earth, I ride on without looking back.

For life, as for the road, there is one rule:

Do not hurry; keep looking forward; gaze into the distance to stay on the road; do not speed downhill, or you will crash at the bottom; to oncoming riders shout, "Keep right!"; when you pass each other, make way; if dogs bark, don't tease them; if a snake crawls out, don't step on it or listen to what it hisses; with fellow travelers, don't tell a clever man that he's clever or a stupid man that he's stupid—you'll never be rid of them; don't display your kindness or your gold—you will be robbed; etc.

But this rule is for ordinary people . . . but who considers himself an ordinary person? I will say no more: extraordinary people, that is, *geniuses*, are *comets*, which follow an undefined path and are not subject to general laws.

312

My horses were exhausted; their harnesses were flecked with foam, and steam floated over them like a fog. The *surugiu*, also tired, vainly shook the hairy end of his whip and cried, "*Hi-me, murgule!*" Thus I drifted down the *Ulița Mare*, across the *Podul Mogoșoaiei*.

My eye was caught on the right and left by *băcălii* with wide windows; then a *cafenea*, through the doors and glass partitions of which I could clearly see the following: straight ahead, a black hearth laden with coffeepots of various sizes; in the middle, a brazier; on the sides, divans; on the divans, wearing *cealmale, cușme, fesuri, fermenele,* and *mintene,* whiskered guests. Here they silently play *concină* and *trictrac*, sip coffee, and envelop themselves in tobacco smoke.

From almost every window of the famous street a woman's face looked out, following the wanderer with curious eyes and the thought: "A Muscovite!" I was amused to notice the variety of the heads exhibiting themselves, now in a hat with flowers—I only saw *eyes*; now in a kerchief tied around a black braid—*freshness and health*; now in dotted lace adorned with pearls and covered with hammered gold netting—*the prolonged word* vos?; now in a white or red fez—*traces of fatigue*; now with huge false curls—*Potiphar's wife looking at Joseph*; now in a transparent veil—*false modesty*; now with smoothed and braided hair—*humble heartlessness*; now with disheveled curls—*a sunburnt child of the gypsy camp.*

But the appearance of the street is gradually improving. After turning to the left by the burned palace of the hospodar, one encounters entirely different objects.

Colorful Viennese carriages scurry back and forth. *Cucoane* and *cuconițe*, decked out in satin, muslin, organdy, *gros de Naples, gros de Berlin, gros de Tours, satin turc, satin de la reine, batiste d'Écosse,* tulle, *kiseya*, crepe, gauze, percale, cashmere—in blondes, laces, shawls, kerchiefs, pelerines, chemisettes, *canezous*, scarves, corsages, veils, collarets, *à la vierge, à la jardinière, à l'anglaise*, in feathers *à l'inca*, in dresses with sleeves shaped like berets, *côtes-de-*

melon, and *oreilles d'éléphant* . . . I am tired! . . . In short, the *cucoane* and *cuconițe* are hurrying somewhere wearing all the variations of ornithology, according to the systems of Vienna, Paris, and London. Carefree, self-satisfied faces with ardent eyes, natural blush and Chinese rouge, natural paleness and lead powder, cast their eyes to the right and left. I go on.

313

In the wood-paved streets there is not much room for pedestrians. Only the common people and the foreigner are unashamed to walk.

314

Qui prouve trop ne prouve rien.
—(Axiome)

But here on the right and left are shops and stores filled with goods from Turkey and Austria. Stamps from Vienna, Leipzig, Istanbul, and Izmir guarantee cheapness and quality.

Not content with the fact that the need and desire to spend money fill the shops and stores with purchasers, hucksters catch you on the street, try to persuade you, drag you violently into their shops, tempt you with low prices and discounts, and before you have decided to buy something you glanced at, the article is already measured, weighed, cut, wrapped, and thrust into your hands, and what remains for you to do? To pay.

After this, trust the abovementioned axiom! Who makes more assurances than a Jew that his goods are *gants fayn*? And you take everything for the *honest truth*.

To those riding by the shops there is the same *severe attention*, the same *forced gratification*.

My tired horses had barely taken a few steps between the long lines of shops before the descendants of *Israel* bestrewed my brichka and threw into it everything that they, being shrewd, thought necessary to sell me. What was I to do? My horses *stopped*, as if bribed by the Jews, and I had to listen to the prices of the goods. "Cambric, cambric!" cried a red-haired Hebrew, "*gants gut, fayn!* Eight chervontsy apiece!" "Dutch canvas!" cried another, with twisted *peyes*, "*akh, finf dukatn eyn shtik!*" "Sedan cloth, fifteen lei an ell!" "Shawl, *bourre de soie,* four chervontsy!" "*Cărți, de vizită, cu caricaturi, optsprezece lei! Cumpără, cumpără, boier! Kaufen Sie, kaufen Sie, mein lieber Herr!*"

Săracul de mine!

315

On *Ulița Mare,* across from the Paşcanu House, which housed the commander-in-chief, was the apartment assigned to me. After eight months of nomadic life in the Bulgarian wilderness, the wide divans of Boyar Ion Neculce-Muta felt gentler to me than friendly embraces. In an instant, I went to each of them and managed to lie down, cross my legs under me *à la turque,* uncross them, stretch out, and find all possible positions of laziness, comfort, and calm.

Here is my trunk! It too will rejoice in the calm, and its sides have been wiped down.

> My servants, as you may presume,
> Have dragged my house into *my room.*

SURUGIU

> "Hei! *Mare dracul*!"*

ORDERLY

> "Heavy, yes!"
> "Of course," I thought, "I must agree!
> For it holds all God's given me,
> All things but cash and happiness!"

316

My affectionate hosts took me in as their own.

---

* Big devil.

Soon a most entertaining person appeared, carrying a tray with wine, *dulceață*, coffee, and a pipe of *dübek*.

"*Poftim, boier!*" he said to me, "*Kaló krasí! Dulceață, cafea si lulea!*"

"Thank you, my friend. Tell me, are you from here?"

"*Eu* Greek man, Captain Micolae; I have wife, *coptil mult!*[*] *N-am cămăsi*, no *straie*![†] *Cucoane si cuconițe* give me *straie si cămăsi; turcii mâncat* everything!"[‡]

"That's a pity; drink some wine for your grief."

"Ah, good! *Kalá eínai krasí!*[§] Captain Micolae sherved empire . . . [¶] Artillery go, big *tunurile*;[**] *eu* show road: battle at Khotin, at Bender, *merge* to Izhmail . . . Commanding *inaral*[††] give Captain Miculae *ena* shertificate . . . what a big paper! . . . *Pețetluit*: et shetera, et shetera, et shetera! . . . [‡‡] Expresh paper! . . . *Hi!* I go to expresh posht offish! . . . Ding-ding-ding-ding! I go, I go! . . . and commanding *inaral* give another paper . . . good! . . . He write: Captain Micolae sherved empire, good . . . give me rank *captain*, good rank, empire! So, you go to Tshargrad?

"Yes, we're going there."

"*Si eu* go! . . . I was in battle, *cu* German[§§] . . . on *Focsani*![¶¶] *Cneaz* send me with supply *căruță* to Coburski . . . [***] German go, go, go! . . . Like that! . . . Hungarian hussar . . . Like that! . . . Good! My God! *Turcii!!!* Many, many!! *Vizir cu cavalerie*, on Anatolian *armasar*!![†††]

---

[*] I have a wife and many children.

[†] No linen, no clothes.

[‡] The Turks ate everything!

[§] Excellent wine!

[¶] Was in the Russian service.

[**] The artillery went, the big cannons.

[††] General, commander.

[‡‡] Printed: etc., etc., etc. (a post-horse order).

[§§] With the Germans.

[¶¶] At Focșani.

[***] The prince sent me with a supply train to the Prince of Coburg.

[†††] A vizier with cavalry on Anatolian stallions.

Go!! I lie on *car.*[*] Boom, boom, boom—*tunurile!* Ah, shcary!! . . . I lie on ground . . . My God, my God! German fall!—Suvorov *venit*!!![†] Boom, boom, boom!!! Pzhee-zhee-zhee-zhee, pzhee-zhee-zhee-zhee!!!—*Fugit dracu turcii!*[‡]

The ardent imagination of the *Greek man,* dissatisfied with this mixture of Greek, Moldavian, and Russian, supplemented the words with all manner of gestures. To represent the vizier's cavalry and the Hungarian hussar regiment, the index and middle fingers of his right hand saddled the index finger of the left.

At the word *go!* Micolae's right hand moved slowly parallel to the ground, and his head rose up proudly, like a rider's. At the words "I lie on ground," he stretched himself on the floor and lay motionless and silent for several moments. At the words "Suvorov *venit,*" the Greek man's whole body shook with the joy of escaping death.

An Italian impresario would pay a great deal for the right to show off Captain Micolae in public.

Having laughed at length, I interrupted his story about the capture of Khotin, the arrival of the Turks at Iași, and the battle of the Hetairists at Skulyany.

"Where does one go out for fun around here?"

"Go out? . . . No shtreet. *Cuconițe mult,* Moldavian, Greek, *Irmen*!"

"Are the *cuconițe* pretty?"

"Pretty? Go out . . . like that . . . heh! Captain Micolae know! . . . My *tata si mama* live in *buric* of Tshargrad.[§] Ee! The girlsh there are pretty! Oh my God! Sho pretty!"

"Farewell then, I'm going out."

"Bun, bun, boierule!"[¶]

---

[*] I lay in the *car.*

[†] Suvorov comes.

[‡] The devil Turks ran away.

[§] *Buric* is Moldavian for "navel"; this expression means "in the very center of Tsargrad."

[¶] Good, good, sir.

317

> Youth, seek your happiness; find it today!
> Tangle yourself in love's chains right away!
> Time, like a lightning bolt, flies quickly by;
> Love will burn up and your youthfulness die.
> —(Epigram)

With this thought I got into the drozhki and started off for Copou. Two rows of carriages were blocking the street, and since I did not want to plod along in the ranks, I passed them by!

Whoever knows Moscow festivities can well imagine that in Iași, every day without exception—excuse me: apart from stormy days—these festivities are a kind of obligation for almost all classes of inhabitants. This is a kind of *exercise* to avoid sedentariness and ennui, a kind of *exhibition* for the industry of the heart, a kind of *far niente* for *doing nothing*; a kind of habit based, like most Moldavian laws and ordinances, on the words *după obiceiul.*[*]

Two rows of carriages stretch from the burned hospodar's palace up and down *Ulița Mare*, across the whole field of *Copou*.

> By people nature is adorned;
> To purest love is life disposed;
> But what is life when we have scorned
> All feeling, to remain composed!

And so I rode, carefully examining everything that filled these moving greenhouses.

[*] According to custom.

Day 45

Cimmeriae tenebrae.

318

In his ardent, inexperienced years, a young man proudly imagines that he was created to unravel the mystery of the universe. "Much time has passed since the beginning of the world," he thinks; "perhaps even more remains before its end . . . There have been great people who have united in themselves the minds and feelings of whole peoples and ages; . . . they have figured out *something* . . . So there must someday be born a genius whose vision is telescopic, whose hearing is like the focus of an ellipse, whose memory is as great as the *book of the universe*, whose mind is as clear and sound as an algebraic formula, and whose reason is as correct as a conclusion . . . Who knows? . . . Perhaps . . . I myself . . ."

Arguing in this way, the young man suddenly meets a little creature, aged . . . but years mean nothing . . . a tender, sensitive creature, full of life and beauty. The high purpose of existence is forgotten! From that moment the youth is trying to unravel no longer the mystery of creation, but rather the heart of this wonderful meeting. With every beat of the pulse, with every word, with every glance, step, and sigh, *she* increases in the youth's eyes and thoughts to infinity and finally transforms into the *universe*, and the whole universe, gradually diminishing, assumes *her* appearance. What a revolution!

319

Lavinia, I will stay with thee!
  But now your face
  Conceals the trace

Of sadness and despondency!
    My love, don't cry!
    For how could I
Leave Italy and heaven here?
    Greek-like, I'm true,
    Always with you!
Don't kill yourself with grief and fear!

Ainsi parlait Énée, les larmes aux yeux:
cependant sa flotte voguait à pleines voiles . . .
—Énéide.

320

I cannot hide from you, my female readers, that the human heart bears a perfect resemblance to the globe. Like the earth, it has poles, and therefore by projecting it on a plane using *Mercator's* method, we shall see that it has *zones* of heat and cold and that *extremes of the heart*, like extremes of the earth, are good for nothing. What do you conclude from this? That it is only pleasant to live in someone's heart when you occupy a temperate zone within it, where neither embraces nor curses will suffocate you.

I think this is true, isn't it?

(Everyone is silent.)

It would be foolish to think, in the present age, that *silence gives consent*.

321

People may ask me what I saw in Copou.

I don't recall what caught my sight:
As on a wheel, spinning by,
I glanced ahead and left and right,
But nowhere could I fix my eye!
Just as in Capricorn are found
So many stars that pierce the gloom;
Here handsome women did abound,
As well as many a bride in bloom.

It was tedious for me to ride alone, without a *connoisseur of Iași beauties*. Fortunately, I came across a comrade.

"Show me everyone; tell me everything!"

"All right," he replied, but his mind was already wandering among the rows of carriages. For a long time we rode back and forth, when suddenly my comrade cried:

> Oh, there is youthful Helen, look!
> A rival of the Syrian rose!

I

> The one whom Paris—I suppose—
> From warlike Menelaus took?

HE

> Oh no, a will-o'-the-wisp is she,
> A skittish steed of Araby! . . .
> In all things wondrous, unsurpassed,
> Soft as a sigh,* and chamois-fast . . .
> The vexing sound of "not for me!"

322

> Comme un vers, qui devient chrysalide,
> aurélie, nymphe, et enfin papillon.
> —Emmanuel Swedenborg

Just so, but . . . Time goes by neither more quietly, nor more quickly. Feelings that had flared up with the joy of finding peace and bliss, feelings that were animated by the newness of Iași life soon returned to their ordinary state. Again they reflected now a temporary satisfaction, now a restless sorrow. They still lacked something: deceived by desires, they saw only tedium in their fulfillment. Once, burdened with thoughts, I descended from the terrace of Mihalache Sturdza's suburban garden, walked around the

* My comrade said "as a sigh of love," but his love did not fit in the verse.

pond, and crossed a light bridge to an island, where acacias concealed a gloomy arbor . . .

323

Amore (solo sedente a pie dell'albero.)
. . . Che bella avventura! che vergogna! che ridicolo! . . .
—*Le Grazie*, commedia del signor di Saint-Foix

324

Δός μοι χαρτί, κονδύλι καὶ μελάνι!
—Γραμματική

(NUBIA)

Imagine, my friends, that after sitting at home for a while, you suddenly think, "I'll go out for some exercise," and have your horse saddled.

"Where are you going?" people ask you.

"Just out!" you answer.

During such a ride you are a *Wanderer*; your impressions are light and inconstant.

325

(MOSCOW)

"My horse is tired, my journey ends!"
"Prrrr/uuuu!!! cried the Wanderer, dismounting.
"Quite long enough, my reader-friends,
Have I amused you with recounting."

1 **Part 2** Indeed included in part 2, chapter 118, but with four new lines substituted for the last three.

1 ***To you*** According to the editor of the Soviet edition, Yuri Akutin, this refers to Yekaterina Isupova, a married woman with whom Veltman was involved, but the vagueness allows for several interpretations (see also chapter 123).

Day 1

6 ***Dübek*** Turkish tobacco variety grown across the Black Sea region.

6 **Pyrrho** Pyrrho of Elis (ca. 365–ca. 275 B.C.E.), Greek philosopher and founder of the skeptical school.

6 **This only proves . . .** This last sentence was not in the 1977 edition.

7 **Podolia** Region of western Ukraine.

7 **Tulchin** Tulchyn, Vinnytsia Region, Ukraine, where Veltman served as an ensign and began a topographical survey of Bessarabia.

7 ***Audaces fortuna juvat!*** "Fortune favors the bold" (Latin).

7 **Instead of a Preface** Just "Preface" in the first edition.

7 **Nubia** Region along the Nile (now southern Egypt and northern Sudan).

7 ***Great Events . . .*** Adrien Richer, *Essai sur les grands événemens par les petites causes, tiré de l'histoire* (Geneva: Hardy, 1758), which tells the story about how salt was discovered by a Tatar khan who dropped a piece of meat on the ground.

8 ***Nec plus ultra*** "No more beyond" (Latin). Before the next chapter the first edition has the title "Continuation of the Journey."

8 **Mogilyov** Mohyliv-Podilskyi, Vinnytsia Region, Ukraine.

8 **City, customs, and quarantine** At Mogilyov, a ferry crossed the Dniester into Bessarabia. Though both sides of the river were Russian at the time, travelers still had to pass through a customs house and a sanitary cordon set up in response to plague that had spread from the Ottoman Empire in 1812.

8 **110 versts** About seventy miles. A verst (Russian *versta*) is a traditional Russian measurement equal to 3,500 English feet (about 0.66 miles or 1.1 km).

8 **Tacitus** Publius Cornelius Tacitus (ca. 55–ca. 120 C.E.), Roman historian. Possibly a misquotation from his *Annals*, 2.39: "Truth acquires strength by publicity and delay, falsehood by haste and incertitudes." Tacitus, *"Histories: Books 4–5," "Annals: Books 1–3,"* trans. Clifford H. Moore and John Jackson, Loeb Classical Library 249 (Harvard University Press, 1931), 445.

8 ***Ataki*** Now Otaci, Ocnița District, Moldova.

9 **Fifty versts** About 33 miles (53 km).

9 **Mereshovka, Oknitsa, Brichany** Mereşeuca, Ocniţa, and Briceni in Moldova.

9 **Khotin** Khotyn, Chernivtsi Region, Ukraine.

9 **Bessarabia** Region between the Dniester and Prut Rivers, formerly part of the principality of Moldavia, ceded by the Ottomans to the Russians in the Treaty of Bucharest (1812), and now mostly in the Republic of Moldova and partly in Ukraine.

9 **Sophia** Zofia Potocka, née Klavoni (1760–1822), Greek courtesan and later Polish noblewoman who was present at the siege of Khotin in 1788.

10 **Rosalinds . . .** Names with various literary associations: Rosalind, the heroine of Shakespeare's *As You Like It* (1599)

10 **Idalide** The Inca princess in Ferdinando Moretti's libretto *Idalide, o sia La vergine del sole* (1783).

10 **Ida** The heroine of various German plays and romances.

10 **Salome** Princess in the New Testament who demanded the head of John the Baptist on a platter.

10 **Nedoboutsy, Sharoutsy** Nedoboivtsi and Shyrivtsi in Ukraine.

10 ***Ținut*** District (Romanian).

10 ***Joc*** Moldavian dance.

10 **Orkhey** Orhei District, Moldova.

10 **Lethe** In Greek mythology, the river of forgetfulness in the underworld.

11 **Arina Makaryevna** The name and description suggest a devout peasant woman.

11 **Parian Marble** Marble stele discovered on the island of Paros in the seventeenth century that includes an inscription referring to the Greek poet Sappho (fl. 600 B.C.E.).

11 **Oh, she is blushing and appealing** These eight lines were first published under the title "Waiting" in the journal *Son of the Fatherland* in 1828 and in *The Northern Star* in 1829.

Day 2

12 **Don Juan, leaving on his journey . . .** See Byron's *Don Juan*, canto 2.

12 **Truth lies at the bottom of a well** A version of this proverb was first stated by Democritus (born ca. 460 B.C.E.): "We know nothing certainly, for truth lies in the deep." *Oxford Dictionary of Proverbs*, 6th ed. (2015), s.v. "Truth lies at the bottom of a well."

12 ***Long box*** From a Russian idiom meaning to postpone a matter indefinitely. The phrase is said to derive from a literal petition box used in the palace of Tsar Alexis, where appeals languished untouched.

Day 3

13 ***The Travels of Anacharsis*** *Voyage du jeune Anacharsis en Grèce* (1788): A fictional account of a Scythian philosopher's travels in Greece in the fourth century B.C.E.; the work contains numerous maps.

13 **Aristotle . . .** Aristotle (384–322 B.C.E.), Greek philosopher, mentioned here for his work on rhetoric; Dionysius of Halicarnassus (ca. 60–ca. 7 B.C.E.), Greek historian and rhetorician; Quintilian (ca. 35–ca. 100 C.E.), Roman rhetorician; Cicero (106–43 B.C.E.), Roman statesman and rhetorician.

14 **Kishinev** Chișinău, now capital of Moldova, then capital of Bessarabia.

14 **Nagoryany, Molodovo, Korman, Vasilevka** Nahoryany, Molodovo (abandoned), Korman, Vasylivka (the original has Vysïlevo), villages in Chernivtsi Region, Ukraine.

14 **Verezhany** Verejeni, a village in Telenești District, Moldova.

15 **Soroki** Soroca, Soroca District, Moldova, once the medieval Genoese colony of Olchionia.

15 **Tsekinovka** Tsekynivka, Vinnytsia Region, Ukraine.

15 **Kamenka** Camenca, Camenca District, Moldova.

15 **Count Wittgenstein** Peter Wittgenstein (1769–1843), Russian field marshal in the war against Napoleon; he was buried in Camenca.

15 **Lacépède** Bernard Germain de Lacépède (1756–1825): French naturalist, musician, and politician. This is a quotation from his work *The Poetics of Music*, in which he writes of a respected old man in a family, "He is a consoling God left in the midst of his children to be a living

image of the God they worship." *La poëtique de la musique* (Paris: Imprimerie de Monsieur, 1785), 269.

15 **Chorna to Sakharna** Ciorna and Saharna, Rezina District, Moldova.

15 **Moldavia** Referring to the broad historical region, which, at the time *The Wanderer* was published, was divided between Bessarabia, from 1812 part of the Russian Empire (present-day Moldova), and the Principality of Moldavia, an Ottoman vassal and, from 1829, a Russian protectorate (now part of Romania).

15 **Tartarus** In Greek mythology, region of the underworld or the entire underworld (Hades).

15 **Milton and Dante** Authors of works describing hell, *Paradise Lost* (1667) and the *Divine Comedy* (1320).

15 **Orpheus** Mythological Greek poet who attempted to retrieve his wife Eurydice from the underworld.

16 **A well-fed man . . .** Russian proverb.

16 **M. Chénier** Marie-Joseph Chénier (1764–1811), French playwright, whose play *Fénelon, ou Les religieuses de Cambrai* (1793) contains the line "Croyez que tout mortel a besoin d'indulgence."

16 **Look askance at Turkey** Veltman fought in the Russo-Turkish War of 1828–1829, which resulted in the independence of Greece and the Russian occupation of the Danubian principalities of Moldavia and Wallachia.

17 **Montecuccoli** Raimondo Montecuccoli (1609–1680), Italian general in the Habsburg army.

17 **Alexander the Great** Alexander III of Macedon (356–323 B.C.E.), son of Philip II (382–336) and Olympias (ca. 375–316). A semifictional account of his life called the Alexander Romance circulated in various versions throughout Europe and the Middle East in the Middle Ages.

17 **Darab** Legendary Persian king identified with Darius II of Persia (died in 404 B.C.E.).

17 **Abul-Faraj** Abu l-Faraj al-Isfahani (897–967), Arab historian.

17 **Sa'id ibn Batriq** Arabic name of Eutychius (877–940), historian and patriarch of Alexandria.

17 **Nectanet, Nestabanus** Legendary figure identified with Nectanebo II (ca. 380–ca. 341 B.C.E.), king of Egypt.

17 **Justin** M. Iunianus Iustinus (fl. ca. 390 C.E.), Roman historian. In book 11 of his *History*, he relates Olympias's confession that she conceived Alexander "by a serpent of extraordinary size."

Day 4

19 **Horace** Quintus Horatius Flaccus (65–8 B.C.E.), Roman poet. The reference is to Horace's *Letters*, 1.18: "Avoid a questioner, for he is also a tattler." Horace, *Satires. Epistles. The Art of Poetry,* trans. H. Rushton Fairclough, Loeb Classical Library 194 (Harvard University Press, 1926), 375.

19 ***Metamechanics*** Apparently an invention of the author, who in the short story "Erotida" says metamechanics is concerned with "the laws of spiritual movements in nature."

20 **Chaldeans** Ancient Semitic people, known for their astrology, who ruled Babylonia in the seventh and sixth centuries B.C.E. Here and below Veltman draws on Berosus's *Babylonian History* (third century B.C.E.), which recounts a great flood like the one in Genesis.

20 **Cronus** Father of Zeus in Greek mythology, who in Berosus stands in for the Babylonian god Ea (or the Sumerian god Enki).

20 **Ocean Sea** Archaic usage based on the ancient Greco-Roman conception of the ocean as a great outer sea (or originally a river).

20 **Elaim** Elohim, one of the Hebrew names for God.

20 **Karkura** Berossus's "Corcyraean Mountains," perhaps located in the region of Gordyene, southwest of Lake Van (modern southeast Turkey, historical Armenia).

20 **Xisuthrus** Ziusudra, hero of the Mesopotamian flood epic and an analogue of Noah.

20 **Sisparis** Ancient Mesopotamian city on the Euphrates, site of a library and the temple of the sun god Shamash.

20 **Stadia** Plural of *stadium*, ancient Greek measure of length, about 158 meters or 173 yards.

20 **Chaldean traditions** Veltman's probable source for this narrative is Volney's *New Research on Ancient History*, which prints the Berossus flood fragment next to the Genesis text. C.-F. Volney, *Recherches nouvelles sur l'histoire ancienne* (Paris: Courcier, 1814), 1:126–129.

20 **Gorodishche Monastery** Monastery of the Dormition of the Mother of God in Ţipova, Moldova.

21 **"The neglect of religion . . ."** *Émile, or On Education*, book 4: "The neglect of all religion leads to the neglect of the duties of man."

21 **Tatars** Here the monk means the Crimean Tatars, who launched frequent incursions into Moldavia from the fifteenth to eighteenth centuries.

21 **Stephen the Great** Stephen III of Moldavia (reigned 1457–1504).

21 ***Muscali*** The Romanian word normally refers to "Muscovites," but in Moldavian regional usage it also means "soldiers."

21 **Cannons** In Romanian, *pușcă* means "rifle," whereas in Russian the cognate *pushka* means "cannon."

21 **Last Turkish war** Russo-Turkish War of 1828–1829.

21 **Eiren** Airyanem Vaejah, or Eran-wez, the mythical homeland of the Aryans (early Iranians).

21 **Scudéry** Madeleine de Scudéry (1607–1701), French novelist. "La vie est si courte, que ce n'est pas la peine de s'impatienter." Quoted in *Dictionnaire de morale, de science et de littérature . . .* (Paris: Capelle et Renand, 1810), 295.

22 **Five versts** About 3.3 miles.

22 **Lalovo . . .** Villages in Rezina and Orhei districts.

22 **Upper, Middle, and Lower Jora** Jora de Sus, Jora de Mijloc, and Jora de Jos.

22 **Orkhey** Orhei, city in central Moldova.

22 **Reut** The river Râut.

22 **Forty versts** About twenty-seven miles.

22 **Twentieth ode of Horace** The closest line is actually in book 1, ode 24: "Endurance can make lighter what no one is allowed to put right." Horace, *Odes and Epodes*, trans. Niall Rudd, Loeb Classical Library 33 (Harvard University Press, 2004), 71.

22 ***Byk*** Bâc or Bîc, river in Moldova, which sounds like the Russian *byk*, "bull."

22 **The first time . . .** In the first edition, this paragraph is moved to the next chapter.

Day 5

24 **Agamemnon** Upon his return from Troy, Agamemnon was murdered by his wife Clytemnestra and her lover Aegisthus.

24 **1,184 years before Christ** Date of the fall of Troy, according to the Greek scholar Eratosthenes.

24 **Only seven years** In fact, Russian law let an abandoned spouse petition for divorce after five consecutive years without any word of the spouse's whereabouts. See *Svod zakonov Rossiiskoi imperii*, vol. 9, *Svod zakonov grazhdanskikh i mezhevykh* (Saint Petersburg: Printing House of the Second Section of His Imperial Majesty's Chancellery, 1832), 8.

26 **Titus** Titus Vespasianus Augustus (39–81 C.E.), Roman emperor.

26 **Amici, diem perdidi!** "Friends, I have lost a day!" Quoted by Suetonius in his *Life of Titus*, 8.1.13. Suetonius, *Lives of the Caesars*, trans. J. C. Rolfe, Loeb Classical Library 38 (Harvard University Press, 1914), 2:317.

28 **Lado, Did, Lel** Supposed gods of love and marriage in ancient Slavic mythology, possibly invented by early modern scholars who misinterpreted folksong refrains. Lado is mentioned again with the spelling *Lada* in chapter 132.

Days 6 and 7

29 **Lucullus** Lucius Licinius Lucullus (117–ca. 57 B.C.E.), Roman consul and commander.

29 **Tigranes** Tigranes II (140–ca. 55 B.C.E.), king of Armenia. According to Plutarch (*Lucullus* 27:7), the Roman general said, "Verily, I will make this day, too, a lucky one for the Romans." Plutarch, *Lives*, vol. 2, *Themistocles and Camillus. Aristides and Cato Major. Cimon and Lucullus*, trans. Bernadotte Perrin, Loeb Classical Library 47 (Harvard University Press, 1914), 561.

29 ***Nu ştiu*** "I don't know" (Romanian).

29 ***Surugiu*** Driver (Romanian), from Turkish *sürücü*.

29 ***La care fartir*** "To which *fartir*?" The driver mishears the narrator's *traktir* "tavern" (Russian) as *fartir* "quarters" (Romanian).

29 **Lakar's** The narrator interprets *la care* "to which" (Romanian) as the name of an innkeeper.

29 **I caught the whiff of Jews** Here *zhidy*, the plural of *zhid*, now an ethnic slur that in the 1830s was still the everyday Russian word for "Jew," though it was beginning to acquire pejorative overtones. In *The Wanderer* Veltman uses *zhid* roughly four times as often as the then-bookish *evrei*, which I translate as "Hebrew." *Evrei* fully displaced *zhid* in polite usage by the late nineteenth century. See John D. Klier, "'Zhid': Biography of a Russian Epithet," *Slavonic and East European Review* 60, no. 1 (1982): 1–15.

29 **Factor** A commercial agent who met travelers, arranged lodging, and brokered goods for a fee.

30 ***Abub*** An ancient Jewish wind instrument. Veltman's source was probably Frédéric de Castillon, "Abub," in *Supplément à l'encyclopédie, ou dictionnaire raisonné des sciences, des arts et des métiers* (Amsterdam: M. M. Rey, 1776), 1:75, https://artflsrv03.uchicago.edu/philologic4/supplement/navigate/1/190/.

31 **Kircher** Athanasius Kircher (1602–1780), German Jesuit scholar, author of the *Musurgia Universalis* (Universal singing, 1650).

31 **Calmet** Augustin Calmet (1672–1757), French Benedictine monk and biblical exegete.

31 ***Ambubaia*** The Latin word actually referred to Syrian courtesans in Rome who sang and played the abub.

31 ***Genii*** Latin plural of genius—in classical Roman belief the tutelary spirit assigned to every person or place.

31 ***Meşti*** Red slippers made from morocco leather.

31 ***Cuşme*** Caps made from Astrakhan fleece.

31 ***Caşcaval*** A yellow cheese (Romanian words of Turkish and Slavic origin).

31 ***Plăcinte*** Pastries filled with cheese, fruit, or vegetables, eaten in Romania, Moldova, and Ukraine.

31 **Calash** Light carriage with a folding top.

31 ***Mazil*** Impoverished nobleman (Romanian).

31 **Boyar** Nobleman (*boier* in Romanian). In Russia *boyar* was a medieval order of nobility that had became obsolete by the eighteenth century, but the title persisted in Wallachia and Moldavia into the twentieth.

31 **Tirynthian** Hercules, from Tiryns, perhaps referring to the moment when he laughs while fighting Achelous in Ovid's *Metamorphoses* (book 9, line 66).

32 **Gaudy dolman** In the Russian a "hussar's dolman." The dolman was a jacket of Turkish origin worn by a hussar (member of a light cavalry unit).

32 ***Căciulă*** Fur cap (Romanian).

32 **Arnaut** A native of Albania (from Turkish *arnavut*).

32 **Metropolitan** In the Orthodox Church, a rank above archbishop and below patriarch. The first leader of the Russian Church in Bessarabia was Metropolitan Gabriel (1746–1821), who was succeeded by Archbishop Demetrius (1772–1844).

32 **Oh, how devout . . .** This poem was published in *Son of the Fatherland* in 1828 and in *The Northern Star* in 1829.

33 ***Cucoane, cuconiţe*** Old and young women, respectively.

33 **Why do the nations rage?** Psalm 2:1. Veltman quotes the verse in Church Slavonic, the liturgical language of the Russian Orthodox Church, creating a play on words, since the Slavonic verb looks like a Russian one that means not "to rage" but "to lounge about."

Day 8

34 **Strabo** (ca. 63 B.C.E.–23 C.E.) Greek geographer.

34 **Livy** Titus Livius (59 B.C.E.–17 C.E.), Roman historian.

35 **Quintus Curtius** Quintus Curtius Rufus (first century C.E.), Roman historian.

35 **Ammianus Marcellinus** (ca. 330–400 C.E.) Roman historian.

35 **Attila** Ruler of the Huns, who died in 453 C.E., so the aforementioned historians could not have written about him.

35 **Ring finger** In Russian, "nameless finger."

35 **Decebalus** Last king (reigning ca. 87–106 C.E.) of Dacia, corresponding to present-day Romania and Moldova.

35 **Moesia** Region in present-day Serbia and Bulgaria.

35 **Peucinia** Region in the Danube delta. In Russian Veltman plays on the similarity between the words *mizinets*, "little finger," and *Miziya*, Moesia.

35 **Plutarch** Mestrius Plutarchus (ca. 45–ca. 120 C.E.), Greek philosopher and biographer, who wrote in his *Life of Pericles*, 13.12: "To such degree, it seems, is truth hedged about with difficulty and hard to capture by research." Plutarch, *Lives*, volume 4, *Alcibiades and Coriolanus. Lysander and Sulla*, trans. Bernadotte Perrin, Loeb Classical Library 65 (Harvard University Press, 1916), 47.

35 **Saint-Réal** César Vichard, abbé de Saint-Réal (1643–1692), French historian and novelist, who argued in *De l'usage de l'histoire* (On the use of history) that a good historian should seek to understand human passions rather than simply record facts; this is probably not a direct quotation.

35 **Thermopylae . . . Marathon** The famous battles of Marathon (490 B.C.E.), where the Greeks defeated the Persians, and of Thermopylae (480 B.C.E.), where the returning Persians defeated three hundred Spartans and a few thousand other Greeks.

36 **Moldavian boyar** The Soviet editor Akutin asserts that this character was based on Yegor Varfolomey (1764–1842), whom Veltman met in Kishinev and described in his *Memoirs of Bessarabia*.

36 ***Iorghi, ciubuce!*** "Georgi, pipes!" (Romanian).

36 ***Poftim, şezi!*** "Please sit!" (Romanian).

36 ***Moldoveneşte . . .*** "'Does he not know Moldavian?' 'No, he doesn't'" (Romanian).

37 ***Bună seara!*** "Good evening!" (Romanian).

37 ***Raluca, şezi!*** "Raluca, sit!" (Romanian).

38 **He that hath a mouth . . .** Compare "He that hath ears to hear, let him hear" (Matthew 11:15 and elsewhere in the Gospels).
38 **Comte de Lignolle** An admirer of charades in Louvet de Couvray's novel *Les amours du chevalier de Faublas* (1787–1790).
39 **The game's . . .** A French proverb, "Le jeu ne vaut pas la chandelle," meaning that something is not worth the cost or effort required.

Day 9

40 **Alcoran** Archaic European form of *Qur'an*, the sacred scripture of Islam.
40 **Houri** One of the maidens who will accompany the faithful in the Muslim paradise.
40 **Entertaining tale** The first and second editions have this, but the Soviet edition has "ninth tale."
40 **Al-Buraq** Muhammad's legendary horse.
40 ***Azar*** Probably the *isra'*, Muhammad's nighttime journey from Mecca to Jerusalem, mentioned in the Qur'an, 17:1, and in other writings connected with the *mi'raj*, Muhammad's journey to heaven.
40 **Rivers of milk . . .** Described in the Qur'an, 47:15.
41 **Raven** In the usual tellings, Prometheus's liver is eaten every day by an eagle.
41 **Abarim** Mountain range in Jordan.
41 **Zamzam** A holy well in Mecca.

Day 10

42 ***Nécessaire*** Small case containing personal articles.
42 ***Savon à la mousseline*** Kind of soap scented with iris and other ingredients.
42 **barber's razors** The original has the English word *barber*.
42 ***cuir de Pradier*** Strop made by the French razor maker Pradier.
42 ***pâte d'amande, pâte minérale*** Almond and mineral pastes used for scrubbing.
44 **Raphael** Either the archangel or the Italian Renaissance painter.
45 **Azael** An angel mentioned in kabbalistic writings.
45 **What happened next . . .** This poem is an excerpt of a draft of Veltman's poem "The Fugitive" (1831). According to Akutin, M—— is Maria Mavrokordatou, a Kishinev acquaintance of Veltman's.

Day 11

46 **Budzhak** From Turkish Bucak, coastal region between the Danube and the Dniester, mostly in present-day Ukraine.

46 **Yalpukh . . .** Yalpuh, Kahul, and Sasyk in Ukrainian, lakes north of the Danube delta.

46 **Prut** River forming the border between modern Romania and Moldova.

47 **Dibuglu** Edib-oglu, a former Ottoman official, who had three daughters, Elena, Maria, and Ralu (see chapter 56).

47 **Krupensky** Matvey Krupensky (1775–1855), vice-governor of Bessarabia from 1816 to 1823.

47 **Field of Mars** A military parade ground.

47 **Malina** A garden area outside of Kishinev.

47 **Getic wilderness** Region of the lower Danube inhabited in ancient times by the Getae, a Thracian tribe.

47 **Calypsița** Romanian diminutive of Calypso, the name of the nymph in the *Odyssey* who detains Odysseus for seven years. In François Fénelon's didactic novel *Les aventures de Télémaque* (1699), she also tries to hold back Telemachus, Odysseus's son.

48 **Mentor** Gray-haired guardian (Athena in disguise) who guides Telemachus, Odysseus's son, in the *Odyssey*. In Fénelon's novel, Mentor pushes the wavering youth off a cliff into the sea to help him escape from Calypso.

48 **Bulbok** Bulboaca, Anenii Noi District, Moldova.

48 **Tighina** Medieval Romanian name for the town and fortress later called Bender (Turkish) and Bendery (Russian).

48 **Parcani** Village in Transnistria.

48 **Tiraspol** City in Transnistria.

48 **Kherson** City in southern Ukraine, quite distant from the preceding places.

48 **Three versts** Almost two miles.

48 **Varnița** Village in Anenii Noi District, Moldova.

48 **The son . . .** Charles XII (1682–1718), king of Sweden, known for his abstinence and strict military habits, hence the opprobrious epithet "corporal." In the Great Northern War he won a series of victories against Denmark, Poland-Saxony, and Russia, before being defeated by Peter the Great at the Battle of Poltava in 1709. He fled and established a provisional court in Bender, then still part of the Ottoman Empire. After the Turks made peace with the Russians, they besieged Charles's residence to force him out.

48 ***Drabant*** Bodyguard of the kings of Sweden; "the foremost drabant in the world" refers to the king as commander of these guards.

48 ***Exerzierhaus*** Drill hall (German).

48 **here, I say . . .** According to Voltaire's biography (probably Veltman's source), during the storming of his residence, Charles accidentally grabbed a barrel of brandy to put out the fire and promoted a guard named Rosen for proposing a retreat to the more defensible chancellery building, but he ultimately suffered defeat by tripping over his own spurs. Voltaire, "Histoire de Charles XII" *Œuvres complètes de Voltaire* (Paris: Garnier frères, 1878), 16:301–2.

48 ***Pro aris et focis*** "For altars and hearths" (Latin), i.e., for hearth and home.

49 **Here noisy joy subsides . . .** Veltman's loose prose translation of Byron's *Lara*, canto 1, stanza 29. In the original:

> Where joy subsides, and sorrow sighs to sleep,
> And man o'er-laboured with his being's strife,
> Shrinks to that sweet forgetfulness of life:
> There lie love's feverish hope, and cunning's guile,
> Hate's working brain, and lull'd ambition's wile,
> O'er each vain eye oblivion's pinions wave,
> And quench'd existence crouches in a grave.
>
> Lord Byron, *The Complete Poetical Works*, ed. Jerome J. McGann (Oxford University Press, 1981), 3:235.

Day 12

50 **Sterlet** A small species of sturgeon.

51 **Oread** In Greek mythology, a mountain nymph.

51 **Melissa** Nymph who is said to have invented the art of beekeeping and fed honey to the infant Zeus.

51 ***Cobză*** Moldavian lute.

51 ***Mititică*** Moldavian dance, literally "tiny."

51 ***Sârbeşti, bulgăreşti, and ciobăneşti*** Serbian, Bulgarian, and shepherds' dances, respectively (Romanian).

51 ***Mult prea mulţumesc*** "Thank you very much" (Romanian).

52 **Tyras** Ancient Milesian colony at the mouth of the Dniester.

52 ***Map*** The map in Veltman's own *Outline of the Ancient History of Bessarabia* (see chapter 149).

52 **Palanka** Palanca, Stefan Vodă District, Moldova.

52 **Immodest migrant** The Venus de Milo statue.

52 **Anacreon** Anacreon (sixth century B.C.E.), Greek lyric poet.

53 **Belgorod . . . Akkerman** Bilhorod-Dnistrovskyi, Odesa Region, Ukraine.

53 **Ovidiopol** Town in Odesa Region, Ukraine.

53 **Ovidius Naso** Publius Ovidius Naso (43 B.C.E.–17 C.E.), Ovid in English, Roman poet who was exiled by Augustus to Tomi on the Black Sea. The location of Tomi was long disputed; current consensus places it at the site of present-day Constanța.

53 **Mankalya** Mangalia, Constanța County, Romania.

53 **Oberon** Epic poem written by Christoph Martin Wieland in 1780, which contains the description of a shipwreck. "*Sie hören nichts*": "They hear nothing." The exact phrase is "sie hören's nicht" (they do not hear it), in *Oberon*, canto 7, stanza 17.

53 **Captain Cook** Captain James Cook (1728–1779), whose journals were first published in 1773.

54 **A stormy poet** Veltman himself, in his fairy-tale poem *Ianko choban* (Yanko the shepherd), written in the early 1820s.

54 **Aquilo** Personification of the Roman north or northeast wind, equivalent to the Greek Boreas.

Day 13

55 **Aurora** Roman goddess of the dawn.

55 **Phoebus** "Radiant," epithet for Apollo, who in Greek mythology came to be equated with Helios the sun god.

55 **Phaeton** Light four-wheeled open carriage; the word derives from Helios's son Phaëthon, who perished while borrowing his father's chariot.

55 **More than seven thousand years** According to Byzantine chronology, the world was created in 5509 B.C.E.

55 **Justin** See note above for page 17.

55 **Arrian** Arrianus of Nicomedia (first–second centuries C.E.), Greek historian.

55 **Quintus Curtius** Q. C. Rufus (first century C.E.), Roman historian.

55 **Plutarch** Plutarchus (first–second centuries C.E.), Greek biographer.

55 **Ptolemy** Ptolemaeus I Soter (fourth–third centuries B.C.E.), ruler of Egypt and historian.

55 **Diodorus of Sicily** Diodorus Siculus (first century B.C.E.), Greek historian.

55 **Firdawsi ibn Farrukh** Abu'l-Qasem Ferdowsi (ca. 940–1020 C.E.), Persian poet.

55 **Muhammad ibn Mir-Khwandshah** Muhammad ibn Khwandshah, also known as Mir-Khwand (ca. 1433–1498), Persian historian.

55 **Hamd-Allah ibn Abi Bakr** Hamd-Allah Mustawfi (ca. 1281–1344), Persian historian.

55 **Yahya ibn 'Abd Allah** Probably Yahya ibn 'Abd al-Latif al-Qazwini (sixteenth century), Persian historian.

55 **Dakhelui** Amir Khusraw Dihlavi (1253–1325), Indo-Persian poet.

55 **'Abd al-Rahman ibn Ahmad** 'Abd al-Rahman Nur-al-Din Jami (1414–1492), Persian poet.

56 **Death of Alexander** Alexander the Great died in Babylon in 323 B.C.E.

56 ***Baharistan*** Book of stories and moral advice, composed in 1487 by the Persian poet Jami (see above).

56 **Eskander** This unrhymed poem, in amphibrachic meter (one stressed syllable between two unstressed syllables), was written in 1828 and published separately in the *Moscow Telegraph* (1831, no. 2). Veltman draws on the medieval tradition of the Alexander Romance, known in the Islamic world as the *Iskandar Nāma*.

56 **The legends are silent** Compare Veltman's comments on Alexander's origins in chapter 27.

56 **Lord of Olympus** Zeus.

56 **Erythraean** The Erythraean (Red) Sea, by which name the ancient Greeks referred to various parts of the Indian Ocean, including the Red Sea and the Persian Gulf.

57 **Ammon** Greek name of Amun, a supreme god of the Egyptians. After Alexander occupied Egypt he was hailed as the son of Zeus-Ammon.

57 **Monument** The town of Alexandria, founded by Alexander in 331 B.C.E.

57 **Ganges** In fact, Alexander never reached the Ganges, as his troops refused to cross the river Hyphasis (Beas) in the Punjab.

58 **Zenda** Veltman's invention, possibly based on the Persian word *zende*, "alive."

58 **Bel** Lord (Akkadian), title given to the Babylonian god Marduk.

59 **Zulmat** "Darkness" (Arabic). In the Persian Alexander Romance, Alexander goes into the Land of Darkness to seek the Water of Life.

59 **Parcae** The three goddesses of fate, the Roman equivalent of the Greek Moerae.

59 **Ab-Hayt** *Ab-i Hayat*, the Water of Life in Persian mythology.

60 **Tair and 'Asad** Arabic names for the brightest stars in the constellations of Aquila and Leo, respectively: al-Nasr al-Tair (the flying eagle, Altair) and Qalb al-'Asad (the heart of the lion, Regulus).

60 **Ka'ba** The holy sanctuary in Mecca, which may have existed before Islam.

60 **Serapis** Greco-Roman name of Osiris-Apis, the Egyptian bull god, whose cult spread throughout the Mediterranean in the Hellenistic period (after Alexander).

60 **Leda** In Greek mythology, Zeus visited Leda in the guise of a swan.

61 **Istakar** Istakhr, ancient Persian city, though Veltman is probably referring to nearby Persepolis, which Alexander looted and burned in 330 B.C.E.

61 **Pontus** The sea, here personified.

61 **Lectonia** According to the fifth-century *Orphic Argonautica*, Poseidon, in a quarrel with Zeus, struck the land of Lectonia or Lycaonia with his trident and scattered the fragments over the sea. Some nineteenth-century scholars took this as evidence of an actual flood.

61 **Phalanges** Plural of *phalanx*, the compact body of heavily armed infantry famously used by Alexander.

61 **Héloïse** Either Héloïse (1098–1164), French writer and lover of Abélard, or more likely the heroine of Rousseau's *Julie, or The New Héloïse* (1761), who dies from sickness after jumping into Lake Geneva to save her son.

62 **Babylon** The historical city in Mesopotamia, identified as the site of the Tower of Babel described in Genesis 11:1–9.

62 **Airy gardens** The Hanging Gardens of Babylon (Akutin has "airy traces," probably by mistake).

62 **Tavernier** Jean-Baptiste Tavernier (1605–1689), French traveler, who argues the contrary—that a structure called Agarcouf near Baghdad was not the ruined tower of Babel, despite popular belief. See *Les six voyages de Jean Bapt. Tavernier* (Henri Scheurleer, 1718), 1:236–237.

62 ***'Aqarquf or Karkuf*** In Iraq, site of the ruined Babylonian town of Dur-Kurigalzu.

62 **Teixeira** Pedro Teixeira (born ca. 1570), Portuguese explorer and author of *Relaciones* (1610) containing a description of his journey from India to Italy. He is mentioned in the entry on "Akerkuf" in the 1776 supplement to the *Encyclopédie*. (Akutin misidentifies this as the French explorer Charles Texier.)

62 **Al-Mansur** Abu Ja'far 'Abd Allah ibn Muhammad al-Mansur (ca. 713–775), second Abbasid caliph and founder of Baghdad.

62 **Mickiewicz** Adam Mickiewicz (1798–1855), Polish poet. One of his *Crimean Sonnets* (1826) is entitled "The Akkerman Steppes."

62 ***Gleich*** "At once" (German). Veltman spells it *glaig*.

62 **Johannisberger barrel** From Schloss Johannisberg, a winery near Wiesbaden.

62 **Kagul** Cahul, Cahul District, Moldova.

62 **Rumyantsev** Pyotr Rumyantsev-Zadunaisky (1725–1796), Russian general who defeated the Ottomans at the Battle of Kagul in 1770 during the Russo-Turkish War of 1768–1774.

62 **Izmail** Izmayil, Odesa Region, Ukraine.

62 **Suvorov** Aleksandr Suvorov (1729–1800), Russian general who defeated the Ottomans at the siege of Izmail (1790) during the Russo-Turkish War of 1787–1792.

62 **Psammetichus** Psamtik I (ruled 664–610 B.C.E.), king of Egypt, who, according to the Greek historian Herodotus, besieged the Syrian city of Azotus (now Ashdod, Israel) for twenty-nine years.

63 **Bessarabian Tartary** Budzhak was once inhabited by the Nogai Tatars.

63 **Vilkovo** Vylkove, Odesa Region, Ukraine.

63 **Kiliya** Kiliia, Odesa Region, Ukraine.

63 ***rahat lokum*** Turkish delight (Turkish).

63 ***dulceaţă*** Jam (Romanian).

63 **Guarinos** Hero of the medieval Spanish "Romance del conde Guarinos," a prisoner of the Moors who escapes after being allowed to participate in a tournament. The Russian historian and poet Nikolai Karamzin translated the romance in 1792.

63 **"Clip-clop . . ."** Quotation from Ivan Dmitriev's poem "Caricature" (1792).

63 **Cromwell . . .** Possibly alluding to a story in Geoffrey le Baker's chronicles (ca. 1356) about a message sent to the keepers of the castle where King Edward II was imprisoned: "Edwardum occidere nolite timere bonum est." Depending on where the punctuation is placed, it can mean either "Do not fear to kill Edward—it is good" or "Do not kill Edward—it is good to fear." Oliver Cromwell was involved in the execution of a different king, Charles I, in 1649.

63 **Prod** Veltman here plays on the name Prut, which means "twig" or "switch" in Russian.

64 **De Lévis** Pierre-Marc-Gaston de Lévis, second duke of Lévis, French politician and aphorist (1764–1830). The original is in his *Maximes, préceptes et réflexions* (1825): "L'ennui est une maladie dont le travail est le remède; le plaisir n'est qu'un palliatif" (Ennui is an illness for which work is the cure; pleasure is only a palliative).

64 **La Motte** Antoine Houdar de La Motte (1672–1731), French writer. This phrase is found in his *Fables nouvelles* (1719): "L'ennui naquit un jour de l'uniformité" (Ennui was born one day from uniformity).

64 **La Bruyère** Jean de La Bruyère (1645–1696), French moralist. This phrase is from his *Les caractères ou les mœurs de ce siècle* (1688): "L'ennui est entré dans le monde par la paresse" (Ennui entered the world through idleness).

64 **Cunegund's young knight** Candide, the protagonist of Voltaire's *Candide* (1759), whose love interest is Cunegund (Cunégonde in French).

64 ***Domovoy*** A house spirit in Slavic folklore.

64 ***Leshy*** A forest spirit in Slavic folklore, said to lead travelers astray.

65 **Charites** The Graces, goddesses of grace, beauty, and happiness.

65 ***Armăsar*** Stallion (Romanian).

Day 14

66 **Adeona** Roman goddess of arrivals.

66 **Even on horseback** Reference to a Russian proverb: "You can't go around your destined husband even on horseback," that is, "You can't escape your fate."

66 **Methuselah** Grandfather of Noah, who is said to have lived longer than any other human being (969 years). The sentence about him is omitted in Selivanovsky's second edition.

66 **Rephaim** A race of Canaanite giants described in the Old Testament (Genesis 14:5; Deuteronomy 3:11, 13).

67 **I'm rummaging through history . . . Good!** In Selivanovsky's second edition, these lines were omitted, and the chapter was shortened to the following:

> I had just lain down with my sultana on the divan, when suddenly my guest came in.
>
> "What are you doing?"
>
> "Oh, nothing."
>
> "What are you reading?"
>
> "Oh, nothing."
>
> Soon my guest left; I headed out too, almost right after him.

67 **Circassians** Ethnic group of the northwest Caucasus, whose native name is Adyghe.

67 **Khazars** Turkic ethnic group who ruled the Khazar Khaganate (ca. 650–969), which spanned parts of today's southern Russia, eastern Ukraine, and western Kazakhstan.

67 **White Ugrians** Medieval designation for a Christianized branch of the early Hungarians living under (or alongside) the Khazars; the color marked social status, not skin color.

67 **Maeotic Sea** Ancient name for the Sea of Azov, though usually described by classical writers as a lake or a marsh.

67 **Lezgins** People of the northeastern Caucasus.

67 **Avars** People of the northeastern Caucasus.

67 **Ancient Albania** Region of the eastern Caucasus, unrelated to the Balkan country of Albania, though the speaker seems to draw a connection.

67 **Khokli and khoklachki** Jocular or derogatory terms for Ukrainian men and women, originating from the word for the traditional Cossack topknot hairstyle.

67 **Six days you labor** Allusion to Exodus 20:9–10 ("Six days you shall labor and do all your work. But the seventh day is a Sabbath to the Lord your God; you shall not do any work," NRSV) and Genesis 3:19 ("By the sweat of your face / you shall eat bread," NRSV).

67 **Keramin** An obscure reference, perhaps to Abel-Keramim, or "plain of the vineyards," an ancient town in what is now Jordan (mentioned in Judges 11:33, NRSV). "Vineyards" suits the talk of drinking, while the phrase "judge and settle their affairs" (*sudit' i riadit'*) recalls the Book of Judges in which the place appears. Akutin's note connecting the name to the Carian town of Keramos seems less plausible.

67 **They're all plain** Stepanov's edition has "Fair maidens . . . yes, fair, but not truly beautiful, all wearing flowers—poor flowers!"

68 ***Good* Garden** The garden of the Potocki Palace, built in the 1780s, called Khoroshe ("good").

68 **How long ago . . . their sovereign rule forgot** These four lines are replaced in the second edition with prose:

> The Good Garden is now empty. Whosoever seeks solitude—it is there.
>
> A long time ago?

68 **In the garden . . .** The sentence is omitted in the second edition.

69 **Roller bird** The European roller (*Coracias garrulus*), a jay-like bird with blue and brown plumage.

69 **Alcamenes** Greek sculptor (ca. 440–400 B.C.E.).

69 ***Revue . . .*** "Revised, corrected, expanded, and illustrated" (French); compare the epigraph at the beginning of part 2.

70 **Saturn** The Roman equivalent of Cronus, often identified with Chronos (time), and depicted with wings.

70 **Raven** In the original Greek myth, Zeus punished Prometheus by sending an eagle every day to peck at his liver.

70 **Susanna** In chapter 13 the book of Daniel, two wicked judges accost the pious married woman Susanna while she is bathing.

70 **Lapushna, past Chuchuleny** Lăpuşna and Ciuciuleni, Hînceşti District, Moldova.

71 **Lozovo** Lozova, Străşeni District, Moldova.

71 ***Casă*** "House" (Romanian).

71 **Măriucă** Diminutive of Maria.

72 ***Mărioliţa*** Another diminutive of Maria.

72 ***mititică*** "Tiny" (Romanian).

72 ***Părinte*** "Father," "priest" (Romanian).

72 ***Muscal*** "Muscovite, Russian, soldier" (Romanian).

72 ***Lei*** "Lion dollars," Dutch coins used throughout southeastern Europe.

Day 15

73 ***Post . . . long-distance*** Post-horses were changed at stages and could be driven fast; long-distance horses had to be driven slowly so they would not wear out.

73 ***Va banque*** "Go bank" (French), a decision, in faro and other card games, to go all in against the banker.

73 **Fălciu** Small town in Vaslui County, Romania.

74 **Published in the *Northern Bee*** Omitted in the second edition. The reference is probably to "Iz pokhodnykh zapisok ofitsera (Okonchanie)," *Severnaia pchela*, April 27, 1829.

74 **Iaşi** Iasi, or Jassy, city in Romania (sometimes spelled Jassy in English).

74 **Cytherea's son** Eros, or Cupid, son of Aphrodite, called Cytherea from the island of Kithira, famous for its cult of that goddess. According to Akutin, this poem refers to Veltman's real plans to meet his lover, Yekaterina Isupova, in Crimea.

74 **Tauric shore** The ancient Greek name for Crimea was the Tauric peninsula (*chersonesos Taurikē*), after the tribe of Tauri who lived there; this name was reintroduced after Russian annexation of the Crimea in 1783.

74 **Chatyr-Dag** Mountain in Crimea.

75 **Cincinnatus** Lucius Quinctius Cincinnatus (born ca. 519 B.C.E.), Roman patrician. According to the Roman historian Livy, when Rome was under threat from the Aequi in 458 B.C.E., Cincinnatus was called from working in the fields and appointed dictator. Within fifteen days, he assembled an army and defeated the enemy, then returned to his plough.

76 **Fields** A pun in Russian (*pole*, "field," also means "margin").

76 **Thus concluding...** This paragraph is omitted in the second edition.

Part 2

77 **Lorsque *quelque*** "When *some* is in front of the substantive *thing*, these two words are often used as one . . . , for example: 'Have you read this book?' 'No, I have read *something* in it that seemed good to me.'" Charles-Constant Letellier, ed., *Grammaire françoise* [*sic*] *de Lhomond*, 12th ed. (Paris: Le Prieur, 1811), 128. This grammar was popular in Russia in the early nineteenth century; it is also mentioned in Dostoevsky's *Poor Folk* (1846).

78 ***Plimbare*** "Promenade" (Romanian).

Day 16

80 **Clothes severe** Rousseau had argued against the practice of swaddling in *Émile*.

80 **Mamunya** A diminutive of *mama* (Russian).

81 **. . . then give a shout!** Compare the poem at the beginning of the book.

81 **Quintus Curtius** Roman historian (see chapters 53 and 85) who attributed these words to Alexander: "Even our glory, although it rests on a solid foundation, is greater in name than in fact." Quintus Curtius, *History of Alexander,* trans. J. C. Rolfe, Loeb Classical Library 369 (Harvard University Press, 1946), 2:379.

81 **Pluto** Greco-Roman god of the underworld. Used here as a poetic rendering of *preispodniaia*, "nether regions, underworld."

82 **Fifth age** The ancient Greeks and Romans divided history into four or five ages. Veltman may be recalling Ovid, who listed four (golden, silver, bronze, and iron), which would imply that Veltman's fifth age is a new, modern age.

82 ***Ciubucci-paşa*** "Head pipe bearer!" (Romanian, from Turkish). The correct Romanian form would be *başa,* which Veltman, perhaps on

purpose, confuses with *pasha*, the Turkish term for a man of high honor or office.

82 **The morning is wiser than the evening** A well-known Russian proverb.

83 **Izuara** Ishvara, "lord" in Sanskrit, a title often given to the Hindu gods Vishnu and Shiva.

83 **Father Paolino . . .** Various scholars of Sanskrit and the Indo-European language family: Paulinus a S. Bartholomaeo (1748–1806) from Austria, Louis-Mathieu Langlès (1763–1824) from France, and William Jones (1746–1794) and Charles Wilkins (1749–1836), both from England.

83 **Let the weak . . .** A loose translation of *Childe Harold's Pilgrimage*, canto 1, stanza 30:

> Though sluggards deem it but a foolish chase,
> And marvel men should quit their easy chair,
> The toilsome way, and long, long league to trace,
> Oh! there is sweetness in the mountain air,
> And life, that bloated Ease can never hope to share.

Lord Byron, *The Complete Poetical Works*, ed. Jerome J. McGann (Oxford University Press, 1980), 2:22.

83 **Byron/Beyron/Biron** Veltman lists three ways in which Byron's name was transliterated into Russian.

84 **Mahmud** Mahmud II (1785–1839), Ottoman sultan.

Day 17

85 **Ezopka** Diminutive of Ezop, that is, Aesop, the possibly legendary Greek fabulist. Veltman may have chosen the name because Aesop was said to have been a slave or because he combined wisdom and simplicity in his fables.

85 **Penelope** Odysseus's wife. Perhaps an ironic reference to Penelope's steadfast fidelity.

85 **Waffles . . . *earl*** Veltman comically rhymes *vafli* (waffles) and *graf li?* (will a count?).

85 **Asphaltic Sea** The Dead Sea, known to the ancient Greeks and Romans as the Asphalt Lake.

85 **Kühlenz** Probably Kühnlenz, a German-Estonian gunmaker.

86 **Vertumnus** Roman god of change and the seasons.

Day 18

87 ***Golmin Šanggiyan Alin*** Manchu name for Paektu (Changbaishan) Mountain, now on the border between China and North Korea. According to legend, the progenitor of the Aisin Gioro clan, who later founded the Qing dynasty, was born to a virgin near this mountain.

87 **Siloam** Pool near Jerusalem where a blind man sent by Jesus recovered his sight, according to John 9:1–12.

87 **Xerxes** Xerxes I, king of Persia (486–465 B.C.E.).

88 **Chimborazo** Mountain in Ecuador, which various Europeans, including German naturalist Alexander von Humboldt, had attempted to climb in the early nineteenth century.

88 **Sumeru** Also called Meru, the mountain at the center of the world in Hindu cosmology.

88 **Karkuf** ʿAqar Quf in modern Iraq; see chapter 87.

88 **Cythera** Island south of the Peloponnese.

88 **Salem** An early biblical name for Jerusalem.

88 **Fifteen sazhens** 35 feet (11 m).

88 **Dalecarlian** From Dalecarlia (Dalarna), a province in Sweden.

88 **Tauric** From Tauric Chersonese (Crimea).

88 **Holm oak** Veltman uses the unusual word *belot*, which I take to mean *Quercus ilex* or *Quercus ballota*, the holm oak.

88 **Sannin** Mountain in Lebanon. Veltman probably found this quotation in Constantin-François Volney, *Voyage en Égypte et en Syrie, pendant les années 1783, 1784 et 1785* (Paris: Volland, 1787), 1:287.

88 **Quli Khan** Nader Shah (1688–1747), also known as Tahmasb Quli Khan, shah of Persia. After routing the Mughal army at Karnal, he entered Delhi in 1739 and carried off its fabled treasure, including the Peacock Throne and the Koh-i-Noor diamond. Veltman's "palace of Quli Khan" seems to be a literary vision inspired by that plunder.

89 **Allatalah** Al-Lat, pre-Islamic Arabian goddess.

89 **Anaya** Probably Anahita, Persian goddess.

89 **Greek Venus** Roman version Aphrodite, Greek goddess of fertility.

89 **Lada** Balto-Slavic fertility goddess.

90 **Dendera zodiac** First-century B.C.E. bas-relief from a temple in Dendera, Egypt.

90 **Palate . . . marrow . . . heart** Veltman's menu is a triple pun on offal dishes. The Russian word for "palate," *nebo*, also means "sky"; the term for "marrow," *amurety*, is a French loanword (amourettes) that also means "little love affairs"; and the pun on "heart," *serdtse*, works in both languages for the organ and the seat of emotion.

90 **Then chaos filled . . .** Veltman wrote this chapter in metered prose, which I replicate here. Specifically, it consists of amphibrachs (one stressed syllable between two short ones).

91 ***Oats . . . oaths*** (emphasis added) In the original Russian Veltman plays on the similarity between the Russian words for dinner (*obed*) and vow or oath (*obet*).

91 **Taihao Fuxi** The founder of the semilegendary Xia dynasty, dated to various years in the third millennium B.C.E.

92 **Sugarplums** Confections containing slips of paper or "mottoes" were common in the nineteenth century.

92 **Pilpai** The name given in Europe to the author of the Panchatantra, an ancient Indian collection of fables that was translated via Arabic into the European languages in the late Middle Ages.

92 **Krylov** Ivan Krylov (1769–1844), Russian fabulist.

92 **Man who burned the temple** Herostratus burned down the temple of Artemis at Ephesus out of a desire for fame.

92 **One talent** A reference to the parable of the talents (Matthew 25:14–30), though in that parable the slave who is entrusted with two talents gains two more.

92 **Yandi Shennong** Mythic emperor and culture hero of China, who supposedly reigned for 120 years in the twenty-eighth and twenty-seventh centuries B.C.E. and taught humanity farming and herbal medicine.

93 **Hundred-mouthed rumor** Compare Virgil's description of the goddess Fama (Rumor) in the *Aeneid*, 4.181–183: "For the many feathers in her body [she] has as many watchful eyes beneath—wondrous to tell—as many tongues, as many sounding mouths, as many pricked-up ears." Virgil, *"Eclogues," "Georgics," "Aeneid": Books 1–6,"* trans. H. Rushton Fairclough, rev. G. P. Goold, Loeb Classical Library 63 (Harvard University Press, 1916), 435.

94 ***Amur*** Play on the French word *Amour* (Love, Cupid) and the Mongol word *amar* "peaceful, happy" (or perhaps the Amur River, near Mongolia).

94 **Eiren** Eden; see note above for page 21.

94 **Alcinous** Legendary king of the Phaeacians in Homer's *Odyssey*, famed for his lush gardens.

94 **The gardens of Alcinous . . .** Paraphrase of a passage from the *Odyssey*, 7.117–121: "The fruit of these [trees] neither perishes nor fails in winter or in summer, but lasts throughout the year; and continually the West Wind, as it blows, quickens to life some fruits, and ripens

others; pear upon pear waxes ripe, apple upon apple, grape bunch upon grape bunch, and fig upon fig." Homer, *Odyssey*, trans. A. T. Murray, rev. George E. Dimock, Loeb Classical Library 104 (Harvard University Press, 1995), 1:263.

96 **Zang porcelain** Perhaps *tenmoku*, a Japanese style that arose in imitation of the Chinese Jian ware of the Song dynasty.

96 **Pashtet** A pastry filled with minced meat and other ingredients.

96 **Aisha** 'A'isha bint Abi Bakr (ca. 613–678), wife of the prophet.

Day 19

97 **Akbah** 'Uqba ibn Nafi' (ca. 622–683), Arab commander.

97 **Omar** 'Umar I ibn al-Khattab (died 644), the second Muslim caliph. This moment is described in Ibn Idhari's history *Al-Bayan al-Mughrib*, and in Edward Gibbon's *History of the Decline and Fall of the Roman Empire*, chapter 51. Gibbon called Akbah the "Mahometan Alexander."

98 **Lt. Gen. Kreutz** Cyprian von Kreutz (1777–1850), commander of the cavalry corps in Moldavia and Bulgaria.

98 ***Bim beşli ağa*** Conflation of two Ottoman titles, the *beşli ağa*, commander of the cavalry and police corps, and the *binbaşı*, a major in the army

98 ***Divan efendi*** Secretary of the divan, the Ottoman administrative council.

98 **Sovereign prince** Ioan Sturdza, prince of Moldavia from 1822 to 1828.

98 **Hetairist** A member of the Greek revolutionary group Filiki Etaireia, or Society of Friends, dedicated to overthrowing Ottoman rule in Greece.

98 **Nicholas** Nicholas I, emperor of Russia from 1825 to 1855.

98 **Agathangelus** Purported thirteenth-century author of a *Vision* describing the coming of a "blond race" to liberate the Orthodox peoples of the Balkans; this was in fact written by a Greek cleric around 1751

98 **John** Author of the Book of Revelation, which inspired Agathangelus's *Vision*.

98 ***Venit, venit . . .*** Romanian, Greek, and Russian, in a Greek accent: "The Muscovite has come! The Emperor's cavalry has come. Glory to God! It is good! Good, good! I too served the prince!"

98 ***Şi eu*** "I too" (Romanian).

99 ***Graikos*** Greek self-designation common in the Ottoman period.

99 **Border crossing** The Russian army invaded the Danubian principalities on April 25, 1828, Old Style (May 7, New Style).

99 **Skulyany** Sculeni, Ungheni District, Moldova.

99 **Vadului-Isakchi** Vadul lui Isac, Cahul District, Moldova.

99 **Four versts** About 2.7 miles.

99 ***Trajan's Wall*** Latin *vallum Traiani,* Romanian *Valul lui Traian,* a series of earthworks attributed by tradition to the Roman emperor Trajan. Veltman discussed Trajan's Wall and questioned its attribution to Trajan in *Nachertanie drevnei istorii Bessarabii* [Outline of the ancient history of Bessarabia] (Moscow: Semen Selivanovskii, 1828).

99 **Galați** Port city on the Danube.

99 **Getic wilderness** Region of the lower Danube; see note above for page 47.

99 **Five and ten sazhens** 35 and 70 feet (11 and 21 m), respectively.

100 **Lipkany** Lipcani, Briceni District, Moldova.

100 **Mamalyga** Mamalyha, Chernivtsi Region, Ukraine.

100 ***Yesaul*** Cossack rank equivalent to captain.

100 **Cossack of the Don** The Cossacks were self-governing frontier warriors—mostly Orthodox Slavs—who organized themselves into regional "hosts," gaining land and tax privileges in exchange for hereditary mounted service on Russia's expanding borders. Foremost among these hosts were the Don Cossacks, settled along the lower Don River.

100 **Punsht** Mispronunciation of *punsh,* "punch."

100 **Ataman** Cossack leader.

100 **A hundred miles** In the original, 150 versts, about a hundred miles—much too far to cover in one day.

100 **Article about the Archipelago** Chapter 233.

Day 20

102 **Kosteshty** Costești, Rîșcani District, Moldova.

102 **Hierasus** Possible ancient name for the Prut (it has also been identified with the Siret).

102 **Five versts** About 3.3 miles.

102 ***Suta de Movile*** Veltman uses the form *Suta Mojile.* These were later determined to be geological formations, not burial mounds.

102 **Potyomkin** Prince Grigory Potyomkin-Tavrichesky (1739–1791), Russian statesman and military leader, who died of a fever on the steppes south of Iași.

102 **Țuțora** Village in Iași County, Western Moldavia, Romania. Peter the Great unsuccessfully invaded Moldavia in 1711.

102 **You, Wanderer** Veltman drew on his real-life crossing of a flooded river (but the Dniester, not the Prut), which he describes in his *Memoirs of Bessarabia.*

102 **740 versts** About 490 miles.

102 **Agenor** King of Phoenicia, whose daughter Europa was abducted by Zeus, who had taken the form of a bull.

103 **Springs . . . machines** Veltman uses the words *samokhod*, "self-walker," and *samolyot*, "self-flyer," which in the nineteenth century referred to various mechanical devices.

103 **228 versts** About 151 miles.

104 **Antonache** Romanian name of Greek origin (originally a diminutive of Antonis), perhaps referring to an acquaintance of Veltman's or an innkeeper.

104 ***Ei, măi . . .*** "Hey, Gypsies, Moldavians, Romanians, Greeks, beautiful girl! Quickly, food!" (broken Romanian).

104 **Plaît-il, monsieur** "What would you like, sir?" (French)

104 **Manger, monsieur** "To eat, sir!" (French)

104 **Gleich, was Sie wollen** "At once, whatever you want" (German).

104 **Wir haben Schnepfen** "We have snipe" (German).

104 ***Sehr gut*** "Very good!" (German)

105 **Lichior poftești** "Do you want liqueur?" (Romanian).

105 **Ghermesut** Turkish *germsud*, fine silk fabric.

105 **Ekh verde enen etvas tsáen!** "I will show you something" (German or Yiddish dialect). In the original this is distinguished from the German phrases by not being in black letter, but it is not standard Yiddish either, which would be "ikh vel aykh epes vayzn."

105 **Poftim, poftim** "Please, please!" (Romanian).

105 **Mazur buyurun sultanım** "Excuse me, please, my sultan!" (Turkish).

105 **Idou kaponi kai salatan** "Here's a capon with salad!" (Greek).

105 **Eunuch** A play on the meaning of capon (a castrated rooster).

106 **Anasına** "To his mother" (Turkish), the curse referred to in the next chapter.

106 ***Slujitori*** Servants (Romanian).

106 **Callimachi** Scarlat Callimachi (1773–1821), who became the nominal ruler of Wallachia in 1821.

106 **Divan** State council.

106 **Râmnic wine** Probably from the region around the river Râmnicu Sărat (see chapter 249).

106 **Derzhavin** Gavrila Derzhavin (1743–1816), Russian poet; this line is from his "Ode to Felitsa" (1782).

Day 21

107 **Xisuthrus** Sumerian analogue of Noah; see chapter 32.

107 **Phidias** Renowned Athenian sculptor (fifth century B.C.E.).

108 **Peri** Supernatural being in Persian mythology.

108 **Fountain of Bakhchisaray** The "Fountain of Tears" in the palace of Bakhchisaray in Crimea. According to a legend retold by Pushkin in his poem "The Fountain of Bakhchisaray" (1824), the Crimean Khan Qırım Geray built the fountain in honor of his deceased concubine.

109 ***Butci*** Open carriages (Romanian).

109 **Fruits of the Hesperides** In Greek mythology golden apples guarded by nymphs and a dragon on an island, assumed to be in the western Mediterranean or the Atlantic. One of Hercules's labors was to steal these apples.

109 ***Nec plus ultra*** See note under day 1; here used in a looser meaning of something extreme. The association with Hercules and the western ocean forms a connection with the first line.

109 ***Sotteuse*** Unclear; a montre-sauteuse is a jumping-hour watch. Veltman's spelling also suggests *sot*, "foolish."

109 ***À l'ange qui vole*** "in the style of a flying angel" (French).

109 ***Madame la marchande de modes*** Madam fashion merchant (French).

109 ***Journal des dames*** *Journal des dames et des modes* (1797–1839), French fashion magazine.

109 **Butca gata** The carriage is ready! (Romanian).

110 **Hetairist cap** A cap such as those worn by the Greek revolutionaries; see chapter 148.

110 **Kali imera . . .** Greetings in Greek ("Good day to you!"); Turkish ("welcome!"); Romanian, Russian, French (all "Good evening!"); and German ("Good evening! How do you . . . you . . . you . . . you . . . do?").

110 **Montesquieu** Charles de Secondat, baron de La Brède et de Montesquieu (1689–1755), argued in *The Spirit of the Laws* that climate influences the temperament of a country's inhabitants.

111 **Réaumur's thermometer** Invented by René-Antoine Ferchault de Réaumur in the 1730s.

111 **Volney** Constantin François de Chassebœuf, comte de Volney (1757–1820), rejected Montesquieu's argument that certain countries were destined by their climate to despotic rule.

111 **Shakyamuni** Another name for Siddhartha Gautama, the Buddha; Veltman spells it *Shige-muni*.

111 **Inches . . .** The poem uses several old Russian units of measurement; I have chosen rough English equivalents. The mustache is 3 *dyuymy* (3 inches, 8 cm), the beard 2 *lokti* (3 feet, 1 m), the amber 1 *arshin* (2⅓ feet, 70 cm), and the chibouk (pipe) an unlikely 5 *sazheni* (35 feet, 11 m).

Day 22

112 **Pecheneg** Member of a seminomadic Turkic people inhabiting Ukraine from the ninth to the eleventh centuries. According to the eleventh-century East Slavic *Primary Chronicle*, the Pecheneg Khan Kurya made a chalice out of Prince Svyatoslav's skull.

112 **Janissary** A member of the elite Ottoman infantry corps that formed the sultan's guard (disbanded in 1826).

112 **Baldogineşti, İbrail** Baldovineşti and Brăila, Brăila County, Romania.

112 **Eight versts** About five miles.

112 **Ataman regiment** The tsarevich, or heir to the throne, was also the honorary ataman (chief) of the Cossack troops.

113 **Emperor Nicholas** Nicholas I was directly involved in the campaigns of 1828 and 1829. Veltman, as senior adjutant, provided the emperor with daily memoranda on combat operations.

113 **Zavadovsky** Ivan Zavodovsky (1780–1837), promoted to counter admiral for this action.

113 **Five-pood** About 180 pounds (80 kg).

113 **Open field** Play on words; the Russian word *pole* means both "field" and "margin."

114 **Foam** Perhaps referring to Aphrodite, who sprang from the foam of the sea and whose symbol was the rose.

114 **Hahnemann** Samuel Hahnemann (1755–1843), German physician, founder of homeopathy, which claimed that minute doses of drugs can cure disease.

114 **Abelite** Or Abelian, member of a religious sect in fourth-century North Africa that renounced sexual intercourse.

Day 23

116 **Hacı Kaptan** Hagi-Căpitan, former village in Brăila County, Romania.

116 **Vauban** Sébastien Le Prestre, marquis de Vauban (1633–1707), French military engineer.

116 **Saint-Paul** Jean-François Gaspard Noizet de Saint-Paul (1749–1837), French officer and politician.

116 **Folard** Jean-Charles de Folard (1669–1752), French strategist.

116 **Bélidor** Bernard Forest de Bélidor (1698–1761), French engineer.

116 **Coehoorn** Menno van Coehoorn (1641–1704), Dutch engineer.

116 **Cormontaigne** Louis de Cormontaigne (1695–1752), French engineer.

116 **George** Order of Saint George, the highest military decoration in the Russian Empire, established in 1769.

116 **A Cossack Rides Across the Danube** "A Cossack Rode Across the Danube," a Ukrainian folksong written by the eighteenth-century poet Semen Klymovsky.

116 **Five versts** About three miles.

117 **Bogatyr** Hero in Russian folklore.

117 **2,336 years** Darius I crossed the Danube (Ister) to fight the Scythians in 513 B.C.E., so actually 2,340 years before 1828 C.E.

117 **İshakçı** Isaccea, Tulcea County, Romania.

117 **Jäger** Rifleman or sharpshooter (literally "hunter" in German).

117 **Vizier's Mound** Mound near İshakçı on which legend says a vizier was punished by being buried alive.

117 **Satunovo** Novosilske, Odesa Region, Ukraine.

118 **Babadağ** Lake in Tulcea County, Romania, near a town of the same name.

Day 24

120 **Aesop's fable** The Cock and the Jewel (or the Pearl), first found in Phaedrus's collection (first century C.E.).

121 **La Rochefoucauld** François de La Rochefoucauld (1613–1680), French writer of maxims, including many on vanity and self-love.

123 **Denistepe** Hill in Tulcea County, Romania.

123 **Razim** Lagoon on the shores of the Black Sea south of the Danube.

123 **Tulça, Maçin** Tulcea and Măcin, towns in Tulcea County.

123 **Hırsova** Hârșova, Constanța County.

123 **Bey Davud** Beidaud, Tulcea County.

123 **Satışköy** Crucea, Constanța County.

123 **Karasu** Medgidia, Constanța County; also the river on which the town is situated.

124 **As Byron says** Perhaps referring to Byron's description of a storm in *Childe Harold's Pilgrimage*, III, beginning with "All heaven and earth are still—though not in sleep." Lord Byron, *The Complete Poetical Works*, ed. Jerome J. McGann (Oxford University Press, 1980), 2:109.

124 **Süleyman Paşa and Cafer Paşa** Commanders of the fortresses of İbrail and Maçin, respectively.

124 **Thirty thousand . . .** numbers given in Edward Gibbon, *The History of the Decline and Fall of the Roman Empire*, ed. David Womersley (Penguin, 1995), 3:237.

124 **Köstence** Constanța, city in Romania on the Black Sea.

124 **Horsetails** Poles with horsetail hairs, symbols of power that originated in the Mongol Empire and were later adopted by the Ottomans.

124 **Sublime Porte** The Ottoman government.

124 **Bouilly** Jean-Nicolas Bouilly (1763–1842), French author of several plays on military themes, as well as one about Peter the Great.

125 **Köstence . . .** The Greeks founded the colony of Istria or Istros; the Romans built the nearby town of Tomis, later renamed Constantiana, which became Köstence (Kustendje) under the Ottomans and is now the Romanian city Constanța.

125 **Valentini** Georg Wilhelm von Valentini (1775–1834), Prussian commander, participant in the Russo-Turkish campaign of 1810, and author of books on the art of war.

125 **Ten versts** About seven miles.

125 **Castrametation** "The art or science of laying out a camp" (*OED*).

125 **Notre veillée . . .** In Montaigne's *Essays*, book 2, chapter 12: "Our waking sleeps more than our sleeping; our wisdom is less wise than our folly; our dreams are worth more than our discourse." Michel de Montaigne, *The Complete Essays*, trans. M. A. Screech (Penguin, 1991), 640.

Day 25

126 **Erebus's grandson** Morpheus, god of dreams, son of Hypnus (sleep), son of Nyx (night) and Erebus (nether darkness).

126 **Leman** Lake Geneva.

126 **Julie** The heroine of Rousseau's *Julie, or the New Heloise* (1761), whose lover Saint-Preux is tempted to drown himself in the lake.

127 **Daughter of heaven and earth** In Greek mythology Eros (Love) was usually considered the son of Aphrodite, but Hesiod claimed he was a primordial god who came into existence along with Gaea (Earth) and Tartarus (the Underworld), and Sappho made him the son of Gaea and Uranus (Sky). The Russian word for love is feminine, hence Veltman's "daughter."

128 **Too long . . .** Veltman had earlier included this poem, with some additional lines, in a letter to his former classmate V. P. Gorchakov, the quartermaster of the Sixteenth Infantry Division.

128 **Rusalka** A water nymph in Slavic folklore, sometimes depicted with a fishtail like a mermaid.

128 **Magura** Name of several mountains, here perhaps one in Lviv Region, Ukraine.

129 **Mamenka** Mommy (a diminutive of *mama*).

Day 26

131 **Fire . . . twelve heads** The Holy Spirit descending on the twelve apostles, commemorated in the holiday of Pentecost.

131 **Haller** Albrecht von Haller (1708–1777), Swiss physiologist and poet, whose poem "On the Origin of Evil" was translated into Russian by Karamzin.

133 **A certain glow** This refers to the phenomenon of foxfire, a kind of bioluminescence created by fungi on decaying wood.

133 **Nakhimov** Akim Nakhimov (1782–1814), poet and satirist; the reference is to his "Tale of Themis and the Foreign Clerks."

133 **Civil servant** *Chinovnik,* an official holding a specific rank (*chin*) within the Russian Empire's state bureaucracy. The scene reflects a common disdain, especially among military officers, for low-level bureaucrats.

133 ***Some . . .*** In the original Russian, the civil servant makes various spelling mistakes, including writing suma, "beggar's pouch," instead of summa, "sum."

134 **Behtirköy** Former village in what is now Constanța County, Romania.

134 **Carriages . . .** A diligence was a French stagecoach; a dormeuse ("sleeper" in French) was a carriage adapted for sleeping on long journeys; a calash was a light vehicle with a folding hood; a droshky was a common Russian four-wheeled open carriage; a brichka was a Polish semicovered wagon; a gig (taratayka in Russian) was a simple two-wheeled cart; and a brașoveancă was a large covered wagon from the Romanian town of Brașov.

134 **Kalmyk kibitka** Portable felt tent (yurt) of the Kalmyks, a Mongolic people of the lower Volga steppe.

134 **Orenburg steppe** Region around Orenburg on the Ural River, at the boundary of Europe and Asia.

134 **Constantinople mission** The Russian diplomatic mission in the Ottoman capital.

134 **Mahmutkuyusu** Izvoru Mare, Constanța County, Romania.

134 **Musubey** Izvorovo, Dobrich Province, Bulgaria.

134 **Azaplar** Polkovnik Dyakovo, Dobrich Province, Bulgaria.

134 **Çelebiköy** Former village in Dobrich Province, Bulgaria.

134 **Pazarcık** In full *Hacıoğlu Pazarcık,* now Dobrich, Bulgaria.

134 **Two days' march** According to an anecdote, when Suvorov asked a soldier how far it was to the moon, the soldier answered, "Two days' march." This is perhaps conflated with the story of the grenadier who saved Suvorov at the Battle of Kinburn in 1787.

Day 27

136 **Champollion** Jean-François Champollion (1790–1832), who played a large role in the decipherment of Egyptian hieroglyphics.

136 **Egyptian toil** An expression referring to the labor of enslaved Israelites in Egypt.

136 **Taban Dere** "Dere" means "stream" in Turkish; the Taban is now dried up.

137 ***Cami*** Mosque (Turkish, from Arabic).

137 ***Elinin karısını arzulama!*** "Do not covet the foreigner's wife" (Turkish).

137 **Kozluca** Suvorovo, Varna Province, Bulgaria.

138 **Chemitszan** Mongolian god whose image the Russian diplomat Yegor Timkovsky saw in a temple on Mount Aburga, as recorded in *Journey to China Through Mongolia in 1820 and 1821*. See Egor Timkovskii, *Puteshestvie v Kitai chrez Mongoliiu v 1820 i 1821 godakh* (Saint Petersburg: Tipografiia meditsinskago departamenta ministerstva vnutrennikh del, 1824), 1:228.

138 ***Hatt-ı şerîf*** In the Ottoman Empire, a decree issued by the government and approved by the sultan.

138 **Şumnu** Russian *Shumla*, now Shumen, Shumen Province, Bulgaria.

138 **Tunca** River flowing from central Bulgaria into Turkey.

138 **Eski Saray** Old palace in Edirne.

138 **Edirne** City in northwest Turkey.

138 **Chabrias** According to Plutarch, the Athenian general Chabrias (fourth century B.C.) said that "an army of deer commanded by a lion is more to be feared than an army of lions commanded by a deer." Plutarch, *Moralia*, trans. Frank Cole Babbitt, Loeb Classical Library 245 (Harvard University Press, 1931), 3:107.

138 **Commander of the Faithful** The caliph, the Ottoman sultan.

139 **Law established by Pope Gregory IX** The formalization of canon law under Pope Gregory IX (r. 1227–1241), which included strict impediments to marriage. This also marks the establishment of the Papal Inquisition, which enforced such laws.

139 **Thunder . . .** "Nor rain, wind, thunder, fire are my daughters." Shakespeare, *King Lear*, 3.2.15.

139 **Torn in two** Probably an allusion to Aristophanes's speech in Plato's *Symposium*, which tells the myth of primeval humans being split in two by the gods, with each half longing to find its soulmate.

139 **This cunning dream . . .** According to Akutin, this is an excerpt from a letter Veltman wrote to Yekaterina Isupova.

Day 28

141 **Cabanis** Pierre Jean Georges Cabanis (1757–1808), French physician, philosopher, and early proponent of evolution.

142 **Beautiful Mouth** One of the mouths of the Danube mentioned by Greek and Roman geographers.

142 **Pontus** Black Sea.

142 **Propontis** Sea of Marmara.

142 **Hellespont** Dardanelles.

Day 29

144 **Chabrias** See note above for page 138.

144 **Telescope** Veltman's jab at the Moscow journal *Telescope* (1831–1836, ed. Nikolai Nadezhdin), a liberal literary-philosophical periodical that had mocked part 1 of *The Wanderer* and was later closed for printing Petr Chaadaev's "Philosophical Letter." Veltman himself had more moderate politics and was content to publish in journals across the ideological spectrum.

144 **Niğbolu** Nikopol, Pleven Province, Bulgaria.

144 **Ziştovi** Svishtov, Veliko Tarnovo Province.

144 **Rusçuk** Ruse, Ruse Province, Bulgaria.

144 **Silistre** Silistra, Silistra Province, Bulgaria.

144 **1810** In May 1810 the Ottoman fortress of Silistre on the right bank of the Danube was besieged by Russian troops under the command of Sergeo Kamensky; the Ottomans eventually surrendered.

144 **Akkadınlar** Dulovo, Silistra Province, Bulgaria.

144 **Emberler** Kliment, Shumen Province, Bulgaria.

144 **Ekizce** Bliznatsi, Shumen Province, Bulgaria.

144 **Varna** City in Bulgaria on the Black Sea.

144 **Franka** Now Kamenar, Varna Province.

144 **Münnich . . .** Russian commanders in the Russo-Turkish Wars: Burkhard Christoph von Münnich (Minikh) (1683–1767), Pyotr Rumyantsev-Zadunaysky (1725–1796), Aleksandr Suvorov (1730–1800); Grigory Potyomkin-Tavrichesky (1739–1791), Mikhail Kamensky (1738–1809), and Mikhail Kutuzov (1747–1813).

145 **Di piacer . . .** "My heart leaps with joy," from Gioachino Rossini's opera *La gazza ladra* (The thieving magpie, 1817).

145 **Haemus** Ancient Greek name for the Balkan Mountains.

145 **Pravadı** Provadia, river and town in Varna Province, Bulgaria.

145 **Hieroglyphs** Possibly referring to various ancient inscriptions found in Bulgaria.

145 **Scyths** Scythians.

145 **Disputed forebears** The origin of the Slavs was much debated throughout the nineteenth century.

Day 30

146 **221** Note that chapter 220 is absent, for no stated reason.

146 **Jingdezhen** Town in southern China, the center of Chinese porcelain production.

146 **Pliny** Gaius Plinius Secundus (ca. 22–79 C.E.). The phrase is from Pliny's *Natural History* 7.7, where he writes that the number of languages is so numerous "that a foreigner scarcely counts as a human being for someone of another race." Pliny, *Natural History*, trans. H. Rackham, Loeb Classical Library 352 (Harvard University Press, 1942), 2:511. Veltman omits the word *paene*, "scarcely."

146 **Devne** Devnya, river in Varna Province, Bulgaria.

146 **Madara** Town in Shumen Province, Bulgaria.

146 **Life-Amazons** A reference to the Russian Imperial Life Guard, the personal guard of the Russian emperors.

147 **Nature sets the term** The "lunar fits" here are probably menstruation. In his *Natural History* (book 24, chapter 59), Pliny described rosemary as an emmenagogue.

148 ***La clemenza di Tito*** Opera by Mozart, which premiered in 1791. Veltman is probably referring to the transition in the overture from the vibrant fanfares of the opening in C to a lighter section in G played by the woodwinds.

148 **Chaos** In Haydn's oratorio *Die Schöpfung* (The Creation, 1798).

148 **Lavater** Johann Caspar Lavater (1741–1801), Swiss writer, pastor, and physiognomist.

149 **I know that you would like to read** In this poem, Veltman addresses his former colleagues at the topographic survey of Bessarabia.

149 **My journey with digressions rife** A more literal version of the final two stanzas would be "My life, my being / My journey, / My Encyclopedia! // May the world pick you up and read you, / And pronounce from the soul, / Truly, what a comedy!"

Part 3

151 **Auteur de . . .** "Author of *St*— [a redacted title]: What do you think of my book? A lady: I do as you do, sir, I do not think at all" (French). From "Lettre sur l'ouvrage de Mme de Staël intitulé: De l'influence des passions," in *Œuvres complètes de Rivarol*, 2nd ed. (Paris: Léopold Col-

lin, 1808), 2:256–257. The article, first published in 1797, was signed "Lucius Apuleius" but was assumed to be by Antoine Rivaroli, self-styled "comte de Rivarol" (1753–1801), a French royalist writer.

Day 31

153 ***Οὐ τὸ μέγα εὖ . . .*** "It is not the great that is good, but the good that is great"; proverb attributed to the Athenian orator Demosthenes (384–322 B.C.E.).

153 ***Phrygia*** Region in west central Asia Minor, often equated by the Roman poets with Troy. According to Homer and others, Apollo and Poseidon built the walls of Troy for King Laomedon.

154 ***Ah! ah! (il rit.)*** "Ha, ha! (he laughs)" (French), a line in numerous French comedies. Veltman is perhaps calling attention to the strange (to Russian ears) representation of a laugh as "ah ah" instead of "ha ha" (Russian *kha-kha*).

155 ***Ida*** Mountain range in the southern Troas (present-day Kazdağları, Turkey), from which, according to Homer, the gods watched the battles on the plain of Troy.

155 **Parian marble** A fine, white marble from the Greek island of Paros, prized in antiquity for sculpture and architecture, not to be confused with the Parian Marble or Chronicle mentioned in chapter 13.

155 ***Smyrna . . .*** Six of the seven cities that claimed to be the birthplace of Homer (the seventh was Argos).

155 ***Batrachomyomachia*** *The Battle of the Frogs and the Mice*, a parody of the *Iliad* from the late Hellenistic period, formerly attributed to Homer.

155 ***Hymn to Ceres*** One of the Homeric Hymns, formerly attributed to Homer. Matthaei discovered a Byzantine manuscript of the hymns in Moscow in 1777. He was accused of stealing manuscripts, so the praise here is perhaps ironic.

155 **Continova . . .** "Continova, feminine noun, continuation." From Giuseppe Martinelli, *Nuovo dizionario portatile italiano-francese* (Paris: Bossange, Masson e Besson, 1797), or one of its subsequent editions.

155 ***Sigean* promontory** Sigeum, northwest of Troy.

155 ***Alexandria*** Alexandria Troas, near the modern village of Dalyan in Çanakkale Province, Turkey.

155 ***Bunar-Bashi*** Pınarbaşı, a village in Çanakkale Province, which Jean Baptiste LeChevalier thought was the site of Troy.

155 ***Süleyman*** Süleyman Pasha (died 1357), son of the second Ottoman sultan, Orhan I.

156 ***Mare calabalâc!*** "What a mess!" (Romanian), but *mare* also means "sea," the topic of this chapter and the next, and *calabalâc* (from Turkish *kalabalık*, "crowd") also refers to the skirmish that forced Charles XII from Bender (see chapter 73).

156 **Several tons** Literally "several hundred poods"; a pood (*pud*) was equal to about 36 pounds (16 kg).

156 **Schwarz** Berthold Schwarz, legendary fourteenth-century German monk credited with the invention of gunpowder.

156 **Sea, O sea . . .** There were many manuals called *Short Rhetoric*. "Sea! O vast sea" is given as an example of climax (though under §44, not §56) in Aleksandr Nikol'skii's *Osnovaniia rossiiskoi slovesnosti: Izdany pri gosudarstvennom admiralteiskom departamente dlia morskikh uchilishch* [Foundations of Russian literature: published at the State Admiralty Department for Naval Academies], part 2 (Saint Petersburg: Morskaia tipografiia, 1807), 36.

157 ***Forster*** Georg Forster (1754–1794), German naturalist and ethnologist who wrote about luminous sea creatures in his *Voyage Round the World* (1777).

157 **Q.E.D.** An abbreviation for the Latin *quod erat demonstrandum*, "which was to be demonstrated" (Veltman uses the Russian equivalent).

157 **Was hat . . .** "What did he say? (A Jew)" (German). From "Die jüdischen Rekruten" ("The Jewish Recruits"), a poem attributed to a certain "Kärner" and published in popular anthologies. See Kärner, "Die jüdischen Rekruten," in *Museum der Declamation*, ed. Karl Friedrich Solbrig (Leipzig: Baumgärtnersche Buchhandlung, 1813), 1:136–137.

157 ***Helen*** Saint Elmo's fire, an electric discharge appearing on the masts of ships. In Greek mythology, this was said to be a manifestation of Helen of Troy or her brothers, Castor and Pollux.

157 **Archipelago** The Aegean Sea.

157 ***Thasos*** Island in the northern Aegean known for its minerals

157 ***Lemnos*** Formerly volcanic island in the northern Aegean.

157 ***Euboea*** Or Evia, large agricultural island close to the mainland.

157 ***Salamis*** Island in the Saronic Gulf, site of a naval battle between the Greeks and Persians.

157 ***Aegina*** Island in the Saronic Gulf, home of the Myrmidons, transformed by Zeus from ants into men.

157 ***Hydra*** Ancient Hydrea, which became commercially important in the eighteenth century.

157 ***Nio*** Ancient Ios in the Cyclades.

157 ***Andros*** Island in the Cyclades, sacred to Dionysus (Bacchus).

157 ***Cythnos*** Kythnos, island in the Cyclades known for its hot springs.

157 ***Delos*** Island in the Cyclades, birthplace of Apollo and site of one of his sanctuaries.

157 ***Myconos*** Island in the Cyclades, supposed to contain an unusual number of bald persons.

157 ***Stampalia*** Astypalaea, island in the Dodecanese, known in antiquity for its greenery.

157 ***Imbro*** Imbros, now Gökçeada, Turkey.

157 ***Milo*** Melos or Milos in the Cyclades.

158 ***Skanderbeg*** George Castriot (1405–1468), Albanian nobleman who led a rebellion against the Ottoman Empire. According to legend, he had a sword that could cut an ox in half with one stroke, but only when he wielded it.

158 ***Hai-hai . . .*** Probably words to drive cattle: "Hey, come on, you!"

158 **Little Russian** From the seventeenth through the early twentieth centuries this was the standard Russian imperial term for the Ukrainian lands and people, ultimately derived from the Byzantine Greek geographic label *Mikra Rhossia* ("Little Rus"). Today it is obsolete and widely regarded as pejorative.

158 ***Isis*** Egyptian goddess of fertility, but Veltman probably means Iris, the Greek goddess of the rainbow.

159 **But whoever you are . . .** "Ô vous, qui que vous soyez (mortelle ou déesse)." Fénelon, *Les aventures de Télémaque*, book 1. Veltman may have found this quote in Lhomond's French grammar (see epigraph to part 2). Charles-Constant Letellier, ed., *Grammaire françoise de Lhomond*, 12th ed. (Paris: Le Prieur, 1811), 200.

159 **For "what it's worth"** A reference to the Russian saying "I'm selling it at the price I paid for it," that is, "I'm just passing on what I heard."

Day 32

160 **Good dawning . . .** From *King Lear*, act 2, scene 2. In Guizot's translation from Shakespeare, note 23 reads "*Good dawning.* Il y a en anglais des souhaits pour toutes les époques du jour" (In English there are wishes for all the times of the day). F. Guizot, trans., *Œuvres complètes de Shakespeare* (Paris: Ladvocat, 1821), 6:202.

160 ***Dragon*** Perhaps the dragon of Revelation 12, which knocks a third of the stars out of the sky.

161 **Le genie . . .** "The genius (alone) / (A sweet symphony is heard.) / But what sweet strains follow the cries of pain?" (French). From Ger-

main François Poullain de Saint-Foix's play *Alceste, divertissement à l'occasion de la convalescence de Monsieur le Dauphin* (performed 1752). In Saint-Foix, *Œuvres complettes* (Maastricht: Jean-Edme Dufour & Philippe Roux, 1778), 2:92.

162 **Mais il est vrai . . .** "But it is true that pure air is not made for man, as is demonstrated in chemistry." Antoine Rivarol, "Lettre à M. le président de ***, Sur le Globe aérostatique, sur les Têtes-parlantes, et sur l'état présent de l'opinion publique à Paris," in *Œuvres complètes de Rivarol*, 2nd ed. (Paris: Léopold Collin, 1808), 2:239. On Rivarol, see the note to the epigraph to part 3.

163 **Il n'y avait rien . . .** "There was nothing so easy as discovering America, since it was only a matter of coming across it. (The envious)." Ibid., 241–242. From an anecdote about Christopher Columbus, who then proposed to the "envious" that they make an egg stand on its end; when they failed, Columbus then tapped it on the table, flattening the tip and making it stand up.

163 ***What he should . . .*** A quotation from Jean-Jacques Barthélemy's *Voyage du jeune Anacharsis en Grèce* (1788), in *Œuvres de J. J. Barthélemy*, vol. 1 (Paris: A. Belin, 1821), 468. Compare Aristotle's *Art of Rhetoric*, 3.1: "It is not sufficient to know what one ought to say, but one must also know how to say it." Aristotle, *Art of Rhetoric*, trans. J. H. Freese, Loeb Classical Library 193 (Harvard University Press, 1926), 345.

163 ***Virtue . . .*** Paraphrase of Aristotle's pronouncement in the *Eudemian Ethics*, 4.5: "But then the best state in relation to each class of thing is the middle state. It is clear, therefore, that the virtues will be either all or some of these middle states." Aristotle, *Athenian Constitution. Eudemian Ethics. Virtues and Vices*, trans. H. Rackham, Loeb Classical Library 285 (Harvard University Press, 1935), 263.

163 **Pudet dicere** It is a shame to say (Latin).

163 **Florus** Lucius Annaeus Florus (ca. 74–ca. 130 C.E.), Roman historian. The quotation is found in Florus's *Epitome of Roman History*, 2.8.

Day 33

164 **Ein armer Teufel . . .** "A poor devil sang and warbled from morning into the night, far from grief and care (German story)." The original poem, by Christian Felix Weiße, has *Schuster*, "shoemaker," instead of *Teufel*, "devil." Christian Felix Weiße, *Der Kinderfreund: Ein Wochenblatt* [The children's friend: A weekly magazine], part 4 (Leipzig: Siegfried Lebrecht Crusius, 1776), 171.

164 **Aleksandr Vasilyevich** Suvorov, Russian general (see notes above).

165 **Oracle** The temple of Amun (Ammon in Greek) at the Siwa Oasis in Egypt, where Alexander the Great was proclaimed the "sun of Amun."

165 ***The Tale of Igor's Campaign*** Twelfth-century Old East Slavic text discovered in 1795 and first published in 1800. Veltman's own translation of the *Tale* into modern Russian (1821) rendered this line as "I'll fly like an unlucky one to the Don!"

166 **201** In fact, the theme of the sun links 248 more directly to chapter 202.

166 **The word of the Old Testament . . .** According to Akutin, this poem is an abbreviated version of a longer poem in a manuscript dated "December 12."

166 **Bel** Title of various Mesopotamian gods, especially Marduk.

166 **Vestals** The vestal virgins, Roman priestesses of Vesta, keepers of the sacred fire.

167 **Armida** Saracen sorceress and seductress in Torquato Tasso's epic poem *La Gerusalemme liberata* (Jerusalem delivered, 1581). Her story inspired many stage works, notably Gioachino Rossini's opera *Armida* (1817).

167 **Maçin** Măcin Mountains, Tulcea County, Romania.

167 **Râmnic** Râmnicu Sărat, tributary of the Siret River, the site of a 1789 battle in which the Russians (under Suvorov) and their Austrian allies defeated the Ottomans.

167 **Suvorov's son** General-Lieutenant Arkady Suvorov (1784–1811), who inherited the title "Count of Râmnic" from his father but by a twist of fate drowned in that same river.

167 **Hippomenes . . . Atalanta** In Greek mythology, Atalanta vowed to marry the man who could defeat her in a foot race, which Hippomenes accomplished by dropping golden apples on the track.

Day 34

169 **Hebe** The goddess of youth (Juventas in Latin).

169 **Haman, Mordecai** In the book of Esther, Mordecai is Esther's righteous cousin and Haman is King Ahasuerus's evil minister.

170 ***Ni, shabas, pane!*** "No, it's the Sabbath, sir!" (Ukrainian).

Day 35

171 **Most honorable sir . . .** Formulaic language required in military reports, possibly adapted from *Obshchee nastavlenie dlia obucheniia i za-*

niatiia sapernykh i pionernykh batalionov [. . .] o garnizonnoi i polevoi sluzhbe [General instruction for training and occupation of sapper and pioneer batallions [. . .] concerning garrison and field service] (Saint Petersburg: Voennaia tipografiia, 1824), 308.

171 ***À la fille d'Yémen*** "In the style of the daughter of Yemen" (the original has *Jemen),* possibly referring to the Queen of Sheba, who came from the region of present-day Yemen.

171 **Numidian** From Numidia (present-day Algeria); but compare also the Nemean lion slain by Hercules.

172 **Jupiter** Zeus (or his Roman equivalent, Jupiter) visited Danaë in the form of a shower of gold, and she gave birth to Perseus.

172 ***Newton's binomial*** The binomial theorem, generalized by Isaac Newton, by which any power of a binomial can be expressed as a series of sums.

Day 36

173 ***Orchomenus*** Town in Boeotia where in 86 B.C.E. a battle took place between a Roman army led by L. Cornelius Sulla and a Pontic army led by Archelaus. According to Plutarch, when the Romans began to flee, Sulla seized a standard and cried, "For me, O Romans, an honourable death here; but you, when men ask you where you betrayed your commander, remember to tell them, at Orchomenus." His troops then rallied and defeated the Pontics. Plutarch, *Lives*, volume 4, *Alcibiades and Coriolanus. Lysander and Sulla*, trans. Bernadotte Perrin, Loeb Classical Library 80 (Harvard University Press, 1916), 395.

173 ***Ternaux*** Guillaume Louis Ternaux, French textile manufacturer.

173 ***Yeni Cami*** "New mosque," the Tombul Mosque in Shumen, Bulgaria, which has a 130-foot minaret.

174 **Aidez-moi Johannot** "Help me, Johannot!" (French).

174 **Johannot** Tony Johannot (1803–1852), French engraver, who illustrated books by Walter Scott and James Fenimore Cooper.

174 **Bulanık** Now Matnitsa, a district of Shumen.

174 **Attack on Şumnu** On July 8, 1828, the Third and Seventh Corps of the Russian army attacked Şumnu (Shumla/Shumen), which was defended by a Turkish army of forty thousand men commanded by Hüseyin Paşa. After a brief battle, the Turkish troops fled into the fortress, and the Russians attempted to blockade the fortress, but failed to take it and finally retreated in September.

174 **Turchonok** The Russian name for the horse means "Turkish boy."

174 **Meanwhile . . . Russian glory** These two last paragraphs are omitted from the second edition and the Soviet edition.

175 **Occupation of the Position at Şumnu** This section is omitted from the second edition and the Soviet edition.

175 **Yenipazar** Now Novi Pazar in Şumnu Province, Bulgaria (Veltman writes Yanibazar).

175 **Diebitsch** Count Hans Karl von Diebitsch, aka Ivan Diebitsch-Zabalkansky (1785–1831).

176 **Rudzevich** Aleksandr Rudzevich (1775–1829).

176 ***Wagenburg*** "Wagon fort" (German), a fortification made of circled-up wagons.

176 **Sysoev** Vasily Sysoev (1772–1839).

176 **Bulanık** Probably Matnitsa, now a district of Shumen (Veltman has *Bulany*).

176 **Vedettes** Mounted sentries.

177 **Mayna, Mayka, or Makak** Makak, now a district in Shumen.

177 **Next chapter** Akutin's edition adds "and what?" here, but this is not present in the first or second editions.

177 **Thirty versts** About twenty miles.

178 ***Bête . . .*** The narrator here, in my interpretation, mishears the letter *bet* as French *bête*, "stupid" or "beast." He then calls him a *duga*, "shaft bow (of a Russian harness)," perhaps alluding to the expression *sognut' v dugu*, "to bend someone into a shaft bow (to one's will)."

178 **German** The narrator hears *gimmel* as German *Himmel*, "sky."

178 ***Alef, bet, gimmel . . .*** Hebrew letters, with some inconsistencies. Compare the standard alphabet in Ashkenazi Hebrew and Yiddish: alef, beys, giml, daled, hey, vov, zayen, khes, tes, yud, kof, lamed, mem, nun, samekh, ayen, pey, tsadek, kuf, reysh, shin, tof.

178 ***Lammed . . .*** "All" is not a letter; the order here should be "lamed, mem, nun, samekh, ayen, pey."

178 **Demon! Sanskrit!** First edition. The second edition has "Demon! Jew!"

179 ***Tuf*** The coachman hears the narrator's *oof* as *tuf*, which is the last letter of the alphabet, hence a signal to stop.

180 ***Zammekh*** The narrator mishears *zammekh* as Russian *zamok*, "castle."

180 ***Leshy*** A Slavic wood goblin; see chapter 92.

180 **Asphalius** "the securer," an epithet of Poseidon (Neptune).

180 **Dagon** Semitic deity assumed to be a fish-god by nineteenth-century scholars.

Day 37

183 **Jetzo . . .** "Now we go further. (Convincing Proof of Immortality.) Chapter 1, Section 2" (German). Israel Gottlieb Canz, *Uberzeugender Beweiß aus der Vernunft, antreffend die Unsterblichkeit sowohl der Menschen Seelen insgemein, als besonders der Kinder-Seelen* (Tübingen: Johann Georg Cotta, 1741), 140.

183 **Forty versts** About twenty-seven miles (43 km).

183 **Bousmard** Henri Jean-Baptiste de Bousmard de Chantereine (1749–1807), French military writer.

183 ***Odessus*** Ancient Greek city on the western coast of the Black Sea, modern Varna.

183 **Hero, Leander** In Greek mythology, Hero was a priestess of Aphrodite in Sestos, whose lover Leander swam across the Hellespont every night to visit her, until one night he drowned.

183 **Ladislaus III** Władysław III Warneńczyk (1424–1444), king of Poland and Hungary, who led two crusades against the Ottomans and died in the Battle of Varna. Veltman has "Vladislav IV"; the numbering varied in the sources.

184 **Murad** Murad II (1404–1451), Ottoman sultan; Veltman has "Amurat."

184 ***Jerid*** Turkish *cirit*, Arabic *jarid*, a wooden javelin used in equestrian games. The first edition has *dzhigid*, probably by confusion with a term for a brave horseman.

184 ***Straja*** Strazha, village in Targovishte Province, Bulgaria.

184 **Hüseyin Paşa** Ağa Hüseyin Paşa (1776–1849), Ottoman commander-in-chief for the first part of the war of 1828–1829.

184 **Cuma** Eski Cuma, now Targovishte, Targovishte Province (Veltman has "Cuma").

184 **Eski İstanbul** Veliki Preslav, Shumen Province (Veltman has "Eski Stambul").

184 **Hezargrad** Razgrad, Razgrad Province (Veltman has "Rargrad"), Bulgaria.

184 **Varna** An important town and Ottoman fortress on the road to Istanbul. After a long siege Varna was conquered by the Russians on September 29 (October 11), 1828.

185 ***Ganjuur*** *Bka' 'gyur* or *Kangyur*, the "Translation of the Word," one of the two divisions of the Tibetan Buddhist canon, redacted in the fourteenth century and said to contain 108 volumes.

185 **Janus** The Roman god of passage, war, and peace, who is depicted usually with two faces but sometimes with four. In the Roman Forum

there was a passageway with a statue of Janus and two gates, which were closed only during peacetime.

Day 38

186 **Le métier . . .** "The craft that is believed to be peculiar to actors and conjurers is the craft of all men (Hippocrates)." *Les Œuvres d'Hippocrate, traduites en françois, avec des remarques, et conferées sur les manuscripts de la bibliotheque du roy* (Paris: Compagnie des Librairies, 1697), 2:42. The original has "Ce métier" (This craft). This is a loose translation of Hippocrates, *Regimen (De victu)*, 1.24.

186 **Gli uomini . . .** "Men make themselves miserable by desiring the superfluous (Minerva disguised as Mentor)." A shortened quotation from an Italian translation of Fénelon's *Les aventures de Télémaque* (1699), possibly this edition: *Le avventure di Telemaco, figliuolo d'Ulisse di Monsignor Francesco di Salignac de la Motte Fenelon* (Livorno: G. P. Pozzolini, 1827), 112.

186 **Ces exagérations . . .** (in footnote) "These exaggerations are permitted in poetry, especially in the manner of writing that I use." From a note at the end of "Les Souris et le Chat-huant." See La Fontaine, *Œuvres complètes* (Gallimard, 1991), 444.

186 **Surugiu** "driver" (see chapter 43).

187 ***Perscriptions . . .*** The italics are in the Russian text, emphasizing the soldiers' uneducated pronunciations of medical words borrowed from western European languages.

188 ***La Dame blanche*** *The White Lady*, opera by Adrien Boieldieu to a libretto by Eugène Scribe based on Walter Scott's novels; premiered in 1825.

188 ***Der Freischütz*** *The Marksman*, by Carl Maria von Weber to a libretto by Johann Friedrich Kind, based on a German folktale; premiered in 1821.

188 ***Quadrille française*** French quadrille or square dance.

189 **Milyon Paşa** Ömer Viryoni (Vrioni) Paşa, Albanian commander who led the Ottoman force to relieve the besieged garrison at Varna.

189 **Kamçiya** River south of Varna.

189 ***Nizam-ı Cedid*** "New Order" proclaimed by Sultan Selim in 1793 creating a regular army; Veltman uses it to refer to the Ottoman soldiers.

190 **Ossian** Oisín, legendary Irish bard, made famous throughout Europe by James Macpherson, who in the 1760s published two epics that he claimed to have translated from Ossian's Gaelic but that were largely of his own invention. Several times Macpherson employs the

image of an oak trunk burning to the accompaniment of poetry, for example, in the poem "Carthon": "They sit round the burning oak, and the night is spent in the songs of old." James Macpherson, *The Poems of Ossian and Related Works,* ed. Howard Gaskill (Edinburgh University Press, 1996), 132.

190 ***Emir Oğlu*** "son of the emir" (Turkish).

190 **Emin** According to Akutin, Veltman had earlier planned to write a separate story in prose about Alme and Emin.

190 ***La 'ilaha 'illa llah!*** "There is no God but God" (Arabic), the first part of the *shahada,* the Muslim profession of faith.

190 ***Hançer*** "Dagger" (Turkish).

Day 39

192 **Celui qui n'a pas . . .** "Whoever does not have a grain of fantasy in his head to console himself in the face of reality—I pity him." The original quotation has "un petit grain" (a little grain). From Henri de Latouche's novel *Fragoletta* (1829), which features a character based on the real-life French geologist Déodat Gratet de Dolomieu. Latouche, *Naples et Paris en 1799* (Brussels: H. Tarlier and Aug. Wahlen, 1829), 2:233–234).

192 **Senegambia, Nigritia** Regions of west Africa.

192 **Zaara** The Sahara Desert.

192 **5,895,760 square versts** 2,590,650 square miles (6,709,740 sq km).

193 **Xerxes** To prepare for invading Greece, Xerxes I of Persia built a pontoon bridges across the Hellespont (Dardanelles) and dug a canal through the Athos peninsula. According the Herodotus, he had the sea whipped after a storm destroyed his bridges.

193 ***Suli*** Mongolian *sul'*; feather grass or needle grass, some species of which are toxic.

193 ***Arashan*** The hot springs of Altyn-Arashan in Kyrgyzstan.

193 ***Tarpan*** Kazakh word for the Eurasian wild horse, now extinct.

193 ***Khutagt*** "High lama" (Mongolian), also spelled *hutuktu.*

194 ***Rehe*** Old name (also spelled *Jehol*) of Chengde, the mountain resort of the Qing (Manchu) emperors of China, who held the Mongolian title *Bogd* or *Bogda,* "holy."

Day 40

195 **Celui qui est assis . . .** "He who is sitting works to rise; he who is in movement works to be at rest. *Les Œuvres d'Hippocrate, traduites*

en françois, avec des remarques, et conferées sur les manuscripts de la bibliotheque du roy (Paris: Compagnie des Librairies, 1697), 2:42. The original is Hippocrates, *Regimen* 1.15.

195 **Du, lieber Berg . . .** "You dear mountain! (*Songbook for Children*, von Stoy)." J. S. Stoy, ed., *Gesangbuch für Kinder* (Nuremberg: gedrückt mit Lenzischen Schriften, 1781).

195 ***Birds of a feather . . .*** The Russian saying translates more literally as "One is involuntarily a friend to one's own."

196 **Sbiten** Hot drink made from honey and spices.

196 **Master** Probably not a feudal landowner here, but rather the proprietor of the business the sbiten seller works for.

197 **Kamensky** Sergei Kamensky (1771–1834), Russian general, who became famous for his victories at Pazarcık, Şumnu, and Batın in 1810.

197 **Balkants** The sbiten seller's mispronunciation.

197 **Yermak** A reference to Yermak Timofeyevich (ca. 1540–1585), Cossack ataman who led the Russian conquest of Siberia.

198 **Nekrasovite** One of a group of Don Cossacks who fled their homeland after being defeated in a rebellion in 1708 and eventually settled in the Ottoman Empire.

198 **Irak Arabi** Lower Mesopotamia, the southern portion of modern Iraq. The first and second editions have "Iran Arabi"; this is corrected in the Soviet edition.

198 **Diyarbekir** Or Diyar Bakr, region of Upper Mesopotamia.

198 ***La 'ilaha . . .*** "There is no god but God!" (Arabic; see note above for page 190).

198 ***Gâvur*** "giaour, unbeliever" (Turkish, from Persian).

198 **Seraskier** Turkish *serasker*, commander of the Ottoman army.

199 **Karnobat** Town in Burgas Province, Bulgaria.

199 **Aydos** Aytos, Burgas Province, Bulgaria.

199 **Kırkkilise** Now Kırklareli, Kırklareli Province, Turkey.

199 **Hic ego . . .** Ovid, *Tristia* 3.3. "I, who lie here, with tender loves once played, / Naso, the bard, whose life his wit betrayed. / Grudge not, O lover, as thou passest by, / A prayer: 'Soft may the bones of Naso lie!'" Ovid, *Tristia, Ex Ponto*, trans. A. L. Wheeler. rev. G. P. Goold, Loeb Classical Library 151 (Harvard University Press, 1988), 115.

199 **Knots** Referring to the legend of the intricate Gordian knot, which Alexander the Great "solved" by slicing through it with his sword.

200 ***Octavius Augustus*** Caesar Augustus (63 B.C.E.–14 C.E.), whose birth name was Gaius Octavius Thurinus. In 8 C.E. he exiled Ovid to Tomis (now Constanţa, Romania), for unclear reasons.

200 ***Hothouse*** Presumably the Baths of Agrippa, near the Pantheon in Rome.

201 **Pomptine Marshes** Marshes south of Rome, infamous for their diseased air.

201 **Eclogues** Several of Virgil's eclogues (ca. 39 B.C.E.) may contain references to Octavian, the future Augustus. Virgil laments the death of Claudius Marcellus, Augustus's nephew, in *Aeneid*, 6.860–886.

201 **One sighed . . .** In the first edition, the author's note has Ovid instead of Virgil, probably by mistake. According to an anecdote, when Augustus was visiting his villa with Horace and Virgil, the former poet's eyes were watering owing to excessive drinking, while the latter was always heaving deep sighs, leading Augustus to joke that he was spending his life "between tears and sighs." Athanasius Kircher, *Latium, id est nova et parallela Latii tum veteris tum novi descriptio* (Amsterdam: Janssonius, 1671), 166.

201 **Aesop's frog** From the fable in which a frog tries to puff himself up to be as big as an ox.

202 ***Art of Poetry*** *Ars Poetica* (ca. 19 B.C.E.), a poetical epistle by Horace.

202 ***Alcaic*** A verse form, attributed to the Greek poet Alcaeus, in which each stanza contains two lines of eleven syllables, one of nine, and one of ten, with a complex meter.

202 **Tibullus** Albius Tibullus (first century B.C.E.), Roman elegiac poet. The third volume of the so-called *Corpus Tibullianum* contains five poems about Sulpicia's love for Cerinthus, possibly by Tibullus, and six poems by Sulpicia herself.

202 **Suetonius** (in footnote) Gaius Suetonius Tranquillus (born ca. 70 C.E.), Roman biographer, records that Augustus wrote a poem in hexameters called "Sicily."

203 **Metis** One of Oceanus's daughters and Zeus's first wife. Zeus, hearing a prophecy that Metis will bear a son mightier than himself, swallows her and then gives birth to Athena (whose Roman counterpart was Minerva) from his head. Augustus is misstating the myth.

203 **Melpomene** The muse of tragedy.

203 ***Medea*** A sorceress who helps Jason the Argonaut obtain the Golden Fleece. When she is rejected by Jason, she kills their children and burns his new bride to death in her palace.

204 **Euripides** (ca. 480–ca. 406 B.C.E.): Greek tragedian who wrote the most famous version of the myth of Medea.

Day 41

206 **Une demoiselle** A young lady (French).

206 ***Swarthy frame*** The original Russian uses the expression "to keep in a black body," which means "to ill-treat." The idiom apparently derives from horsebreeding. The implication is that the poet is unattractive.

208 **Mon amie . . . :**

> My friend—may this eye call back to you the eyes
> That loved to seek you out, to contemplate, to understand;
> May you always remember their gentle glances
> And the tears they shed at the moment of farewell.

208 **Deux choses . . .** Two things make the heart suffer / And torment it throughout life / One is remembrance, / The other, forgetting.

209 **Chapter 107 . . .** Corrected from the first and second editions, which refer incorrectly to chapter 106.

209 **Junker** In early nineteenth-century Russia, this could refer to any junior officer.

209 **A simple table . . .** A more literal translation is "Where there is only a corner, and a table, / And the well-disposed female sex." The original includes a pun on the word *pol*, which means both "sex" and "floor."

211 **Abbé l'Épée** Charles-Michel de l'Épée (1712–1789), pioneer in education for the deaf.

211 ***Pontus Euxinus*** Black Sea.

211 **Istros** Also Istria or Histropolis, Greek colony near the Danube estuary.

211 **Torks** Turkic tribe who fought as mercenaries for the princes of Kievan Rus, an East Slavic state centered on Kyiv and ruled by the Rurikide dynasty from the ninth to the thirteenth centuries. Veltman seems to identify the descendants of the Torks as the Bulgars or the Ottomans.

211 **Köstence** Constanța. Veltman links Istros with Constanța, but modern scholars place it thirty miles (48 km) to the north.

211 **P. P. L.** Pavel Petrovich Liprandi (1796–1864), lieutenant colonel of the thirty-second Jäger Regiment.

212 ***Băcălii*** "Grocery shops" (Romanian).

212 ***Balyk*** Cured filet of sturgeon, from Turkish *balık*, "fish."

212 **Turkish victories** Between the fifteenth and seventeenth centuries, the Ottoman Empire conquered significant territory in central Europe.

212 **Alaric** Alaric I (ca. 370–410), king of the Visigoths, was buried with a great hoard under the bed of the river Busento.

212 **Istros** See chapter 297.

Day 42

213 **Pour ne rien . . .** "To leave nothing behind, I will tell you, sir, that . . . (Letter on talking heads. Rivarol.)" "Lettre à M. le président de ***, sur le Globe aérostatique, sur les Têtes-parlantes, et sur l'état présent de l'opinion publique à Paris," in *Œuvres complètes de Rivarol,* 2nd ed. (Paris: Léopold Collin, 1808), 2:216–217. On Rival, see the note to the epigraph to part 3.

213 ***Sancak*** "District" (Turkish) subdivision of an *eyalet,* or province.

213 ***Köy*** "Village" (Turkish) found in many place-names.

213 ***Karamuratköy, Danaköy*** Mihail Kogălniceanu and Nicolae Bălcescu, Constanța County, Romania.

213 **Three versts** About two miles (3 km).

213 **Two versts** About 1.3 miles (2 km).

214 **Demyan's fish soup** In Ivan Krylov's fable by this name (1813), Demyan offers his guest bowl after bowl of rich fish soup despite the latter's complaints that he is full; the moral is that writers should learn to hold back when necessary.

Day 43

217 **Forster** Johann Reinhold Forster (1729–1798) or his son Georg (1754–1794), German naturalists who accompanied Captain James Cook on his second Pacific voyage.

217 **Gay-Lussac** Joseph Louis Gay-Lussac (1778–1850), French chemist, who made a hot-air balloon ascent with Jean-Baptiste Biot to a height of 23,018 feet (7,016 m).

217 **Poetic tale** Veltman's narrative poem *The Fugitive.* A. Vel'tman, *Beglets: Povest' v stikhakh* (Moscow: N. Glazunov, 1831).

218 **Archipelagic** Aegean.

Day 44

219 **Vulcain . . .** "Vulcan (aside): Ah, nature, nature! Go, I abandon you to whoever wants to take you!" In Saint-Foix, *Œuvres complettes*, vol. 2 (Maastricht: Jean-Edme Dufour & Philippe Roux, 1778), 312. Veltman

omitted a word: The source text has "je t'abandonne volontiers," "I willingly abandon you."

220 **Mes regards . . .** From a French translation of Ossian's poems (see chapter 275): *Ossian, fils de Fingal, barde du 3e siècle; Poésies galliques*, trans. Letourneur (Paris: J. G. Dentu, 1810). Here is the English original: "I look into the times of old, but they seem dim to Ossian's eyes, like reflected moon-beams, on a distant lake. Here rise the red beams of war!—There, silent, dwells a feeble race! They mark no years with their deeds, as slow they pass along." James Macpherson, *The Poems of Ossian and Related Works*, ed. Howard Gaskill (Edinburgh University Press, 1996), 319.

220 **Bordea** Village in Iași County.

220 ***Cai*** horses (Romanian).

220 ***Ulița Mare*** "Great Street," Bulevardul Ștefan cel Mare, Stephen the Great Boulevard.

220 **Burnt princely palace** Built by Alexandru Moruzi, hospodar (ruler) of Moldavia in 1806 and destroyed by fire in 1827.

220 ***Copou*** Park north of Iași.

220 ***Mititică*** Romanian dance (see chapter 77).

220 ***Po-o . . .*** Line from a Romanian folksong about Tudor Vladimirescu, leader of the Wallachian uprising of 1821. The original is "Pom, pom, pom eram eu, pom!" (A fruit tree, a fruit tree, a fruit tree I was, a fruit tree!).

222 ***Căruță*** Wagon (see chapter 24).

222 ***Surugiu*** Driver (see chapter 43).

223 ***Hi-me, murgule!*** "Giddyup, you (bay) horse." This seems the most likely reading of the original *murile*, which Akutin translates instead as "carrion."

223 ***Podul Mogoșoaiei*** Now Calea Victoriei, street in Bucharest, which Veltman seems to have transplanted to Iași.

223 ***Băcălii*** "grocery shops" (see chapter 298).

223 ***Cafenea*** "coffeehouse."

223 ***Cealmale*** Turbans.

223 ***cușme*** Fur caps.

223 ***fesuri*** Fezzes.

223 ***fermenele*** Embroidered jackets.

223 ***mintene*** Jackets or vests, worn especially by Albanians.

223 ***Concină, trictrac*** Card games of Greek and French origin, respectively.

223 **Vos?** "What?" (Yiddish). The original has "wus?" printed in black letter.

223 ***Potiphar's wife*** In the book of Genesis, Potiphar is an Egyptian officer whose wife tries to seduce Joseph and then falsely accuses him of trying to rape her.

223 ***Cucoane . . . cuconițe*** Ladies, young ladies (Romanian).

223 ***Gros de Naples . . .*** Heavy silk fabrics made originally in Naples, Berlin, and Tours.

223 ***satin turc*** Turkish satin; *satin de la reine*: more commonly *satin à la reine*, "queen's satin."

223 ***batiste d'Écosse*** Scottish cambric.

223 ***kiseya*** Cotton muslin of central Asian origin.

223 **Blondes** Silk lace.

223 ***Canezous*** Muslin or cambric blouses.

223 ***À la vierge . . .*** Different styles of bodices: "virgin," "gardener," and "English."

223 ***Côtes-de-melon, oreilles d'éléphant*** Melon slices, elephant ears.

224 **Lead whiteness** Faces whitened with ceruse or white lead.

224 **Qui prouve . . .** "He who proves too much proves nothing. (Axiom)" (French). François Para du Phanjas, *Théorie des êtres insensibles, ou Cours complet de métaphysique, sacrée et profane, mise a la portée de tout le monde* (Paris: L. Cellot & A. Jombert, 1779), 1:78.

224 **Istanbul and Izmir** Veltman often favors Turkish forms of Ottoman place-names; in the Russian, he uses *Stambul* and *Izmir* instead of *Konstantinopol'* (Constantinople) and *Smirna* (Smyrna). The choice foregrounds the modern Turkish character of the cities rather than their ancient and Greek history.

224 ***Gants fayn*** "Very fine" (Yiddish).

224 ***Gants gut, fayn*** "Very good, fine" (Yiddish).

225 **Chervontsy** Gold or platinum coins worth between three and twelve rubles.

225 ***Peyes*** "Sidelocks" (Yiddish).

225 ***Akh . . .*** "Ah, five ducats a piece!" (Yiddish).

225 **Sedan cloth** Black-dyed fabric from Sedan in northeastern France.

225 ***Bourre de soie*** Floss or waste silk.

225 ***Cărți . . .*** "Cards, visiting cards, with caricatures, eighteen lei! Buy, buy, sir! (Romanian).

225 ***Kaufen . . .*** "Buy, buy, my dear sir!" (German).

225 ***Săracul de mine!*** "Poor me!" (Romanian).

225 **Ion Neculce-Muta** The name is probably drawn from Ion Neculce (1672–1745), a chronicler from Iași who spent several years in Russia.

226 ***Dulceață, dübek*** See notes to chapters 91 and 1, respectively.

226 ***Poftim, boier . . .*** "If you please, sir!" (Romanian) "Good wine!" (Greek) "Jam, coffee, and a pipe!" (Romanian). The captain's speech is a mixture of Russian, Romanian, and Greek, all in a Greek accent, which is mostly shown in his mixing of the sounds *s* and *sh* (*ș*).

226 ***Eu*** "I" (Romanian).

226 ***Cucoane si cuconițe*** "Ladies and young ladies" (Romanian).

226 ***Merge*** "Go" (Romanian).

226 ***Enu*** "A, one" (Greek).

226 **Tshargrad** Tsargrad, Slavic name for Constantinople.

226 ***Si eu*** *Și eu*, "I too!" (Romanian).

226 ***Focșani*** Town in Vrancea County, Romania, and site of a battle in 1789 between the Ottomans and an alliance of Russians and Austrians.

227 **Prince** Frederick Josias of Saxe-Coburg-Saalfeld (1737–1815).

227 ***Car*** "Cart" (Romanian).

227 **Hetairists** Greek revolutionaries (see chapter 148) who fought the Ottomans at Skulyany in Moldavia on June 29, 1821.

227 ***Irmen*** "Armenian" (maybe Turkish *Ermeni*).

227 ***Tata si mama*** *Tata și mama*, "papa and mama" (Romanian).

228 ***Far niente*** "Doing nothing" (Italian).

Day 45

229 **Cimmeriae tenebrae . . .** "Cimmerian darkness" (Latin). In the *Odyssey*, 11.14, Homer says the Cimmerians lived in a land of perpetual darkness; later historians record that they lived in the Pontic-Caspian steppe (present-day Ukraine and Russia).

229 **Lavinia** In Roman mythology, Latinus's daughter and Aeneas's last wife.

230 **Ainsi parlait . . .** "Thus spoke Aeneas with tears in his eyes; meanwhile, his fleet was running under full sail . . ." French translation of Virgil's *Aeneid*, book 6, line 1. This line, however, occurs before Aeneas has met Lavinia. The translation is probably from a note in an edition of Montaigne's essays, *Essais de Michel de Montaigne* (Paris: Lefèvre, 1823), 2:233n2.

230 ***Mercator*** Gerardus Mercator (1512–1594), Dutch cartographer who developed the map projection named after him.

231 **Comme un vers . . .** "Like a verse, which becomes a chrysalis, a pupa, a nymph, and then a butterfly." Veltman substitutes *vers* (verse) for *ver* (worm). Paraphrase of a passage in Emmanuel Swedenborg's *Conjugial Love, or Marriage Love* (1768). The French source is probably Swedenborg, *Les Délices de la sagesse sur l'amour conjugal, et les vo-*

luptés de la folie sur l'amour scortatoire, trans. J. P. Moët (Paris: Treuttel and Würtz, 1824), 414.

231 **Mihalache Sturdza** Mihail Sturdza (1794–1884), then minister of finances in the Russian administration of the Danubian principalities, later hosopdar of Moldavia.

232 ***Amore . . .*** "Love (sitting alone at the foot of the tree): What a beautiful adventure! What a shame! What ridicule! (Comedy by Mr. Saint-Foix)." *Œuvres de théatre de M. de Saintfoix* (Paris: Charpentier, 1762), 4:263–264. For Saint-Foix, see note above for page 161.

232 **Δός** . . . "Give me paper, a pen, and ink!—Gramm." From a Greek-Turkish grammar and phrasebook: Dimitrios Alexandridis, *Grammatiki graikiko-tourkiki* (Vienna: Ioan. Varth. Tzvekios [Johann Zweck], 1812), 121.

232 **Prrrr/uuuu** Representing a lip trill, the Russian command to stop a horse ("whoa").